'*Mother for Dinner* is laugh-out-loud funny. In addition to challenging a tribalism that prioritizes what sets us apart over what we have in common, Auslander considers the burdens of history and captures the fraught dynamics in families of all origins. Underlying the dark humour, it is, dare I say, a tender tale'   *Financial Times*

'Auslander's greatest strength is the zip and ping of his dialogue . . . uproariously funny'   *Literary Review*

'Auslander is an *enfant* even more *terrible* than Philip Roth . . . [*Mother for Dinner*] provides plenty of dark laughs and inspired comic riffs'

TLS

'A book that's funny enough not just to make you nod to show you got the joke, but to make you laugh and laugh'   *The Critic*

'Written in fast-moving, deadpan prose, this novel pokes fun at the contemporary obsession with the "immigrant experience", while holding dear the importance of preserving tradition'   *New Statesman*

'Auslander's brilliantly written, often hilarious but also deeply thoughtful story, riffs on the cultural conflicts within second- and third-generation immigrant families'   *Jewish Chronicle*

'Consistently funny, consistently wise and consistently disturbing in ways that probably only Shalom Auslander could arrange. It is a rare and agile narrative, part deftly written cannibal satire, part moving exploration of identity and part truly concerning recipe book. Perhaps not a perfect gift for Mother's Day, but then again, it could be just the thing'

A. L. Kennedy

MOTHER FOR DINNER

Shalom Auslander was raised in Monsey, New York. Nominated for the Koret Award for writers under thirty-five, he has published articles in *Esquire*, the *New York Times Magazine*, *Tablet* magazine, the *New Yorker*, and has had stories aired on NPR's *This American Life*. Auslander is the author of the short-story collection *Beware of God*, the memoir *Foreskin's Lament*, and the novel *Hope: A Tragedy*. He is the creator of Showtime's *Happyish*. He lives, sadly, in Los Angeles.

ALSO BY SHALOM AUSLANDER

Hope: A Tragedy

Foreskin's Lament: A Memoir

Beware of God: Stories

Mother

for

Dinner

Shalom Auslander

PICADOR

First published 2020 by Riverhead Books, an imprint of Penguin Random House LLC

First published in the UK in paperback 2020 by Picador

This edition published 2021 by Picador
an imprint of Pan Macmillan
The Smithson, 6 Briset Street, London EC1M 5NR
EU representative: Macmillan Publishers Ireland Ltd, 1st Floor,
The Liffey Trust Centre, 117–126 Sheriff Street Upper,
Dublin 1, D01 YC43
Associated companies throughout the world
www.panmacmillan.com

ISBN 978-1-5290-5209-1

Grateful acknowledgment is made for permission to reprint the following:
'Walls' by C. P. Cavafy, translated by Kwame Anthony Appiah, from *The Lies That Bind:
Rethinking Identity* by Kwame Anthony Appiah. Copyright © 2018 by
Kwame Anthony Appiah.
Used by permission of Liveright Publishing Corporation and Profile Books.

Photograph on page viii from the Collections of The Henry Ford.
Gift of Ford Motor Company. Object ID: 84.1.1660.P.O.7227.

1 3 5 7 9 8 6 4 2

A CIP catalogue record for this book is available from the British Library.

Printed and bound by CPI Group (UK) Ltd, Croydon, CR0 4YY

MIX
Paper from
responsible sources
FSC® C116313
www.fsc.org
FSC

Visit **www.picador.com** to read more about all our books
and to buy them. You will also find features, author interviews and
news of any author events, and you can sign up for e-newsletters
so that you're always first to hear about our new releases.

For my children.

And for Ike,

who helped me unchain them.

Americanization Day, Ford Factory, Detroit, 1917

Without reflection, without sorrow, without shame,
they've built around me great, high walls.
And I sit here now and despair.

—CONSTANTINE CAVAFY

Two Cannibals sit beside a campfire.
I really hate my mother, says one.
Says the other: Then just eat the rice.

—OLD CAN-AM JOKE

M others taste awful.
They're revolting, head to toe (the head is the worst part). No amount of seasoning will change that, ask anyone who's consumed one. You can broil them, you can sous vide them, you can dehydrate them and turn them into jerky. It won't help. Even their smell is awful; toss one on the grill and you'll think someone has been burning car tires, which, with a bit of aioli, would probably taste better than mothers.

It's not a gender thing. Don't get excited. Women in general taste no worse than men, and they often taste better; much depends on the preparation, of course, but men tend to live sedentary lives, which gives them a smoky flavor that's not to everyone's liking. Women, on the other hand, tend to be more active and live longer, their meat more lean, their flavor more subtle.

But mothers—specifically, women who have borne a child—are a very different story.

Mothers tend to live much longer, which leaves them gamy and dry, their years seasoned with disappointment and heartbreak, their deaths often precipitated by long terms of confinement to bed, which stiffens the muscles and joints.

As they said in the Old Country: *When a dead mother beckons, no one wants seconds.*

Not that fathers taste good, mind you, but men on average die younger, and often suddenly. They're no Peter Luger, but they beat the hell out of mothers.

What about mothers who die young? you wonder. Do they taste good?

Yes, they do.

They're delicious.

It is a terrible irony of which only the ancient Cannibalian people are aware:

The younger the deceased, the sweeter the meat.

The sweeter the meat, the more bitter the heartache.

. . .

Seventh Seltzer was at work in his office, high above Manhattan's bustling Soho district, wondering how many Burger King Whoppers (double bacon, extra cheese, no lettuce) his mother could eat before she dropped dead. She had been eating them for years now, often as many as twelve a day, every day, trying, as was the tradition, to fatten herself up for death.

A hundred? he wondered.

A thousand.

Tops.

No way she could eat more than a thousand Whoppers, he thought.

He was way off.

Seventh had been dreading his mother's death for years, even before she started eating Whoppers. He knew the moment was coming, approaching like a storm he could not elude but could only hope to endure, to survive in some fashion, and he knew what she was going to ask of him when her last moment arrived.

She was going to ask . . . *that.*

It.

If he would . . . *y'know.*

She would say the words—she'd been waiting to say them her whole life—but Seventh could not; he wouldn't even think them. But he knew what they would be, and he knew that despite every promise he'd made to himself over the years, despite his burning determination to move on, despite his desperate need to turn his back on her and their unique cultural heritage, he was going to weep, and he was going to wipe his tears and he was going to say, Yes, Mudd, yes.

Mudd? Dr. Isaacson had asked early in their consultations.

It's what we called our mother, said Seventh.

Why?

Well, said Seventh. There's a few versions of that story.

There's a few versions of every story, Dr. Isaacson said.

Seventh hadn't seen his mother in over a decade. Then, three years ago, his sister Zero had phoned and told him that Mudd had begun eating Whoppers (double bacon, extra cheese, no lettuce), a dozen a day, every day, in order to fatten herself up for death. Zero was concerned by her behavior, and asked Seventh to phone her and intervene.

Don't phone her, Seventh thought.

He phoned her.

Fuck, Seventh thought.

Mudd, Seventh said, what are you doing?

I'm dying, she said.

You're dying, he replied, because you're eating Whoppers.

I'm eating Whoppers, she said, because I'm dying.

Dr. Isaacson had cautioned Seventh against engaging with his mother, pointing out that Seventh was always more depressed when he spoke to her than when he didn't. Seventh's guilt had overwhelmed him, though, and he phoned her despite Dr. Isaacson's advice. He took it as a minor victory that he had resisted going to see her; Mudd took it as a major victory that he had phoned, and knew that he'd eventually show up at her door.

Fine, he had said to her. Do what you want. Eat your Whoppers. But I am *not* coming over.

Implying that he hadn't lost.

You phoned, she said. That's all that matters.

Implying that she had won.

Fuck, he thought.

Now, three years later, he sat in his office doing the grisly math of a dozen Whoppers a day, every day, for a year.

Hey Siri, he said to his phone, what's twelve times three hundred and sixty-five?

I have found what you're looking for, said Siri. Twelve times three hundred and sixty-five equals four thousand three hundred and eighty.

Four and a half thousand Whoppers a year? thought Seventh.

No way she's eating four and a half thousand Whoppers a year.

It was morning, but outside his office window the sky above the

4

Hudson River was already turning the dull, oxidized gray of slaughtered meat left out too long. An early winter snow was approaching, catching the city off guard, but Seventh had too much work to worry about it; his desk was buried beneath a mountain of unread manuscripts, each of them, he knew, another tedious version of what he had taken of late to calling the Not-So-Great Something-American Novel. It was all anyone wrote these days, and all Rosenbloom, his boss, cared to publish.

The Not-So-Great Something-American Novel had a few essential elements, which Seventh, in his loathing for the genre, had taken to rigorously codifying. The Something-American Hero's Journey, he determined—they were all journeys, God help him, and they were all heroes—consisted of six basic steps. Step One was *Arduous New World Journey*, the dangerous, misery-laden voyage from the Somewhere to the America (occasionally by car, sometimes by train, usually by boat, the less seaworthy the better; rafts are a favorite ever since Twain, second only to the ever-popular Clinging to a Piece of Driftwood), with a fifty-fifty split between protagonists who are Victims Fleeing Some Greater Evil and those who are Innocents Propelled by Unrealistic but Noble Dreams. This step is followed by the brief but critical Step Two, *Dashed Dreams Leading to Utter Hopelessness*—dreams of freedom, wealth, safety, or love; any dream will do as long as it's shattered (in the real critical darlings of the genre, all four types of dreams will be crushed, a technique Seventh referred to as the Hardship Royal Flush). Immediately following *Dashed Dreams Leading to Utter Hopelessness* comes Step Three, *Determination in the Face of Systematic Repression*. This and Step Four, *Fight for Acceptance*, make up the bulk of these stories, wherein the main character, pure of heart and wide of eye, learns that the New World he has adopted is a filthy toilet down which he is inevitably going to be flushed. Noble these people are, though, and they do not relent, eventually reaching Step Five, *Desire Revealed as Tragic Flaw*, in which the main character learns that the problem is not the New World, but rather his desire to be there, a spiritual lacking within the hero that causes him to prefer the shallow, vacuous, superficial rewards of the New World to the deeper, more spiritual rewards of the Old. This step is critical to the book's success, for nothing so assures the cultural acceptance of a book these days as the rejection of the culture that gave birth to it.

The endings of these books are the most changeable element, and they have adapted with the times. For a long period, before the sun began to set on the American Empire, these stories ended with a step Seventh called *Defiant Resumption of Hope*, in which despite all his hardships and travails, the protagonist refuses to give up hope, for himself and for America. They were very popular in their time, suggesting as they did that all you needed to make it in America was hope (they also suggested, conversely, that if you didn't make it in America, it was your own damned fault, but this didn't seem to bother readers as much as it did Seventh). More recently, though, the writers of Not-So-Great Something-American Novels were opting for an ending that irritated Seventh even more than *Defiant Resumption of Hope*, one he referred to as *Triumphant Rediscovery of Unique Cultural Heritage*, in which the beleaguered immigrant comes to the not unexpected realization that America is a vast cultural and spiritual wasteland, and that the culture he was fleeing is the one he needs to return to, Marcus Garvey–like, minus the whole Supporting-the-Klan and Blaming-the-Jews bits.

It wasn't that Seventh denied the horrors of the world; his people had experienced the immigrant struggle firsthand, for hundreds of years and in dozens of nations. On the contrary: so familiar was Seventh with man's inhumanity to man that it galled him to see it so homogenized.

Seventh rejected every manuscript he read. It wasn't their predictability—he was in publishing, after all, he was used to predictability. It was part of a larger problem with which he had struggled his entire life: identity.

The I-word.

For Seventh, identity had always been a prison he longed to escape—white, black, brown, American, European, Russian, male, female, straight, gay, They, Them, atheist, monotheist, polytheist—the ever-growing list of cellblocks from which there was no release. And yet lately, all around him, the prisoners were proudly raising their shackles overhead and cheering their own bondage. Seventh worked on the eighth floor of his office building, and if he was certain the impact of his skull with the sidewalk would kill him, he'd have jumped out the window twenty Not-So-Great Something-American Novels ago.

He hadn't bought a new manuscript in months, and Rosenbloom had been in to see him about it that morning.

But they're terrible, he said to Rosenbloom.

All of them? Rosenbloom asked.

Yes. All of them.

Well, we have to publish something.

Why? asked Seventh.

Because we're publishers, said Rosenbloom.

That's unfortunate.

What'd you think about that Croatian-American one? Rosenbloom asked. I thought that showed promise.

Which Croatian-American one?

The Pro-Choice-Lesbian-Croatian-American one.

Seventh shrugged. It's no different from the Heroin-Addicted-Autistic-Christian-American one, he said.

The Heroin-Addicted-Autistic-Christian-American-Hemophiliac one, you mean?

No, said Seventh. The Heroin-Addicted-Autistic-Christian-American-Diabetic one.

The Type-Two one or the Type-One one?

Both, said Seventh.

Rosenbloom sighed.

We're a tribal creature, Seventh, he said. Division is the way of man. And woman. It's in our blood. Have you ever looked at a map of human migration? We began in Africa, as one, and got the hell out as soon as we could, braving storms, oceans, beasts, famine. Why? Wanderlust? To see Paris in the springtime? No—because we couldn't stomach each other, not for one more minute. Hell is other people, Sartre said that, but early man would have said it sooner if he had developed language. Or she. Someday, Seventh Seltzer, mark my words, everyone will have a nation of their own. Not every people—every *person*. It's the only way he'll be satisfied. Or she. Seltzerland. Rosenbloom Village. Abdullahville. Hernandez Town. One-foot-by-one-foot squares, evenly divided, all around the globe, surrounded by walls ten feet high, topped with razor wire and colorful flags, everyone in their own square singing rousing marches about how their square is Number One, how God chose their square over all other squares, how this square foot is their square foot and

God help the person who tries to take it from them. And you know what we'll want then?

Guns?

We already have those, said Rosenbloom. We'll want stories. Tales! Legends! About *our* square's suffering and oppression, about *our* desperate journeys, about *our* founder's valiant struggle to make our square the Number One square that it is, and about the evil enemies that to this very day try to take our square away from us. In Seltzerland they'll tell stories about the dirty Rosenblooms; in Rosenbloom Village, they'll dream of wiping the Abdullahs off the map; and Abdullah will peer over his wall, watch Hernandez move into the square beside him, and think, *There goes my property value*. We're obsessed with our squares, with our people, with our pasts. That's why mankind has no future. Or womankind. That's the bad news.

What's the good news?

It's a growing market, said Rosenbloom.

He picked up a manuscript from Seltzer's desk.

Is this the one about the Blind-Alcoholic-Latinx-Sri-Lankan-American? he asked.

Yeah, said Seventh. It read just like the one about the Gender-Neutral-Albino-Lebanese-Eritrean-American.

Just find something, Rosenbloom demanded, tossing the manuscript on Seltzer's desk before stomping out the door.

And then Seventh's phone rang.

He glanced down and saw the familiar name on the screen: *Mudd.*

Mudd said that when First was a baby, he couldn't pronounce the word *Mother*, and it came out as *Mudd*.

Bullshit, First said.

He swore early.

If I had named her, First insisted, it would've been something a hell of a lot worse than Mudd.

Second agreed with First. Third agreed with Mudd, but Third always agreed with Mudd. Fourth, the smartest of the bunch, stayed out of it, declaring simply that a myth becomes truth if enough people believe it.

First despised Mudd—only Second hated her as much, but he hated her mostly because First hated her—and the names he called her were indeed worse than 'mud.' He called her the A-word and the B-word, the C-word and the D-word, the E-word and the F-word— he called her every word, in fact, but the M-word: Mother. He was the first to be born and the first, eighteen years later, to leave.

Don't answer the phone, Seventh thought.

He answered the phone.

Fuck.

Hello, Mudd, he said.

There was a long pause before she whispered weakly: It's time.

Time for what, Mudd? he asked.

You know what, she said. Your sister is here. So are your brothers.

First is there?

Yes.

First is there? In your house?

He's downstairs, she said. With the others.

Which others?

Everyone, she said. It's time, Seventh. Will you come?

Say no, thought Seventh.

Yes, he said.

Fuck.

And so Seventh Seltzer put down the memoir of a Paraplegic-Pescatarian-Presbyterian-Conjoined-Filipinx-Arab-American, and headed for Brooklyn.

. . .

The immigrant experience of Cannibals in America has been much the same as any other minority community, albeit more clandestine and precarious. They too came here long ago with dreams of acceptance; they too were met with rejection and hostility; they too were systematically and institutionally excluded from the promise of this country; they too were forced to hide their traditions and ceremonies. And soon they, too, melted. Tired of not belonging and lured by the seductive gleam of capitalism and materialism, the younger generations began to assimilate. They intermarried. They moved out, moved up, and moved away, and the Can-Am community began to dwindle. For a time, their culture was sustained by their local butcher shops, which in the Cannibal-American diaspora often served as their community center. But when those, facing competition from national supermarket chains, began to shut down, it was the death blow Can-Am leaders knew was coming.

What was once a thriving community in Brooklyn was soon reduced to little more than a few dozen families. Their people's very existence was threatened. Drastic measures were needed, and so were heroes—heroes who would do whatever it took to save their people. Which was why Mudd, soon after she and Humphrey married, vowed to have as many children as she could.

A dozen, she said.

A dozen? asked Humphrey.

Sons, Mudd insisted, for Cannibals are a patrilineal people. Sons who will carry on our name and build our nation.

Yeah, but a dozen?

Mudd got to her feet; she was an enormous woman, six foot four in her bare size-twelve feet. Humphrey was a slight man, and she liked to remind him of that whenever she sensed resistance.

There is a war going on, Humphrey Seltzer, she said, wagging her finger in his face, her hand the size of his head. A covert war, a guerrilla war, undeclared but undeniable. The battleground is not in the Middle East or Europe or Africa. No, Humphrey. It is in the wombs and testicles of the people of the world. We are engaged in an international, winner-take-all fuck-a-thon. A war for existence, a war for domination. The strategy is fucking, Humphrey, and the weapons are babies.

I know, he sighed, for this was not the first time she had espoused this worldview. But a dozen?

From Brooklyn to Palestine, she continued, from the Ukraine to China, people are fucking themselves into majorities—Mexicans, Jews, Muslims, Chinese, Japanese, brown, black, white, polka-dot, you name it—fucking themselves into power while fucking their enemies into irrelevance. Do you know how many kids the average Muslim has? Ten. Jews have even more. And don't get me started with the Chinese. You drive through their communities all the time, Hump, you see them. They're crawling out the goddamned windows.

But twelve sons, Mudd, said Humphrey. On a taxi driver's salary?

But Mudd was adamant—the Ancient Spirits will provide, she insisted—and Humphrey was in love, and so he dutifully performed as she had commanded.

Nine months later, Mudd gave birth to a healthy boy, and she named him First.

First? Humphrey asked.

First, she said. And the next shall be Second. I'm keeping count, Humphrey. I'm keeping score.

Humphrey was concerned that such a naming scheme would harm the child's sense of self-worth; to think of himself as just a number, as mere ballast, the valuation of his individual being reduced to membership in a group—surely that would create emotional problems further down the road.

Just a number? she asked. What could be more important than to be a number? They're our people's new tribes—our future, Humphrey, like the tribes of Abraham.

Jacob, he corrected her.

Were *they* just numbers? she asked. Were the *apostles* just numbers?

No, said Humphrey. They had names.

Name them.

Luke. John.

Keep going.

I don't know. Steve.

Mudd scoffed. You'd remember them if they were numbers, she said. Our people are going to remember our children, Humphrey, for our children shall repopulate our people, as God Himself has promised.

Promises, promises, Humphrey grumbled.

Mudd gasped to hear her husband speak so. Cannibal-Americans have always been a religious people, but damned to secrecy as they were, for as long as they were, the specifics of their spiritual beliefs were now lost, and nobody was certain any longer just what religion it was they followed. Some claimed Cannibals were Christian, some claimed they were Jewish, some claimed they were Muslim, a difference of opinion that resulted in predictably divisive results. The enmity between Christian Cannibal-Americans, Jewish Cannibal-Americans, and Muslim Cannibal-Americans fractured their already small community, and so the Ancients in their great wisdom declared that while it was forbidden to deny the existence of God, it was even more forbidden to say with any certainty who that God was, or what He might want of us, except to say for certain that He didn't want anyone to say for certain who He was, or it might cause people to come to blows. Cannibals are thus unique among the religious peoples of the world in that the most devout vehemently deny knowing anything, often referring to God as Whoever or Someone to underscore their pious uncertainty; it is only the despised heathens who destructively preach the doctrine of the Trinity, for example, or claim that the Quran is the literal word of God. Humphrey, personally, preferred the Old Testament to the New; he didn't think himself a Jewish Cannibal-American, but the Judaic concept of an Asshole God fit his generally negative view of the universe. Mudd, meanwhile, while not declaring herself a Christian Can-Am, preferred the New Testament, which told the story of Jesus, who she said was a Cannibal.

Eat my flesh and drink my blood? she said to Seventh. Jew, my ass. Christ was a Cannibal, just like you and me.

Mudd's naming system worked as planned for the first five children, until the terrible night when Sixth died. He was just five years old, his death sudden and without warning. Mudd wept, not because of the loss of her child, but because Seventh, who was four at the time, and Eighth, who was two, were now no longer her seventh and eighth children. Sixth was dead, so Seventh was now sixth, and Eighth was now seventh, and Mudd was pregnant with Ninth, who would be eighth. The whole naming system was fucked.

Her plan ruined, or at the very least made infinitely more complex, Mudd took to bed in debilitating sorrow, a sorrow from which she refused to emerge. Humphrey begged her to think of the health of the child in her womb, and, hoping to relieve her spirits, promised that they would now have thirteen children (including Sixth), thereby netting twelve in the end. Ninth was born a few months later, without incident, but when a child dies, so often does the marriage that created it, and that is what happened to Mudd and Humphrey Seltzer. Gloom, blame, and recrimination filled the Seltzer home, and Humphrey swore loudly and often that as soon as his promise of husbandry was fulfilled, he would leave Mudd and never see her again. A year later Mudd gave birth to Tenth, two years after that she bore the twins Eleventh and Twelfth, and when she announced, two years after that, that she was pregnant with Thirteenth, Humphrey raised his hands overhead, said, I'm out, packed his bags, and left that very night. That was not the end of the story, though, for a few months later, a routine sonogram revealed that Mudd's thirteenth child was, tragically, a girl.

What have I done to Someone, Mudd wept as she looked at the sonogram, to deserve such punishment?

Mudd was furious with Humphrey for not delivering his promised dozen males, but Humphrey wouldn't accept her calls, and eventually changed his number. She declared him a traitor, an enemy of his people, and worse than Jack Nicholson.

When the baby was born a few months later, the thirteenth child who should have been her twelfth boy but was instead her first girl, Mudd named her Zero.

Because, Mudd said, she didn't count.

. . .

Picture a candelabra, Mudd used to tell Seventh when he was a child. A beautiful, silver candelabra, crafted by the world's finest silversmiths, with a tall ornate stem atop of which sit three beautiful candles. One is red, one is white, and one is blue. The candles, too, are the finest of their kind, tall and without blemish and tapered gently from their strong bases to their elegant tips. Everyone who sees them gasps at their beauty, each one a work of utter perfection.

And then the candles are lit, said Mudd. Fire scorches the wicks. Black smoke rises from their tortured bodies. They begin to melt, to weaken, to die. They cry out in anguish. What was once beautiful becomes grotesque, a dull pool of molten wax with no shape or form, no identity or character. The blue mixes with the red, the red with the white, the white with the blue, until there is nothing left of any of them but a dull colorless mass, which entombs the once-beautiful candelabra within its stiffening remains, destroying all that was perfect and good.

She took Seventh's hands in hers.

The flame, said Mudd, is America.

With her enormous finger, she delicately brushed the hair from his brow.

And you, my son, she said, you are the beautiful candle.

. . .

Sixth died from an unspecified disease. Flu, maybe. Maybe something worse. Nobody knew for sure. One day he was there, Mudd said, the next day he was gone. She wept when she told Seventh the story:

She had done everything she could. She had called the doctor, called the hospital. They all told her the same thing: It's just a bug; he'll get over it. Rest and fluids, they said.

I was alone, she said. I was terrified. Your father was off who-knows-where, while every minute our poor child inched closer and closer to death. I closed Sixth's door, afraid you or your brothers would catch whatever he had. And then one night, the coughing stopped. The coughing stopped and I thought he was better, but in the morning . . . he was gone.

Seventh was only four at the time of Sixth's death, and didn't remember much about it. All he knew for sure was that after Sixth died, the family was never the same again.

And that he couldn't have been happier.

Sixth's death was a devastating blow to Mudd, and something changed in her after. She weakened, softened. Once bellicose and abusive, she was now merely melodramatic and pathetic. She stayed in bed for weeks at a time. The family battles, which she often instigated, suddenly ceased. The house, once filled with shouting, was now blissfully silent. There was no love, but there was less hate, and for that Seventh was grateful.

And for that Seventh berated himself.

What kind of a person is happy their brother has died? he chastised himself.

What kind of a person is happy their mother has broken?

He knew what kind:

A bad person.

And so young Seventh resolved to be good, and he devoted himself ever after to saving his family, and to saving Mudd, and to saving all his people.

Even if it meant destroying himself.

. . .

Like most New Yorkers, the first thing Seventh did when he climbed into a taxi was turn off the damned taxi TV, jabbing furiously at the filthy touch screen until the screeching demon turned black and died. Of course because every other passenger did exactly the same thing, the screen itself was covered in every disease known to man, along with a few unknown, a screen you were required to touch, with a bare finger, if you hoped to silence it.

This was the choice modern man was faced with, thought Seventh as the cab pulled away from the curb and headed for Brooklyn: succumb to the spiritual death of celebrity news and lame talk-show comedy, or expose yourself to the physical death brought on by whatever virus covered the screen.

It was Jimmy Kimmel or the plague.

Tough call.

Seventh hated TV, and he wondered now if he learned this hatred from Mudd. Ever since he could remember, she had preached that television was the enemy of their people, a weapon of propaganda used to spread negative Cannibal stereotypes. The series she hated most was *Gilligan's Island*, which presented the Cannibal people—headhunters, they called them—as easily duped face-painted savages dressed in straw hula skirts, their noses pierced with the ghastly bones of their victims.

We're the savages? Mudd would rail. Our people invented the wheel! We invented the knife, we invented the book! We invented fire! They toss their mothers into a filthy pit, six feet in the ground, in the dirt and the mud. To worms they give their beloveds, to vermin, to maggots. And we're the savages? Lousy Sherwoods.

Mudd was a hateful woman who, like other hateful people, insisted her bigotry was well-founded. It was impossible to say which people she hated the most—her hatred went through phases: she hated black people in the Eighties, Latinos in the Nineties, back to black people at the turn of the century, then Muslims and Chinese ever since—but whoever was in first, Jews were always somewhere in the top three. She called them Sherwoods, after the Jew she despised most of all, Sherwood Schwartz, the creator of *Gilligan's Island.*

Can you imagine if I made a TV show that called Jews money-hunters? she raged. A show where all the characters lived in terror that the evil *Jews* might show up? They'd lock me up. They'd throw away the key. But these lousy Sherwoods can say whatever they want about us.

As the taxi headed across town, Seventh texted Carol.

You good? he asked.

Yep, she replied. *You?*

Good, he lied. *Heading into a meeting.*

Seventh hated lying to Carol, but he didn't have much choice; she would have been surprised to hear that he was on his way to see his mother, given he told her when they met that his mother was dead.

She died when I was a child, he said.

How? Carol had asked.

He shrugged. Nobody knew for sure, he said. One day she was there, the next day she was gone.

Carol's eyes filled with the boundless compassion he had fallen so deeply in love with.

So you never knew what it was like to have a mother? she had asked.

No, he had said.

That, at least, was the truth.

How was Reese this morning? he texted.

Seventh recalled phoning Dr. Isaacson the night their daughter, Reese, was born, beside himself with anxiety and racked with doubt about his ability to be a good father.

What does a father do, Doctor? Seventh had begged him. Tell me, please; I have no idea.

You love her, Dr. Isaacson had said. Unconditionally. For who she is, not for what you want her to be.

Seventh didn't buy it.

That sounds too easy, he had said.

Then why do so few people seem able to do it? Dr. Isaacson asked.

With no other option, Seventh and Carol decided to give the whole love thing a shot. Reese was six years old now, and the Unconditional Love Experiment, as he and Carol had referred to it, was thus far proving Dr. Isaacson right. Reese was already everything Seventh was not: confident, self-assured, brave.

Carol texted back: *She was great. Show starts at 8. You gonna make it?*

Seventh was determined to be the father his father had not been, and so, like every father determined to be the father their father had not been, there wasn't a single event in Reese's life he missed: birthdays, doctor visits, firsts of any and every kind. Most of these he attended happily, but school functions were brutal, and tonight was the Roosevelt Elementary talent show. Short of the even more heinous Grandparents' Day, no school function was as dispiriting as the talent show. He wasn't sure if that was because so few of the children had talent or because so few of the parents seemed aware of it. Or maybe it was just because the parents cheering their children reminded him of those things he had never received himself—love, freedom to be himself, encouragement to follow his dreams. It was difficult to be happy for the winners of the Functioning Family Sweepstakes when you grew up emotionally broke.

Reese, having recently fallen under the spell of a YouTube influencer, had gotten into contortion. Backbends, chest stands, splits. For the talent show, she would be cramming herself into a cardboard box.

She spends her time getting into boxes, thought Seventh. *I spent my life trying to get out of one.*

He looked up; ahead of him loomed the Brooklyn Bridge, which he was never able to look at without remembering the childhood he'd spent on the other side of it.

Of course, he texted Carol.

I can't wait.

. . .

First, Second, Third, Fourth, and Fifth grew up in what Seventh referred to as the BD era of the family—Before the Death, referring to the tragic passing of Sixth. Those early BD years were the years when Mudd was at her loudest and most domineering, years marked by terrible feuding and volatility, the house a war zone. Then Sixth died, and the fire went out of her. She was still manipulative, combative, and controlling, but that toxic stew was now seasoned with heavy doses of grief and self-pity. And so Eighth, Ninth, Tenth, Eleventh, Twelfth, and Zero grew up in a somewhat different family—AD, Seventh called it, After the Death—than First, Second, Third, Fourth, and Fifth. The BD siblings (except for Third and Fifth) hated Mudd and couldn't understand why their AD siblings did not, and the AD siblings (except for Ninth, Eleventh, and Twelfth) pitied Mudd and could not understand how their BD siblings could be so cold and uncaring.

Seventh, the middle child, was trapped both chronologically and emotionally between both Mudds—between the cruelly domineering and the pathetically controlling—and it was this, Dr. Isaacson suggested, that was at the root of his ambivalence. If Sixth hadn't died, Seventh's sense of guilt would have been less severe; Mudd would likely have remained mean instead of pitiful, and Seventh would have been able to walk away from her more easily. Perhaps then he would have known happiness. Perhaps then he wouldn't have called her when she started eating Whoppers. Perhaps then he wouldn't have answered the phone when she called.

Perhaps then he wouldn't be in this cab now, heading to Brooklyn to see her.

Is it love that binds a family together, Seventh wondered, or just the guilt estrangement would cause? BD or AD, the Seltzers had always been a fractious family, and as the taxi rumbled across the ancient Brooklyn Bridge, Seventh grew increasingly anxious about seeing them all again. What would they talk about? Most families talked about the good old days, but the Seltzers had no good old days; there were only bad old days, and worse old days, and many days young Seventh wished he had the courage to run away and never see his family again. Some days the depression overwhelmed him, and he would cry to his mother, wondering why they couldn't just be a happy family like everyone else. He hoped she would hug him, say she was sorry, and assure him she would try harder to be the family he needed.

It's First's fault, Mudd said. That little bastard's impossible.

First, being first, was the canvas upon which Mudd projected all her hopes and dreams, for her family and for their people, and he was thus the victim of the worst of her tyranny.

She wanted him to become their people's leader, their statesman, their chief. First just wanted to play with Malika, the little girl down the street.

She's black, said Mudd.

So? asked First.

You'll do anything to hurt me, said Mudd.

She scolded him and rebuked him, slapped him when he disappointed her and slapped him harder when he disappointed his people. And so First grew to despise Mudd, and he rejected her, and he rejected their people. He left home at eighteen, and never spoke to anyone in the family again.

Second, who idolized his older brother, watched the violence from the top of the stairs, peering through the prison-bar posts of the handrail and wishing he had the courage to go to his brother's defense. But he did not. Instead, he consoled First afterward, hugged him when he cried, brought him tissues when Mudd bloodied his nose, and grew to hate his mother as much as First did. At eighteen, Second followed in his older brother's footsteps, which led straight out the front door, and he too never spoke to Mudd or anyone else in the family again.

Mudd went no easier on Third than she did on First and Second, but Third was physically enormous, a giant from birth, larger even than she was. She struck him, as she did the others, but due to his size, the physical abuse had little effect, on him or on their relationship. Third's body had always been that of a man, but his mind remained developmentally that of a child, and like a child, he could never be angry with his mother, for a mother could do no wrong. Because of his size, Mudd decided early on that Third would be the warrior of their tribe, the defender of their people who would lead them to freedom. But Third was no fighter. He was no conqueror. He was too simple to be angry, even when he should have been, and he never raised a hand to anyone, even when he should have leveled them. He never left Mudd's house, and to this day, despite being in his midthirties, he still lived with his mother in the Brooklyn home in which he was born.

Fourth, born two years later, was the opposite of Third in every way. He was slight, the smallest of the four, pale, sickly, scrawny, and utterly brilliant. Fourth was the smartest Cannibal anyone could ever recall being born in the New World or even the Old Country.

He's off the charts, said the school administrator as he handed her Fourth's intelligence assessment.

My God. Mudd beamed at the paper in her hand. If he lied and cheated he could be a Jew.

Fourth read by the time he was two, did long division by the time he was three, and questioned Mudd's every word by the time he was four. He couldn't throw a football, he couldn't run ten feet without tripping, and he couldn't stay silent in the face of her ignorance.

When we consume the bodies of our beloveds, Mudd told her children, our love carries their nutrients into our cells, and so they live on, within us, forever.

Mitochondria carry nutrients into our cells, said Fourth, not love.

Mudd clopped him on the head with the back of her hand.

Stop being stupid, she said.

Knowledge was Fourth's rebellion, intelligence his weapon. First and Second fought Mudd with shouts and violence; Fourth quietly read Goethe, knowing how much Mudd hated when Cannibals read the books of other peoples. She would have preferred shouts and violence.

Go-thee? she demanded. What the hell kind of name is *Go-thee?*

It's pronounced *Ger-ta*, he said. He was a German writer and a statesman, a scientist and a dramatist. His first novel was so affecting that many Germans who read it took their own lives.

Well, said Mudd with a shrug. Anyone who can make a bunch of Krauts kill themselves can't be all bad.

Fourth rebelliously read the Irish, insolently studied the Russians, brazenly surveyed the Chinese, and truculently investigated the French; then he taught himself the languages and defiantly reread them a second time in the original. All these provocations Mudd stoically bore, but when he entered college at the age of sixteen and announced his intention to study anthropology, she'd had it.

Maybe you should worry a little less about mankind, she said, and a little more about *your* kind.

Mankind *is* my kind, he said.

Mudd scoffed.

And *you're* the smart one? she asked.

They were the last words she ever spoke to him.

Fifth was six years old when Sixth died, and he blamed himself for his younger brother's death.

I should have checked on him, he reproached himself. I should have brought him medicine; I should have called an ambulance.

Mudd held him.

We all make mistakes, she said to him. Not as big as yours, but we make them.

Fifth would have hated Mudd as much as the others did had he not been so busy hating himself. He couldn't forgive himself, and the cancer of his guilt spread to every other area of his life. He felt guilty for eating too much and he felt guilty for eating too little; he felt guilty for not cleaning his bedroom, and then when he did clean his bedroom, he felt guilty for how slovenly his clean bedroom made his brothers look in comparison; when he got a B, he felt guilty for not getting an A, when he got an A, he felt guilty for not getting an A+, and when he got an A+, he felt guilty for ruining the grading curve for everyone else. He saw himself as a failure— both as a son and as a Cannibal.

I'm sorry, Mudd, he would say, twice a day, if not more, every day of his youth. Perhaps unsurprisingly, he went on to become a psychiatrist, which Mudd interpreted, as she did most things her children did, as an attack on her.

Professional mother blamers, that's all you shrinks are, she said to him at his medical school graduation.

I'm sorry, said Fifth.

Sixth, said Mudd, was perfect in every way. He never cried, not when he was hungry, not when he was tired, not even when he was born.

He came out, she said, with a smile on his face. Doctors, they'd never seen anything like it. My angel.

First, who had been waiting just outside the delivery room at the time, remembered it differently.

I heard crying, he scoffed when she told the story, which she did often.

Well it wasn't Sixth, Mudd said. He never cried, not once.

Must've been the doctor, First whispered to Second. When he saw her fat cooch.

Mudd smacked them both.

Stop being stupid, she said.

Seventh was just four years old when Sixth died, and Mudd, traumatized and wracked with grief, threw her full attention into protecting Seventh and keeping him from harm, afraid that he might die too. She made him sleep in her bed, beside a large, gilt-framed photo of Sixth—Father, by then, had already taken to sleeping in the den—so that she could keep an eye on him.

Don't you die on me, she said to Seventh. Don't you hurt me.

I won't, he promised.

Young Seventh made his mother's happiness his life's mission. She became his needy child, and he, her doting parent, did all he could to please her. When his brothers fought, Seventh made peace. When they cursed Mudd, Seventh defended her. His own wants and needs, meanwhile, were measured by the degree of hurt or pleasure their fulfillment might cause her: he ate dinner when he wasn't hungry so she wouldn't feel her work was for naught, he excelled at school so as not to disappoint her, and when he fell sick, he told her it was nothing, not to worry, then went and suffered silently in his bed, coughing into his pillow so as not to remind her of the terrible coughing of Sixth the night he passed away.

Eighth, the first of the AD children, followed the lead of Seventh and also made Mudd's happiness his mission. But Eighth was a child of severely limited competencies—neither as defiant as First, nor as determined as Second, nor as strong as Third, nor as smart as Fourth, nor as sensitive as Fifth, nor as selfless as Seventh—and so, utterly lacking in any discernible skills, talents, or competencies, Eighth became a clergyman. He modeled himself after his beloved uncle Ishmael—their father's brother, known by all as Unclish, the spiritual leader of the entire Cannibal-American community. While his brothers wasted their days learning the rules of Monopoly and Dungeons & Dragons, Eighth studied their people's ancient rules of Consumption, the myriad stipulations of the traditional Victuals, the history of their people, the benefits of charcoal versus propane, and how to set up a two-zone grill. He memorized whole sections of The Guide—the codification of all their laws and traditions, codified by Unclish himself—and repeated them by heart to Mudd, who swelled with pride.

Through you, she said to Eighth, our unique cultural heritage will be passed on.

Ninth was a child of incomparable sensitivity to the world around him, with a love of nature and a near mystical connection to her many creatures. The most vicious dog would cuddle at his feet, the most aloof cat would leap into his arms. It was as if they knew they could trust him, that they sensed within him a spiritual being like none other. But Mudd cared not a whit about any of that. She cared only that Ninth was gay, an identity that revealed itself early in his life. His friends were all girls, and he never showed much interest in sports. Mudd scowled with contempt as she watched young Ninth brush his Barbie doll's hair.

He's just having fun, Seventh said.

It isn't natural, she grumbled.

Mudd didn't have any particular concern for the norms of nature; her only concern was for her people, and Ninth's nascent sexual orientation meant that he would never reproduce, and thus never contribute to their people's dwindling numbers. Ninth sensed his mother's disapproval, and struggled to hide his feelings as best he could. But on the eve of his fourteenth birthday, he decided he could lie to her, and himself, no more.

Mudd, he announced, I'm gay.

Today I shall mourn a second son, she sobbed, and all the sons he might have given us.

She felt cheated, and she felt betrayed, and so she blamed the Jews.

The Sherwoods in Hollywood, she shouted at Ninth, that's who's got you all confused! With their vile TV shows and movies, men dressing up like women, women dressing up like men. Animals! You think they want us to reproduce? You think they want us to survive? Nothing would make them happier than to turn us into a nation of queers, Ninth. They *want* us to be sick—and you, you're Patient Speedo.

You can berate me all you want, Mudd, Ninth said. It isn't going to make me like girls.

Oh, honey, she said sweetly, thinking perhaps this had all been a terrible misunderstanding. I don't care who you *like*. I only care who you have sex with.

Ninth never believed for a moment that Mudd's concern was for reproduction, and claimed she was a casualty herself—of homophobia, of hatred, of narrow-mindedness. They fought day and night until he was old enough to leave.

I don't hate you, Mudd, he said. I just pity you.

Well I hate you, she said, and slammed the door behind him.

Tenth, listening to Mudd's jeremiads about Ninth's selfish destruction of their people, was inspired to come to their defense, to become the warrior Third wasn't, to devote his life to protecting his people from the countless enemies whose names Mudd daily cursed. He bought karate magazines to learn how to fight, dumbbells to put on muscle, headbands to look like Rambo.

They won't be expecting it, he said when Seventh discovered him hiding steak knives around the house: under the couch, behind his headboard, on top of the bookshelf in the living room.

They who? Seventh asked.

They everyone, said Tenth.

Eleventh and Twelfth were twins, and Mudd celebrated their miraculous births, saying the Ancient Spirits had made amends for Sixth's death by blessing her with two sons for the price of one.

From one birth came two sons, she sang with joy, and from these two sons will come many more.

But that wasn't the way it turned out. Before the twins were out of elementary school, they were already suffering the devastating psychological agony of gender dysphoria. They had been born in the wrong bodies, there was no doubt about it, female spirits trapped in male forms, and they longed for release from the prison of their physical selves. Something had gone wrong at the factory; God had accidentally installed the complex engine of a Ferrari into the frame of a clunky Jeep, and there was nobody in Customer Service who could help. And so they took it upon themselves to become the people they knew they were: they began dressing like girls, growing their hair long, wearing makeup, and saving every penny they could, dreaming of the day they would be able to afford the surgery that could make them the women they were meant to be.

Don't be ridiculous! Mudd said when they wept and begged her not to throw out their dresses and shoes. You can't just *decide* to be something new. Can a tree just *decide* to be a bird? Can a bird *decide* to be a tree? The tree has leaves, the bird has feathers, no matter how much the tree wants feathers and the bird wants leaves.

We're not trees, said Eleventh.

That's what the tree said, Mudd replied.

Tenth, defender of his people, mocked his twin brothers—Sisters, they demanded, but he didn't care—pulling on their braids and calling them sissies who were destroying their people, but this only strengthened their resolve, and Eleventh and Twelfth grew to hate the mother who denied their pain, and Tenth, who abused them, and Eighth, who told them, again and again, that it was forbidden for them to change who they were.

Says who? asked Eleventh.

Yeah, said Twelfth. Says who?

Says the Elders, said Eighth.

And how many of those Elders, Eleventh asked, are men I wonder?

And how many, Twelfth asked, are LGBTQ?

LG what? Eighth asked.

Exactly, said Twelfth.

And then there was Zero. Zero loved her family with all her heart and all her soul. She forgave their shortcomings, met their disdain with smiles, and responded to their bitterness with love. But Zero was of no use to the Cannibal community, reproductively speaking, and so Mudd ignored her. When she was a baby, it was left to Seventh to care for her, to feed her, to change her, to go to her at night when she cried out in fear. Mudd didn't see the point of teaching Zero their rules and traditions, and so Zero grew up more American than Cannibal, more New World than Old. But no matter how much Mudd rejected Zero, Zero loved her, and no matter how much Tenth ignored her because she wasn't male, she loved him too, and no matter how much Eighth refused to answer her questions about their history and tradition because she was just a girl, she loved him too. Her equanimity drove them insane, and Mudd was certain there was something wrong with her, beyond her useless gender. One morning, Seventh came into the living room to find Mudd at the front window. Zero, still just a little girl, was outside in the pouring rain, jumping up and down in the sidewalk puddles and standing with her arms outstretched, her bright smiling face turned up to the heavens, laughing with boundless joy. Seventh smiled to see her, her bright face lighting up the gray day, her joy a rebuke to the clouds themselves, which, seeing her below, soon lightened and cleared and set the sun to shining upon her.

Mudd sighed and shook her head.

It's bad enough she's a goddamned girl, she said as she turned away from the window with disgust. Did she also have to be a fucking retard?

. . .

Asked the Elders: May a girl become a boy?

Yes, said the Elder Elders.

May a boy become a girl? asked the Elders.

No, said the Elder Elders.

But why may a girl become a boy but a boy not become a girl? asked the Elders.

Because one may not go from something, said the Elder Elders, to nothing.

. . .

Seventh had moved away, said Dr. Isaacson, but he had never moved on. Seventh agreed, but felt that Dr. Isaacson couldn't possibly understand the burden placed upon him by his unique cultural heritage.

Dr. Isaacson sighed.

Not the headhunter thing again, he said.

Cannibal, Seventh corrected him. Cannibal-American, actually.

There are no cannibals in Brooklyn, Seventh.

Not anymore.

Where did they go? Dr. Isaacson asked. Gilligan's Island?

Away.

Mm-hmm, said Dr. Isaacson. And where did they come from?

From the Old Country, said Seventh. My great-grandfather Julius came over when he was eighteen.

What Old Country?

I don't know.

You don't know.

We forgot.

So you remember that your great-grandfather was a cannibal, but you can't remember where he came from?

He was Cannibal, he corrected the good doctor. Not *a* Cannibal.

Seventh's ancestry was a sore point between him and Dr. Isaacson, who never believed Seventh's story and attributed his outrageous claims to his need for individuation from his narcissistic mother.

I give you credit, Seventh, he said. I've had many patients consumed with their mothers, but I've never had a patient who actually wanted to consume her.

I don't want to consume her, Seventh bristled. That's the whole point.

Eventually Seventh stopped seeing him, his heritage an impasse that doctor and patient could not overcome. Now, though, as the taxi made its way through Brooklyn and Seventh felt anxiety clench like a fist around his heart, he wished that he could phone Dr. Isaacson, right now, wished someone, anyone, would tell him to turn around and go back to Manhattan, back to Carol and to Reese and to the new family he had built on the ruins of his old one.

Wrote the great French essayist Michel de Montaigne:

I have broken my chains, you say. But a struggling cur may snap its chain, only to escape with a great length of it fixed to its collar.

Seventh first encountered Montaigne in college when his English professor assigned the class the famous essay "On Cannibals." He was terrified at first, assuming the secret of his identity had somehow been revealed. But the professor was unaware of Seventh's heritage, and had simply chosen the piece as an early example of something he called *intertextuality*, the very sound of which caused Seventh's eyes to glaze over. Hearing the names Bakhtin and Barthes soon sealed the non-deal for Seventh, their being the two surest signs to any college student that time was about to slow to an imperceptible crawl and make one long for the sweet release of death. But as he read Montaigne's words, he was struck by the Frenchman's passionate humanism, by his defiant open-mindedness, by his contrarian wisdom—by his difference, in every possible way, from the people he had come from. Seventh meant to read more of him, but he was in college, a time of life when gaining knowledge takes a distant second importance to getting laid, and he never pursued Montaigne further. Then, a few months ago, after discontinuing his treatment with Dr. Isaacson, just as Seventh was looking for direction, for insight, for some guidance through the dark forest of his life, a manuscript he was reading by a Jewish-Fourth-Wave-Lesbian-Socialist-Pro-Immigration-Anti-Vax-Latinx-American mentioned Montaigne, attacking him as a Bourgeois-European-Patriarchal-Franco-Roman-Catholic-Cisgendered-Male-Monothesistic-Apologist.

Perhaps, thought Seventh, it was time to read him again.

Brooklyn, USA, the taxi driver called out as they passed the WEL-COME TO BROOKLYN sign at the end of the bridge. I grew up here.

Me too, said Seventh.

Couldn't afford it now, though.

Me neither, said Seventh.

The driver glanced in his rearview mirror, taking note of the color of Seventh's skin.

They get rid of us, said the driver. One way or another, they get rid of us.

They who? Seventh asked, but the driver just waved his hand as if the question wasn't worth considering.

Seventh hadn't been back to the old neighborhood in years. Like most everywhere, it had changed dramatically. Gone were the small corner shops and local markets. In their place he found trendy coffee shops, high-end restaurants, gourmet doughnut bakeries, and artist lofts that no artist could ever afford. Hipsters replaced the homeless, and Seventh gasped as they drove past an Apple Store where once a fruit market stood—selling, he thought wryly, actual apples. Still, though, as he looked up here and there, he could spot occasional remnants of the old Can-Am community: an old Cannibalian frieze above the doorway to a vegan cupcake shop, or perched above the entryway to an old renovated bank (now a coworking space, whatever the hell that was). Here, three figures sitting cross-legged consuming a human leg; there, a prone figure being eviscerated by a standing figure; and everywhere, if you knew where to look, the telltale bas-relief cauldrons non-Cans thought were simple decoration, but which Can-Ams knew to be the traditional markings of the homes of their people.

To see them only fanned the flames of Seventh's already smoldering guilt. He had always considered himself a 'cultural Cannibal,' a designation that meant nothing to Mudd but cowardice, but which allowed Seventh to perform the delicate high-wire act of ambivalence: I am neither a backward leaver of modern people, he could claim, nor a modern leaver of backward people. But to see from the back seat of the taxicab just how the neighborhood had changed caused him to stumble, to lose his footing, and to fall headlong into doubt and regret.

He had left. He had disappeared. And the community had disappeared with him.

Melting, Mudd used to say, is for candles.

But melt most of his family had. Seventh well remembered the day his brother First left home. He watched from the stairs, his small heart breaking, as his beloved eldest brother slung a backpack over his shoulder and walked out the front door, never to return. It was the middle of the night, the neighbors long asleep, but Mudd stood on the front porch, shouting after him into the darkness.

Would that Julius had sunk at sea! she called. Better for him to have drowned in the Atlantic than to watch you drown in the sea of America. Let me tell you a little something about melting pots, young man; our people know a thing or two about melting pots! They don't start with your head or your feet or your hands, I can tell you that. They start with your soul; that's the first thing they cut off! Your spirit! When your spirit is dead, they take your body and boil you down until you're indistinguishable, until you're nothing but muck and bones, no different from the million other dead fools in that miserable bastard pot. And while you thank them for letting you boil, they stoke the fire and cheer that you're gone, you and your whole history with you. Go, you bastard! Go and never darken my doorway again!

She said the same thing when Second left two years later, and again when Fourth left a few years after that.

Seventh could still hear her voice, echoing down the darkened street, as his taxi slowed to a stop in front of Mudd's house.

Fifteen dollars, said the cab driver.

Don't get out, Seventh heard Dr. Isaacson say. *Do* not *get out.*

Seventh got out.

Fuck.

. . .

Skin color, sadly, is one of humankind's primary identity markers. This is primitive and disheartening, to be sure, but perhaps also to be expected, as we are, despite our baseless high estimation of our-selves, just one more species of animal trying to survive. For a zebra, Lion = Death, and none would lecture her for profiling the king of the jungle in such a reductive manner. Still, one can only imagine the heights we humans might rise to if more essential characteris-tics like kindness and intelligence were as immediately discernible and valued as the stripes and spots of our coats. It is painful and demeaning to be judged by the color of one's skin, as anyone who has been knows. But if there's anything worse than being judged by one's own skin, it is being judged by the color of *everyone's* skin. This, though, is the terrible situation Cannibals today suffer, as they are neither black skinned nor white, neither light nor dark, neither Eastern nor Western. Having fled and assimilated and fled again so many times throughout their beleaguered history, they have reached something of a racial absolute zero in terms of their features; their unique characteristic is that they possess no unique characteristic, and their coloring is of such a particularly ambigu-ous shade that they can be taken for—and hated by—every race and every people in every nation of the world. Second, whose early interest in art led to a career in advertising, once remarked that thousands of years of history had left them with no homeland and no treasures; all it had left them with was skin the specific Pantone color of which assured they would be hated by everyone, every-where, for the rest of time. Seventh had been taken for Mexican in Texas, white in South Central Los Angeles, Palestinian in Jerusa-lem, and Israeli in the West Bank. In New York City alone he'd been assaulted in Staten Island by a group who thought he was black, in Crown Heights by some Hasidim who thought he was Hispanic, and in Queens by some white supremacists who thought he was a Jew. If there was any upside for Seventh for what Unclish called their 'accursed ambiguous identity,' it was the chance it provided Seventh to pursue women from ethnicities who might not have dated him otherwise—an upside Seventh, in his youth, took full advantage of.

Black? he'd said to Jada, a Pro-Choice-Liberal-Democratic-Baptist-African-American-Dominatrix. Of course I'm black.

Jewish? he'd said to Leah, a Pro-War-Orthodox-Neoconservative-Zionist-Jewish-American-Nymphomaniac. I'm as Jewish as they come.

Persian? he'd said to Yazmin, a Bisexual-Communist-Dyslexic-Persian-American. Don't I *look* Persian?

The ruse wasn't easy to sustain, though, and as the murky waters of his numerous fictional identities rose up around him, he wished he could meet someone who identified simply as Human. But such a person was not to be found, and Seventh was soon drowning in such a deluge of nationalities and designators that he often couldn't recall whom he was dating, where she was from, or what he had claimed to be. Keira was the final straw, the Nigerian-Irish-Ukrainian-Egyptian poet/accountant/producer he met at the book party for a recently released memoir by a Gender-Fluid-Hearing-Impaired-Liberal-Democratic-Palestinian-Canadian-American (It's about time! the *Times* had raved). Seventh was relieved when their relationship finally fell apart; his shoulders ached from carrying protest placards with her every weekend, and he often couldn't remember what cause he was supposed to be claiming to support and which cause he was supposed to be claiming he was protesting. He was fairly certain Keira didn't know either, and pointing that out to her brought their relationship to a swift end. He swore off women, cursed relationships, rejected human beings, and proclaimed the impossibility of love, which is precisely when he met Carol.

What are you? he asked, awaiting the usual deluge of identifiers.

What am I? she asked. Or who am I?

Let's start with what, he said.

I'm a human, asshole. How about you?

Seventh was smitten. Carol was even more beautiful inside than out, and he found her endlessly fascinating: her fiery opinions, her dark humor, her jade green eyes that seemed to burn brighter when she spoke of the things she loved and which blackened when she railed against that which she disdained. And her laugh—a laugh so uninhibited, so lustful, that he knew the first time he heard it that he wanted to hear it every day for the rest of his life. But alas, so cluttered was his mind with tags and adjectives by then that though he loved her dearly, the only thing about her heritage he could recall two months into their relationship was that she was Dominican-Something-American, and to ask her now would be impossible. As for what he had told her about himself, all he could be certain of was that it was a lie.

Dad, this is Seventh, Carol had said when first introducing him to her father. Seventh, this is Dad.

Hello, her father said, eyeing Seventh's skin tone for clues. Are you . . . Colombian?

Yes, sir, said Seventh.

You said you were Dominican, said Carol.

I'm Dominican-Colombian, said Seventh.

But you said your father was Guatemalan, she said.

My father was Guatemalan, Seventh said. Guatemalan-Colombian.

My mother was Dominican. I'm Dominican-Guatemalan-Colombian-American.

Carol shrugged, not particularly concerned either way, and when she went to the kitchen to get drinks, her father gave Seventh a hearty slap on the back.

As long as you're good to my daughter, he said, I don't care what you are.

Then he winked, nudged Seventh with his elbow, and whispered, Just as long as you're not a goddamned Haitian.

Heh, said Seventh.

Seventh didn't know what Carol's father's issue with Haitians was, but if he hated Haitians, he wasn't going to like Cannibals very much, and he worried Carol shared her father's prejudices. And so Seventh never said a word to her about his people, or about his traditions, or about who he really was, and to this day neither Carol nor Reese knew about his actual heritage. Now looking for the first time in over ten years at his childhood home—at the lawn where he once tossed a ball with his father, at the second-floor window from which he and First dropped plastic parachuted army men, at the front door Sixth had once bounded out to greet him when he walked up the path, at perhaps the last home of the last Cannibal-American family in existence—he wondered if he should tell them. If they should know. If he should just sit Carol and Reese down and say, Guys, I have something important to tell you. You know the fat guy on *Gilligan's Island* with the bone through his nose? The one holding a spear and shouting Ooga Booga? Well, that's me.

Maybe it was time.

To accept who he was.

To *own* his story, wasn't that what the kids were doing these days? Owning their stories?

He'd been afraid when he was younger; afraid he would be rejected, that he would never belong to the larger world beyond his doorstep. But what larger world? he now wondered. There was no larger world, just a collection of warring mini-worlds of nationalities, genders, politics and religions, of ists and isms, neo-this's and ultra-that's.

Maybe Rosenbloom was right.

Maybe if everyone else was retreating to their cages and calling it freedom, maybe he should too.

Maybe it was time to embrace his shackles.

Maybe the only people left to belong to anymore were your own.

. . .

Seventh Seltzer was drowning in stories. The damned things were everywhere: old stories written by dead masters overflowed the shelves of his home; new stories piled up in his office, screaming, shouting, demanding to be heard; but worse than any other, there in the dark corners of his mind, were the stories about his people—hundreds of them, thousands of years long, stories of suffering and oppression, of persecution and accusations, of shattered dreams and broken bones, maudlin and grim, the miserable tales of yesterday that waylaid his every today.

The horror story, Mudd called it, of Us.

Mudd told her children stories. Day and night she told them, horrible stories, stories she forbade them to forget and commanded them to retell; stories of misery and torture, of victimization and slaughter, of endless suffering at the bloody hands of the hateful nations of the world. *Once upon a time, fuck.*

No child was too young to hear them.

You kids, she began every tale, have it easy.

Everything was worse in the past, she said, unimaginably worse, and the further back in the past one went, the worse things became. Two hundred years ago, said Mudd, they raped and killed our babies in front of their mothers. Three hundred years ago they raped our mothers in front of their babies, and then, when they were done, they raped the babies in front of the mothers. Then they killed them both.

What did they do four hundred years ago? Third had asked.

Mudd clopped him on the head with the back of her hand.

Stop being stupid, she said.

Mudd was a strict authoritarian even in the most casual of times, but never more so than when she was telling her people's stories. Then she brooked no disrespect, allowed no questions, suffered no childish levity. Not even First dared challenge her when she was telling of their past.

At least back then they killed you honestly, she said, with a knife to your throat or a sword through your belly. Here in America, they cut you up one piece at a time: they change your name, they ban your traditions, they belittle you on TV, until all that's left of thousands of years of heritage is a television set and a pair of Levi's.

What are Levi's? asked Second.

Pants, said Mudd. Made by some New York Jew.

Levi Strauss was from San Francisco, Fourth pointed out.

Pardon me, Mudd said. Made by some Jewish fag.

Mudd loved her people, so much so that, as a matter of pride, she despised all others: she hated blacks, Asians, Latinos, Caucasians, Indians, Germans, Sumerians, Macedonians, Canaanites, Hittites, Babylonians, homosexuals, cross-dressers, leathermen, tops, bottoms, vegans, hippies, Christians, Catholics, Jews, Muslims, Baptists, Catholics, Jainists, Manichaeans, Ashurists, pagans, and atheists, and she was unabashed in her declarations, privately and publicly, that they were stupid, lazy, criminal, unethical, cowardly, imperialistic, deceitful, manipulative, dirty, cheap, ugly, foul smelling, uneducated, and sexually perverse.

There must be *something* good about them, Fifth had said.

Yeah, said Mudd. They die.

Seventh often worried that he would contract her hatred, inherit her bigotry, like a virus, like a birth defect, despite his best efforts to resist, a sort of Fetal Asshole Syndrome; but he was thirty now and thus far he hadn't seen any symptoms. But you had to be vigilant; you never knew when it might appear, and you'd suddenly find yourself one Sunday afternoon at the local Klan Depot, getting the wife and kids fitted for the Robe-N-Hood Combo.

Stories were Mudd's way of inoculating her children from the influence of these despised and dangerous others. She used stories to treat her children the way physicians use medication to treat their patients, examining her offspring for signs of moral infection, of cultural poisoning, and deciding, based on their symptoms, which story to administer, how frequently, and in what form.

When First came home with a black girlfriend, she told him the story of Julius marrying his sister, Julia, just to have Cannibal children and save their people.

When Second came home with a Jewish girlfriend, she told them stories of how the Muslims raped and killed their people.

She's Jewish, Second said, not Muslim.

Six of one, Mudd said, shrugging, half a dozen of the other.

But the story she told the most often, the story all Cannibal-Americans told and retold, was the story of their great-grandfather Julius, who came to America with little more than the shirt on his back.

And it was this story, nearly thirty years after he'd first heard it, that haunted Seventh Seltzer to this day.

. . .

The year was 1914, said Mudd, when Julius Seltzer, son of Samuel Seltzer, son of some other Seltzer, left the Old Country for the New World, mere days after his eighteenth birthday.

What was the Old Country like? young Seventh had asked.

The Old Country, said Mudd, was a paradise, filled with tall trees and babbling brooks and lush meadows, with grapes the size of apples, apples the size of grapefruits, and grapefruits the size of a Chevy. But behold, one day, it was time to leave. A new king had come to power, and it was no longer safe for their ancestors to be there. And so one night, Samuel took his son, Julius, and daughter, Julia, to the dock, where he handed Julius a brown leather valise with a wooden handle and heavy golden clasps, inside which lay the ancient Knife of Redemption, with which the sacred rite of Consumption is performed, and which had been passed down through the family for generations.

Take this with you, Samuel said to Julius.

But Papa, said Julius, wary of such responsibility, are you sure?

Yes, said Samuel. Take it with you, and never forget who you are, or where you came from.

Four harrowing weeks at sea later, Julius and his sister, Julia, sat huddled on the deck of the SS *Endeavor*, waiting for the New World to appear on the horizon. With them sat hundreds of other hungry, desperate immigrants, from dozens of Old Countries of their own. The golden sun was beginning to rise in the east, the sky ablaze with violets and pinks; they had departed the Old Country in the dead of winter, but now, as they drew close to the New World, it was early spring. They had braved storms, illness, and deprivation, but at last they were drawing close, in this season of rebirth, to a nation that had itself been born little more than a century and a half before.

The ship lumbered through the heavy waves of yet another endless sea, the dark waters crashing against its weary hull, when suddenly, an elderly man standing to Julius's left stood up tall at the rail, pointed over the side of the ship, and cried:

America!

Julius and Julia craned their necks and stood on their toes, and there she was, the robed goddess they had been waiting to see with their own eyes, the Statue of Liberty, emerging from the fog, her magnificent torch a beacon of freedom for all.

At once the passengers began to weep with joy. Those who believed in God raised their voices and sang unto Him songs of praise and thanks, and even those who did not believe joined the faithful in their ecstatic hymns of gratitude. Husbands hugged wives, brothers hugged sisters, stranger danced with stranger. There on the deck of that exhausted, weather-beaten ship, people came together without regard for race or creed or religion or color, for here on the soil of the New World they could live without fear of hatred or oppression.

You some kinda Negro? the immigration official asked Julius, eyeing his ambiguous pigmentation.

No.

Jew?

No.

Arab?

No.

Asian?

No.

Italian?

No.

French?

No.

Communist?

No.

Socialist?

No.

Gay?

Gay? asked Julius.

Homosexual.

I know what gay means.

Well, are you?

No.

Jew?

You asked me that already.

The official eyed him.

Then just what the hell are you, boy? he asked. You gotta be something.

But Julius knew that it was forbidden to reveal who his people were or where they were from, for when they did, pitchforks and torches always followed.

I'm from the Old Country, Julius said.

Which old country?

The oldest one.

How old?

Very old.

Does this country have a name?

Yes.

Do you know the name?

No.

The official sighed with exasperation.

Well, you're sure as shit not from here, he said.

No, Julius agreed. This is the New World.

You're goddamned right it is, said the official, pleased to have asserted his authority in some fashion. I'll put down Other.

Perfect, said Julius.

Married? asked the official.

Julius paused, for it was well-known that immigration officials preferred the married to the unmarried. Julius could have lied and claimed his wife was arriving on a later ship, but it wouldn't have helped; if the immigrant's spouse wasn't present, the officials considered the immigrant single. And so Julius had no choice.

No . . . , he began to say, when Julia suddenly stepped forward, took his hand in hers, and said, Yes.

You're his wife? the official asked.

Yes.

You look like his sister.

Julia's heart sank, for Cannibals share strong family resemblances. Hopeless and thinking to just run for the door, she turned around, and there in that immigration center, she saw a shocking sight: brothers kissing sisters, mothers kissing sons, and fathers kissing daughters, all of them desperate to prove they were married, to become, one and all, Americans. And so Julia turned to her brother, took his face in her hands, and kissed him, as passionately and deeply as she had ever kissed anyone before.

Julius stammered, Julia blushed, the official stamped their papers, and behold, Julius and Julia passed through the door marked WELCOME, and took the family's first steps into the New World of their dreams.

But their joy, Mudd said heavily, was short-lived. The streets weren't paved with gold. Most of them weren't paved at all. New York City was a toilet. There was too little work and not enough food. And so when Julius heard that a great man named Henry Ford was promising to pay his workers five dollars a day, a fortune in those times, he decided to pack their few belongings and head west for the land of Michigan, where he took a job, like so many other new immigrants, at the Ford Motor Company in the city of Detroit.

There too, though, the reality was not as Julius had hoped it would be. The work was brutal and dangerous, the overseers cruel, the machines relentless; should a worker's cuff get caught in one of the gears or hooks, the machine would consume him in seconds. But for these men, cold and hungry, the risk to their lives was worth the five dollars a day to care for their families. And so they came, day in and day out, by the thousands. So many workers came, in fact, that Ford changed the rules. To be eligible for the five-dollar daily salary, he decreed, each immigrant first had to be *Americanized*, a demanding process that included mandatory classes, random home inspections by Ford overseers, and the following of strict regulations. It was arduous and intense, and often demeaning, and many did not successfully complete the process. But once a year, on what he called Americanization Day, Henry Ford held a ceremony for those who did.

The event, fittingly, took place on the Fourth of July. Friends and family of those being Americanized would arrive at the appointed time to a strange sight: the plywood façade of a black cauldron, thirty feet wide by fifteen feet high, the words *Melting Pot* scrawled in large white letters across the front. After a few brief introductory comments, the ceremony began. One by one, the employees who had successfully completed their courses at the Americanization Academy would emerge, dressed in the traditional garb of their native countries. As their families watched, they would, by way of a ladder, climb up and 'into' the Melting Pot. Once inside and out of the view of the audience, each employee would shed his traditional garb, underneath which he would be wearing the black suit and necktie of the respectable American worker. He would then be handed a small American flag, and directed to the ladder on the opposite side of the Melting Pot, by which he would emerge, to the cheers of the crowd, a proud suit-wearing, flag-waving American.

Here Mudd's voice would crack with emotion.

Julius emerged from that infernal pot in tears, she said. A broken man he had entered that pot, desperate for money, but he emerged not a man at all. For what is a man but his past and his people? Without them, he is only a ghost, a shadow, a featureless shape without depth or substance. And so poor Julius climbed out the other side of that damned pot, stumbled down that damned ladder, whereupon Julia took him in her arms, and wept, saying, America: it was not worth it.

It was, said Mudd, the most woeful story in the most agonizing chapter of the entire heartbreaking history of Cannibal-Americans. Ever since, it has been the tradition that on the day of their eighteenth birthdays, young Cannibal-American men go about in black suits and ties, carrying brown leather valises with wooden handles and heavy golden clasps, to commemorate the terrible day Julius was forced to become an American.

And you kids, Mudd would say as she wiped the tears from her face, you're diving into that pot headfirst.

. . .

Seventh Seltzer opened the door to his mother's house and fell backward in time. Here history lived on, like the slasher in a horror film one thought was dead but who always manages to return for one final bludgeoning.

Hello? he called. Mudd?

Nothing had changed since he'd left: not the photos of Sixth beside the armoire, not the floral-print couch mummified for eternity in a clear vinyl slipcover, not the fading four-foot-tall poster of the University that had dominated the room since his childhood.

The sight of the University caused Seventh to shudder.

The University had been Unclish's greatest project, a vast, multimillion-dollar Cannibal-American center of learning located in New Jersey, the first of its kind in Cannibal history. The poster was composed of an artist's watercolor rendering of the exterior of the grand main hall, Cannibal-American students passing in and out through its tall arched doors, while others sat in the shade of a nearby oak, debating their people's laws and customs, longing for the Old Country, and telling stories of their blessed forefathers.

One day you'll go there, Mudd said to Seventh, and you'll be the pride of the whole university.

But that dream, like so many of Mudd's dreams, never came to be, and again the foul taste of guilt filled his mouth.

Hello? he called again. Anyone here?

The kitchen door swung open and Zero emerged, a cold compress in her hand. She stopped in her tracks to see him.

Seventh? she asked.

Zero? he gasped. Zero, my God, is that you?

Seventh hadn't seen his sister in years. She was twenty now, and had grown into a striking young woman, tall and olive-skinned with deep, dark eyes. But within those eyes, Seventh detected a weariness that he hadn't known in her before. Mudd's infirmity had no doubt taken a toll, but it was the weariness of a parent he sensed in Zero, and he remembered that just as he had taken care of her when she was a child, Zero, for years now, had been taking care of Third, who, even in his midthirties, was still developmentally just a child. Zero fed him and clothed him, took him for walks in the park, to playgrounds she didn't play in and to children's movies she had no interest in seeing. Seventh's childhood may have been marked by dysfunction and discrimination, but Zero had never had a childhood at all.

Sev, she said, hugging him tightly.

Zero-Hero, he said, using the name he'd called her when they were young. How is she?

Not good.

Was it the burgers? he asked.

She shrugged.

How many? he asked.

In total? Third was keeping count. Around thirteen thousand.

Thirteen *thousand*?

She's been eating them for three years . . .

What's a Whopper cost these days, he asked, four bucks? Five?

Six, said Zero. Double bacon, extra cheese.

That's gonna take a chunk out of the inheritance, Seventh joked. Better not tell First.

Zero smiled, and once again, for a brief moment, she was the sunny child he remembered.

Come, she said, taking him by the hand. There's not much time.

Zero led Seventh upstairs to Mudd's bedroom, where the rest of the Seltzer siblings were already waiting, all ten of them, crammed into Mudd's small bedroom around her extra-large bed.

Seventh couldn't remember the last time they had all stood in a room together. He wasn't sure they ever had; as the youngest Seltzers were just learning to stand up, the oldest were already running away.

The room reeked, a putrid combination of Whoppers and urine, like a bathroom at a truck-stop Burger King. The air was thick and heavy, suffocating, a situation made worse by the dozen adults pressed so tightly together that from the doorway Seventh couldn't even see the bed they were gathered around.

First, standing closest, as always, to the door, turned to him and nodded a dutifully somber hello. First was approaching middle age now, his hair beginning to recede and gray, but his eyes with the same intensity Seventh remembered from their youth. Seventh spotted Tenth across the way, the grief on his face a bizarre contrast to the garish, multicolored tracksuit he was wearing; he seemed to have come straight from the gym, where, judging from his physique, he spent a considerable portion of his time.

Still the warrior, thought Seventh, still waiting for war.

(I lifted two hundred pounds today, Tenth once bragged to Fourth after a triumphant afternoon at the gym, flexing his arms and chest.

Why? Fourth had asked. We have machines to do that for us now.

It was a genuine inquiry, but Tenth had tackled him and held him in a headlock until Fourth admitted that lifting heavy weights was a reasonable pursuit despite mankind's significant mechanical progress.)

Beside Tenth stood Eleventh and Twelfth—the twins, as they were known to all—wearing somber black dresses and black felt hats draped with black netted veils, delicately dabbing tissues to their noses and the corners of their mascara-stained eyes. They stepped aside to let Seventh through, their high heels clicking on the floor as they did. Seventh cringed, wishing they hadn't moved, knowing Mudd would hear their heels too. It was a vestigial reaction from his childhood, one he thought he'd left behind: wanting the twins to be free to be themselves, but worried at every turn about Mudd being hurt.

Third, towering a full two feet taller than anyone else in the room, stood at the foot of Mudd's bed, inconsolable. Zero held his huge hand in hers, trying to comfort him. Third stepped aside to let Seventh through, and there in her bed, at the center of them all, he saw Mudd, the rusty hub of the dilapidated wheel of his family.

And she was enormous.

Beyond enormous.

She had grown utterly, unfeasibly, impossibly obese, as wide now as she had always been tall; her breath was shallow and labored, and she seemed to Seventh to be asphyxiating to death beneath her own impossible mass. He wondered not how she could be dying, but how she could possibly be alive.

Discarded Burger King bags were piled high on the nightstand. Empty ketchup packets lay strewn about the linens. French fries littered the floor, as if trying to escape their certain fate.

Mudd? he asked, coming closer to her, unable to hide his shock. Mudd . . . ?

It was customary among their people for those in the late stages of their lives—and, more importantly, early stages of death—to gorge themselves with food, to put on as much weight as possible before dying, a tradition known as the Cornucopiacation, so that all who wished to Consume them could do so without limit. It began many years ago, following the Great Deprivation, the terrible time in the Old Country when their people were so hungry and poor that when they finally wasted away and died, there was little left of them to Consume. Determined to continue their traditions, the Cannibals created a dish called *Zubets*, though to call it a dish was optimistic— it was basically just a pile of the deceased's salted bones the family would gnaw on until someone lost a tooth, at which point the Consumption would be declared complete.

That was why Mudd had been eating a dozen Whoppers every day. Certain that death was approaching, she was beginning her Cornucopiacation. But death had been slower to arrive than she expected—or was unable to kill her when he did—and she had put on so much weight over the past few years that Seventh wouldn't have recognized her had he passed her on the street, assuming she could fit out the front door.

Seventh? Mudd moaned. Is that you?

Seventh took her enormous, bloated hand in his.

I'm here, Mudd, he said. I'm here.

Mudd looked up at him, her eyes glassy and dim.

You're late, she said.

There was traffic, he said. On the bridge.

What kind of an idiot takes the bridge on a weekday? she said.

Mudd, said Seventh, what's going on?

Ninth stood opposite Seventh in his white doctor's lab coat; he too must have come straight from work, but from where he stood, Seventh couldn't make out the hospital name embroidered on his chest pocket. Ninth took Mudd's other hand in his, feeling her wrist for her pulse. He looked to Seventh and shook his head. It was bad.

Mudd, Seventh said, please—let me call an ambulance.

But Mudd refused.

No, she said firmly. No cops.

No cops, said Seventh. Not no ambulances.

Where is Fifth? Mudd groaned. Is Fifth here?

Fifth was standing in the corner beside her bathroom door, his face streaked with tears.

I'm here, Mudd, he called. I'm here. Mudd, I'm so sorry . . .

You have apologized enough, my son, she said. You have apologized when your brothers wouldn't. And so to you, Fifth, I leave my heart, since you gave me yours.

Mudd, don't . . . , Fifth begged.

Mudd, said Seventh, I'm calling an ambulance. This is ridiculous. But Mudd ignored him.

Where is my Eighth? she moaned.

Eighth stood at the foot of the bed, his tearful eyes fixed on the digital clock beside Mudd's bed. Seventh knew that Eighth, ever the guardian of their laws and regulations, was watching to note the precise time of her death. Time of death was critical.

For, y'know.

That.

I'm here, Mudd, Eighth said without taking his eyes from the clock. I'm here.

Eighth, she said, you alone were my scholar. You alone studied the ways of our people. You alone committed our traditions to memory. And you alone will one day lead our people, the way your dear Unclish has. And so to you, my son, I leave my head, since it is with your head that you will redeem us.

Tears ran down Eighth's cheeks, but his eyes remained fixed on the clock.

Mudd now turned to Tenth.

Tenth, she said, her voice weak.

Mudd, said Tenth, his lip trembling. You need to hydrate . . .

My warrior, said Mudd. *Our* warrior. To you, my hero, I leave my hands, since it is with your fists that you shall protect us long after I have gone.

At this, Third fell to pieces. He simply could not bear to hear the mention of his mother's death. His shoulders hunched up around his ears, and his face grew red as he tried to hold back his grief, until he could withstand it no longer and he threw his head back and wailed. It pained them all to see Third cry—he was, in his innocence and guilelessness, the beating, unprotected heart of the family—and the others now, too, began to weep.

To you, Third, Mudd said, to you who stood by me until my very last hour, to you who stayed with me when the others walked away, to you I leave my arms, since with your own mighty arms you always supported me.

Mudd, said Seventh, enough of this. I'm calling for help.

And now to you, my dear Seventh, she continued, who made it your mission since youth to hold this family together, to you, my son, I leave my skin, as it held me together. May you hold our people together ever more.

She began to cough, wincing as pain tore through her.

If we're going to call a doctor, Ninth said to Seventh, it has to be now.

You *are* a doctor, Seventh said.

I'm a veterinarian, said Ninth.

That seems appropriate, said First.

Tenth glared at him.

Watch it, he said.

Blow me, said First.

The sound of First's voice seemed to pull Mudd back from death's dark door. She lifted her head to lay her eyes on him, and whatever small flame was left in her was suddenly rekindled.

And now, she said with renewed vigor and disgust, her gaze

fixed upon him, for the rest of you. The deserters. The traitors. The melters. You who left me. Who left your people.

She turned her head to Second.

To you, Second, who married a Sherwood, I leave my feet, since you ran from your people to someone else's.

Married a Sherwood? thought Seventh. *Second?*

Seventh felt a sudden surge of anger rise within him.

Second had married a Jew?

Why?

And why, more importantly, did he care? He himself had left his people, why shouldn't Second? And yet somehow—perhaps because Mudd was dying, perhaps because Third was crying, perhaps because Eighth wouldn't take his eyes off that damned bedside clock— Seventh felt somehow betrayed.

Betrayed?

Yes, betrayed.

Did he have to marry a *Jew*?

And then, immediately, Seventh shuddered, hating himself for thinking it.

Fetal Asshole Syndrome.

Good, Seventh thought. Good for Second. Good for him. I'm happy for him, good.

To Fourth, Mudd continued, the man of *science* (she said this word with the same contempt she had since their youth), the one who could have written books about our people but chose instead to write about others, to you I leave my tongue, since you used yours against us. To Ninth, the lover of men, who chose pleasure over preservation, to you I leave my legs, since you pulled mine out from under me. To Eleventh and Twelfth, who might have brought forth a new generation but chose to become women instead, I leave my genitals. Since you hate yours so much, maybe you'll like mine. And to Zero, who gave me zero, I leave nothing.

Pain tore through her once more, and she twisted, wracked with agony.

The end was close. All that sustained her now was her rage.

And lastly, she growled through her clenched and yellowed teeth, to my First. The first who left me, the first who betrayed me, the first who dove headfirst into the melting pot the great Julius so disdained, the first to be worse than Jack Nicholson—to you, First, I leave my ass.

She winced again.

So you can kiss it, she said.

First smiled bitterly.

Aw, Mudd, he said. You shouldn't have.

She closed her eyes, concentrating on her uneasy breath.

Children, she said, you were born in this house, and now I will die in it. It has stood, while so many of you have fallen. I bought it for a pittance, many years ago, and now it is worth a fortune. And if you want your share of that fortune, you will honor this, my final request.

Of course, said Eighth.

Anything, wept Tenth.

A fortune? First asked.

Mudd, stop this, said Seventh. You're not dying, for God's sake. Let me call someone.

He reached for his phone, but Mudd grabbed his wrist, locking it in place beside her, and she looked up at him, her eyes growing wide as her soul began to depart this world. With her great hand she pulled him close, and with her final breath, whispered the words he knew she would say, the words she'd been waiting her whole life to say, the words he couldn't even think, let alone utter.

Eat me, she said.

She pulled him closer, her dying eyes burning into his:

Eat me.

And Seventh, despite every promise he'd made to himself over the years, wiped his tears and said what he had always known he would:

Yes, Mudd, he said. Yes.

And only then did Mudd release his arm, and her hand dropped back to the bed, and the pain disappeared from her face.

And Mudd was dead.

. . .

Three years ago, after learning that Mudd had been eating Whoppers, Seventh phoned Dr. Isaacson. This was some time after Seventh had stopped his treatment, but he was at a loss as to how to deal with the news and needed help. He felt himself spiraling, and couldn't go to Carol for support.

It's my mother, he said to Dr. Isaacson. She's trying to kill herself.

Then call the police, Dr. Isaacson said.

She's eating Whoppers.

The malted milk balls?

The burgers, said Seventh. Double bacon, extra cheese, no lettuce.

Then call a nutritionist, said Dr. Isaacson.

It's a tradition.

Eating Whoppers is a tradition?

Fattening yourself up is a tradition, said Seventh. Before you die.

A tradition for who? Dr. Isaacson asked.

I told you, said Seventh. For . . . us.

Your unique cultural heritage, said Dr. Isaacson.

Seventh hesitated.

Yes, he said.

He could hear Dr. Isaacson sigh heavily.

I don't see any reason to resume your therapy, Mr. Seltzer, said Dr. Isaacson, if you're not willing, at minimum, to tell me who you are.

And Dr. Isaacson hung up.

But that, thought Seventh, is precisely what I'm trying to figure out.

· · ·

It was following the death of his father that Montaigne locked himself away in his library to begin his project of writing about himself—his thoughts, his fears, his loves, his insecurities.

Others form Man, he wrote. *I give an account of Man and sketch a picture of a particular one of them who is very badly formed.*

Who am I? Montaigne essentially wondered five hundred years ago. *What's my story?* And now Seventh, in the wake of the death of his mother, wondered the same thing. Because for all of Montaigne's honesty and self-awareness, for all his humanity and insight, what most interested Seventh about him had always been this:

His name wasn't Montaigne.

His name was Eyquem.

Michel had given up the name of his ancestors.

He had turned his back on his people.

Did Michel de Montaigne, one of the most significant figures of the Enlightenment, the paragon of free thought and independence, the man who influenced everyone from Descartes to Emerson to Shakespeare—did Michel want to melt?

I am not portraying being, Montaigne wrote, *but becoming.*

Sounds like melting to me, thought Seventh.

. . .

Father told his sons a very different version of the Julius-Coming-to-America story from the one Mudd had.

The year was 1914, said Father, when Julius Seltzer, son of Samuel Seltzer, son of some other Seltzer, left the Old Country for the New World, mere days after his eighteenth birthday, with little more than the shirt on his back.

What was the Old Country like? young Seventh had asked, wanting to hear again of the meadows and the hills and the oversize fruit.

The Old Country, Father said, was a toilet, with dirt roads and open sewers and pestilence and misery. At last, Samuel decided it was time to leave.

Because of the king? offered Seventh.

What king?

The new king.

There was no king, said Father. The Old Country was governed by a loose alliance of tribal leaders organized around a powerless executive branch propped up over the years by various global super-powers.

Oh, said Seventh.

It was time to leave, Father said, because Samuel wanted a better life for his children than the Old Country could provide. And so one night, under the cover of darkness, he took Julius and his younger sister, Julia, to the dock, where he handed Julius a brown leather valise with a wooden handle and heavy golden clasps, inside which lay the ancient Knife of Redemption, with which the sacred Consumption rite had been performed throughout the ages.

Take this with you, Samuel said to Julius.

So that I never forget who I am or where I came from? asked Julius.

No, said Samuel. Because it's the only thing we have of any value. Take it with you, hock it for some cash, and move on with your life. Forget who you are, Julius, and forget where you came from.

Julius resisted. He had been raised to love his traditions and his past, and his people defined who he was. He was not just Julius Seltzer. He was a proud Cannibal-Whatever-Country-They-Were-Inian, and he always would be.

But Father, Julius begged, how can I just throw away all those years of history and ignore all that our people have been through?

Samuel clopped him on the head with the back of his hand.

Don't be stupid, he said. The past is an anchor, my son, chained at one end to our ankles and buried in the mud of history at the other. It drags us down; it keeps us from moving forward. Darwin, who was Cannibal, said we come from monkeys. Should we then climb into trees and swing from vines because our ancestors did?

Should we eat bugs, throw shit at each other, and fight over bananas? No—we move ahead. We progress. We leave the jungle behind. Now go! If you want to help your people, help all people, because all people are your people. Go. Go and go forward, Julius. The future awaits.

How difficult it was for Julius to do as his father had commanded! He resisted, and spent the first days and nights on that ship clutching that brown valise to his chest, refusing to let it go. But soon, said Father, he did forget, and he did move on. Because what he discovered there on that old ship was something far more valuable than any ancient valise.

You see, Father explained, Julius and Julia were not the only ones on that ship looking for something new. They were not the only ones looking to escape their past. All the passengers, they soon learned—from different pasts and different nations and different races and different religions—shared a common dream, a crazy dream, a beautiful dream, a dream that in all the history of mankind had never been dreamed of before: the dream of a shared future. While the rest of the world fixed their eyes on the past, the huddled immigrants were defiantly looking forward. Where they had come from individually was less important than where they were going together.

Mad, they were, said Father. Insane, even. But all prophets are.

And so, Father continued, eight harrowing weeks at sea later, as Julius and Julia stood on the deck of the SS *Expedition* and peered up at the Statue of Liberty, they wept, strangers hugging strangers, because the bleak, bestial world of difference and division was far behind them, and here in the New World, mankind would live as one. Without so much as a single question, the immigration official stamped their papers and welcomed them with a smile to the New World.

Wherever you are from, he said, now you are home.

And with that, Julius and Julia Seltzer took the family's very first steps into America. Soon after, needing money, Julius remembered his father's words, and he brought the old valise to a pawnshop to try to sell the Knife of Redemption as his father had commanded him. He lifted the valise onto the counter, and explained that what lay inside it was a cherished and antique family heirloom that it broke his heart to part with, but that his father had commanded him to sell.

The shopkeeper offered him a nickel.

A second shop offered him a dime.

A third shop offered him a pair of shoes in trade, and threw in a straw hat, badly in need of blocking, for Julia.

Julius couldn't do it. To part with such an important piece of his unique cultural heritage for so little was more than he could bear.

I would rather starve, he snapped at the shopkeeper.

That's always an option, the shopkeeper replied.

The customer behind him, though, realizing Julius was in need of work, took him aside and told him that a man named Henry Ford was promising to pay his workers five dollars a day—a fortune in those times—in exchange for helping him build his cars. Julius couldn't believe his good luck. He decided to keep the valise, and the very next day, he and Julia set out for Michigan.

Julius's experience at the Ford factory, said Father, was as inspiring as the one on the ship had been. There on the assembly line, Germans worked beside Japanese who worked beside Russians who worked beside Africans. None thought himself better than the rest, and all worked together to build their dream. And so when Julius was at last accepted into the Americanization program, he wept with joy. Americanization Day came, and when the ceremony was over, Julius held Julia in his arms and wept with joy, saying, America: was it not worth it?

Hang on, Seventh asked.

What?

I thought he said, America: it was not worth it.

Father shook his head.

No, said Father. He said, America: was it not worth it?

Seventh was confused.

But wasn't this the most painful story in the most agonizing chapter of the entire heartbreaking history of Cannibal-Americans? he asked.

No, said Father. It was the most uplifting story in the most miraculous chapter of the history of Cannibal-Americans.

So uplifting was it, Father said, that ever since, it has been a tradition among Cannibal-Americans that young men, on the day of their eighteenth birthdays, go about in black suits and red ties, carrying brown leather valises with wooden handles and heavy golden clasps, to commemorate the wonderful day Julius finally became an American.

Mudd and Father held fast to their particular versions of the story. In fact, Seventh would later learn, it wasn't just his parents who disagreed about the Julius-Coming-to-America story, it was all Can-Ams; the conflicting narratives bitterly divided the Cannibal-American community, some holding by the It-Was version, some holding by the Was-It version, and both having nothing but contempt for those who held otherwise. The infighting might have eventually destroyed the community but for the fortunate happenstance that the commemorations of both versions were identical in practice—suits, ties, valises—so that nobody could say for certain who was commemorating what, or for what reason. Disaster was thus avoided, but the conflict between the two groups was never resolved and the enmity never waned, and so it was that the foundational story of the Cannibal-American people not only held them together, it also drove them apart.

As Father finished his tale, his voice cracked with emotion.

Your great-grandfather Julius was a great man, he said, wiping a tear from his cheek. In his entire life, he only made one mistake.

What was that? asked Seventh.

He never did sell the Knife of Redemption, Father said. He just couldn't do it. He kept it, in that ancient valise, and took it with him wherever he went. That was his only failing, Seventh; even with all his courage, he still held on to the past. He should have thrown the damned thing overboard.

Into the sea, Father said as he got to his feet.

And then, with a heavy sigh, he added:

With the rest of that ancient bullshit.

. . .

Of the BD children, only Third agreed to celebrate his eighteenth birthday in the traditional manner. Mudd bought him a black suit at the Big & Tall Shop, and a red tie, and found an old brown valise at the Goodwill store in Fort Greene.

Look at me! Third said excitedly as Mudd fixed his necktie. I'm Julius!

Mudd clopped him on the head with the back of her hand.

It's a *sad* day, she said.

Oopsie, said Third, fixing his expression appropriately.

First, Second, Fourth, and Fifth had, on their eighteenth birth-days, flatly refused to perform the ritual. Seventh would have re-fused too, but he was the first child after Sixth, and on what would have been Sixth's eighteenth birthday, Mudd wept so bitterly that when Seventh's time came, a year later, he agreed to wear a suit even though he didn't want to.

He sat inside the whole day, refusing to go outside for even a moment.

But you have to go about, Mudd scolded him. The Elders said you have to go about!

I'm not going about, said Seventh. I'm going to my room.

A disgrace, Mudd growled. You children are a disgrace to your people.

She stormed upstairs, stamping so hard that the walls trembled and the poster of the University tilted on its hook.

What would Julius say? she asked as she slammed her bedroom door.

Seventh, slumped in his ill-fitting suit on the vinyl-covered couch, thought what he always thought when she said that:

Which one?

. . .

Some say Montaigne locked himself away in his library not be-cause of the death of his father, but because of the death of his friend Étienne de La Boétie. Others say Montaigne locked himself

69

away in his library not because of the death of his father or because of the death of his friend Étienne de La Boétie, but because of the many wars in France at the time. Others say that Montaigne locked himself away in his library not because of the death of his father or because of the death of his friend Étienne de La Boétie or because of the many wars in France at the time, but simply because his political career had fizzled out.

It was this last theory, part of a six-hundred-page biography he was reading, that rankled Seventh the most (A new Montaigne, the *Times* had raved. It's about time!). Montaigne, the author claimed, was merely a political opportunist trying to become a nobleman; he only wrote his *Essays* because that was what noblemen were expected to do, and he only wrote about the self and identity because he didn't have the courage to write about politics.

This was part of another publishing trend Seventh disdained, one he referred to as Contemporary Assholization Studies, in which an author chooses the most beloved historical figure one can find and ascribes to him or her the most contemptible motivations one can imagine.

One star, he wrote on the book's Amazon page, *because I couldn't give it none*.

He hated people who left that review.

But sometimes, he knew, you had to fight asshole with asshole.

. . .

Seventh first started seeing Dr. Isaacson because he suspected he was an asshole.

You're not an asshole, said Dr. Isaacson.

Seventh vehemently disagreed. On paper, sure, he was a good person: a loving father, a good spouse, a loyal friend. But that didn't tell the whole story. He'd hurt his mother, he'd failed his family, he'd hurt his people.

Dr. Isaacson tried to convince Seventh that he wasn't bad. And that he wasn't a cannibal. In fact, it was his professional opinion that Seventh's claim of cannibalism was merely the external manifestation of a damaged inner child that saw itself as fundamentally evil— a self-image created by his narcissistic, overbearing mother and the coward father who abandoned him.

You're a good person, Seventh, said Dr. Isaacson.

I'm an asshole.

Dr. Isaacson sighed.

Do you cheat on your wife? he asked.

No.

Do you beat your child?

No.

Have you ever killed a person?

Seventh thought a moment.

No, he had said.

Now, standing in Mudd's bedroom staring down at her corpse, he thought otherwise.

He thought: I killed a whole people.

Eighth cranked open the window above Mudd's bed, letting the bitter winter air fill the room.

It will keep the body cold, he said. Until we figure this out.

The Seltzer siblings traipsed down to the living room in silence. Second went straight to the kitchen, emerging a moment later with a bottle of whiskey his grateful siblings began to pass around.

Third sat stricken on the couch, his hand in Zero's. Seventh sat beside her, Mudd's last words still warm against his ear.

Eat me.

Is that a thing? Zero asked Seventh. What she was doing up there? Giving out . . . parts?

Seventh nodded.

It's called the Allocation, he said.

The Apportioning, Tenth corrected him.

It's called the Assigning, said Second, taking a pull of the whiskey. I'm pretty sure it's called the Assigning.

It galled Seventh to hear Second opine on their traditions.

Thanks, Rabbi, he thought.

It's called the Disbursement, Eighth said definitively as he searched the living room bookcase. It has to be here somewhere . . .

What? asked Second.

The Guide, said Eighth.

The Guide? asked Ninth. I thought you knew that thing by heart.

That was a long time ago, said Eighth.

The Guide—its official title was *The Complete Guide to Field-Dressing and Processing Your Deer*—was a complete compendium of Cannibal law in the guise of a simple hunting handbook. It had been composed by Unclish when he was just a young man, but even at that early age he was already considered to be the preeminent authority on their people's rules and regulations. It was an ingenious way for their people to commit their traditions to paper—to hide, as it were, in plain sight—codifying their laws and educating their young without risking either prosecution or persecution. It quickly rose to number one in Amazon's Survivalism category, as without revealing their identity, Cannibals seeking guidance and information could simply consult The Guide, replace the word *deer* with *Mother* or *Father* or *Sally* or *Bob*, and none would be the wiser.

The deer must be killed quickly, with little or no pain or fear; fear triggers the release of adrenaline, which can affect the quality of the meat. (14:2–3)

The deer must be drained of its blood immediately, or risk contamination by bacteria. (7:14)

Heat butter in a large skillet over medium heat. Add deer and sauté until browned. (3:16)

First reached for the whiskey.

It's freezing in here, he said. Someone turn up the heat.

We have to keep her cold, said Eighth.

I thought she was pretty cold to begin with, First said with a grin.

Tenth glared at him. You didn't deserve a mother like her, he said.

Who does? asked First. Stalin. Mao, maybe . . .

Second snickered.

Tenth ground his teeth.

Seventh could hear Mudd's voice in his ear:

Eat me.

Did she really expect him . . . them . . . to do . . . that? It was insane. Forget insane, it was a felony: improperly disposing of a body. He remembered the day last year when the governor of New York, Governor Cuomo, signed it into law. Mudd phoned him that evening, beside herself.

Does that goddamned guinea think I was born yesterday? she railed. I should make eating a cannoli a felony, let's see how he likes it. He'd have his Mafia thugs after me in a heartbeat.

Although, Seventh knew, there were ways.

To do . . . it.

Without being caught.

Without leaving a trace.

Certain . . . methods.

Theirs was an ancient people, after all. They knew things. Techniques. It had never been easy to practice their rituals; only in the Old Country were they free to openly perform their sacred funerary rites. Everywhere else, in every other time, they had to do so in the shadows. But perform it they did, Seventh knew, for centuries, without incident. Without arrest. Without prosecution.

Her ass, you believe that? First was saying. That's what she left me. Eighth, you're the big scholar—are we talking cheeks or asshole?

You're the asshole, said Tenth.

The buttocks, Eighth replied, still searching the bookcase.

He looked behind the books, on top of the case. Nothing.

The anus and rectum are removed during Purging, he said.

Well, that's some relief, said First. Who does the removing? Because I'm telling you now, I'm not doing any fucking *removing* . . .

Eighth stepped back from the bookcase, concerned.

It's not here, he said. I'm going to check the kitchen.

Don't complain about getting her ass, Fourth said to First. I got her tongue. Comparatively speaking, you got off easy.

Seventh couldn't believe that he was even considering her request. He was an editor, for Christ's sake; he cut up sentences, not people. Besides, how could they do it, even if they wanted to? Not a single one of them had ever even witnessed an actual Consumption before, let alone performed one themselves—to say nothing of

Draining, Purging, and Partitioning. Sixth had been Consumed, sure, but Unclish had performed those Victuals alone; Mudd had expressly prohibited the brothers from attending, saying they were too young. Mudd's last wish or not, Seventh knew they had no idea what to do, or how to do it. And they were in the middle of Brooklyn. Crazy shit went down in Brooklyn, but not cannibalism-crazy.

How is tongue worse than ass? First asked Fourth. Two bites and you're done.

It's not a question of quantity, said Fourth. That tongue was my mother's. It's practically incest.

We got her vagina, said Eleventh. Don't talk to me about incest.

You're not supposed to fuck it, said First, just eat it.

Just eat it? said Twelfth.

I got her feet, said Second. Did you *see* her feet? Tongue's gross, but at least a mouth is sterile.

That's a canine mouth, said Ninth. The human mouth is a cesspool.

Seventh went to the living room window and opened the blinds. Outside, pedestrians hurried back and forth, buried in their coats and hats, leaning into the biting wind.

How long he had longed to be one of them.

The Others.

The living room window had been through changes; it was the only part of the house that had. In the early days, when the Can-Am community was thriving and friends waved to Mudd through the window and asked about the family, she had hung about it the sheerest of curtains, and sunlight filled the room. But as the community dwindled, the window treatments grew heavier. Sheers were replaced by solids, solids by blackouts. But even blackouts weren't enough to hide Mudd from black people; when they moved in, so did the venetian blinds, solid strips of metal that were forever closed, day and night, from the moment they were installed.

Only good thing those lousy Italians ever did for us, Mudd said as she twisted them shut for eternity.

Venetian blinds aren't from Venice, Fourth informed her. They originated in France.

My mistake, said Mudd. Only good thing those lousy *French* ever did for us.

When Latinos appeared, so did the iron security bars, and at last, Seventh's prison, built from the inside out, was complete.

Then again, Seventh thought, Brooklyn did have a history of lunatics chopping up bodies and cooking them. It certainly wouldn't be the first time. There was that cop they arrested a few years ago for planning to eat women. And Albert Fish, back in the twenties.

But they were caught, you see?

That's the whole point.

You don't eat someone, call for the check, and just walk away. Fish got the fucking *chair*.

But then Fish wasn't Cannibal. He was *a* cannibal. A real Cannibal wouldn't have been caught. Anytime you hear about a cannibal being caught by police, trust me—he isn't Cannibal.

You want to trade? First offered Second.

Feet for ass? said Second. No way.

I'll take feet for tongue, said Fourth.

You can't trade, said Tenth.

Why not? asked First.

It's not allowed, said Tenth.

I'm surprised she didn't give *you* her ass, First said to Tenth. You've been kissing it long enough.

Tenth stood and unzipped his track jacket, preparing to fight.

Keep pushing me, First, he said. Just keep pushing me.

Forget about if they could get away with it, thought Seventh. Forget about if he could get them all to agree to it. The real question was, did she deserve it? According to the Ancient Ones, it was among the greatest of honors to be Consumed, and among the greatest of dishonors to be buried. Seventh didn't think Mudd deserved either. Who did, after all? How many people deserve the greatest honor or the greatest dishonor? A handful, tops, in all the history of man. Most of us fall somewhere in the middle, with our heads neither held high with pride nor hung low in shame; we are, on average, average. But those were his only choices; if he didn't give her the greatest honor, he was giving her the greatest dishonor.

Did she deserve that?

The greatest dishonor?

Mudd wasn't perfect, Seventh thought, far from it. But she had her moments, and as he stood staring out the living room window, he recalled a story from his youth that he hadn't thought about in years.

It happened not long after Father had left. Seventh, just ten years old at the time, had become anxious and withdrawn. Between the death of his older brother Sixth and the abandonment by his father, his whole world had been upended, and he grew fearful and timid. The fourth-grade bully, Oscar Kowalski, sensing weakness as bullies do, targeted Seventh for abuse. As part of that abuse, he decided that Seventh was a cannibal.

There had been rumors of cannibals in Brooklyn for years. The rumor was true but unproven, and nobody could ever produce any evidence that such a community existed. Oscar, though, thought it fun to accuse Seventh of being one of the mysterious despised savages, and so day after day, he and his minions terrorized Seventh, stole his lunch, knocked his books to the floor, and called him a dirty cannibal.

Seventh begged Mudd to let him stay home from school, but she wouldn't hear of it.

Last time I checked, she said, this was a free country. That'll change soon enough, like all the other countries before it, but until it does, you've got as much right to go to school as the next boy. Now get dressed, you're going.

Seventh trembled as he walked to school that day. He considered running away, disappearing. But Mudd had always taught her sons that a Cannibal never runs away from a fight, and if she ever heard that one of them had, they were going to have to run away from her too.

How will running away from you teach us not to run away from others? Fourth had asked.

Mudd clopped him on the head with the back of her hand.

Don't be stupid, she said.

When Seventh got to school, he found Oscar was waiting for him in the schoolyard, together with his grinning, knuckle-dragging minions.

All right, cannibal, said Oscar. It's you and me.

Leave me alone, begged Seventh.

But Oscar just shoved Seventh to the ground, and his henchmen laughed and cheered him on.

I'm tired of you animals ruining our neighborhood, Oscar said.

He straddled Seventh's chest, pinning his arms beneath his knees. He grinned down at Seventh, whose tears betrayed him and ran down his cheeks. Oscar raised his fist overhead, and was about to start pummeling Seventh, when a long dark shadow fell across them. It fell across Oscar and it fell across his gang. It fell across the schoolyard, it fell across the school, and it fell across all of Brooklyn.

Seventh opened his eyes.

It was Mudd, blocking out the sun, her massive arms crossed over her massive bosom, glaring down at Oscar with a thousand years of oppression in her eyes.

Mudd didn't leave the house very often, even before Sixth's death, and she never left at all once he passed away. Few in the community had ever seen her. And so when Oscar Kowalski turned around to find, looming over him, the largest human being he'd ever seen, his grin disappeared and the blood ran from his face.

Good morning, boys, Mudd said.

Whooaaa, said one of Oscar's henchmen, stepping backward as he did.

What the *fuck?* whispered another. They turned and ran for the safety of the school door.

Oscar climbed off Seventh and scrambled to his feet.

Wh-who are you? he asked.

I'm Seventh's mother, Mudd said pleasantly. You must be Oscar. Kowalski—that's a Polack name, isn't it?

She held out her hand to him, and Oscar, afraid to refuse the fearsome giant, slowly took it. She closed her hand around his, engulfing his arm from fingers to elbow.

That's a nice shirt, she said, squeezing his hand tightly. You look positively *delicious* in it.

Oscar swallowed hard, and began to tremble. Now the rest of his gang turned and ran screaming into the school, the heavy steel door slamming loudly behind them.

Oscar tried to pull his hand from hers, but Mudd held him fast.

I'm famished, said Mudd. I better get going. It was very nice meeting you, Oscar. We'd love to have you for dinner.

Now Oscar began to panic. His chin trembled and his eyes filled with fear, and he tried with all his might to free himself from her grip, but to no avail. Just then the front door of the school opened and a group of indignant faculty members emerged, all shirtsleeves and loosened ties and hands on hips, wondering just what all the commotion was about. Their perturbation disappeared, though, the moment they laid eyes upon Mudd, and the principal, stopping dead in her tracks, said, Whoa.

Mudd smiled politely at the teachers.

Such sweet children, she said, then leaned over and pinched Oscar's cheek. Why, she said, looking him dead in the eye, I could just eat . . . you . . . *up*.

And then she released his hand, turned, and headed for home.

Seventh, still peering out the living room window, remembered standing in the front yard of the school, long after the bell for class rang, watching her lumber away. Passersby gawked. Dogs barked. Children pointed and laughed.

He felt an arm around his shoulder.

You okay? Zero asked.

He shrugged. Okay, he said.

She was a good mother, said Zero.

He shrugged again. Okay, he said.

Zero smiled.

Well, she said, she was a mother. Let's leave it at that.

. . .

We need a novel, Mudd said to Seventh. He was fifteen years old.

We need a novel, and you're going to write it.

Mudd primarily bore children so that they would in turn bear children of their own, but reproduction was not their only duty to their people. Each child had their own secondary mission, which Mudd assigned them based on their specific talents and abilities: those born with indomitable strength she expected to be their defenders; those possessing charisma she expected to become their leaders; those gifted with sensitivity she expected to get over it; and those with a facility with words she expected to tell their people's story.

Our people aren't going to get an ounce of respect until we have a novel, she said. A great Cannibal novel. Sherwoods have novels, blacks have novels, Sumerians have novels, hell, even the gays have a novel or two.

She assumed Fourth would write it, what with his early acumen and love of reading. Once he entered college, though, he decided to pursue anthropology instead of literature—or, as Mudd phrased it, to write about monkeys instead of his own people. Seventh was just beginning high school at the time, and she turned to him for the novel she believed would deliver them from the shadows.

Write it, Seventh. For me. Full of romance and adventure, of war and heroes, of oppression and survival. Like that mick, what's-his-name, James Michener.

James Michener wasn't Irish, Fourth corrected her. He was an orphan. It's impossible to say where he was from.

Well then he wasn't *not* Irish, was he, Monkey Boy? said Mudd.

Seventh was never good at saying no to Mudd, and so he said yes. He spent hours after school at the library, reading every family saga he could find. He studied their structures, he studied their character arcs, he studied their themes. In the end, though, they weren't the inspiration he'd hoped for. In fact, they bored him. It may have just been adolescent cynicism, but he found their stories tediously alike and thus tediously unlikely, overly full of romance and adventure, of war and heroes, of oppression and survival, laden with self-aggrandizement and victimization, with hagiographic tales that beggared belief, and with the same bigotry by the heroes that the heroes decried being subjected to themselves.

Mudd smiled to hear him describe them, and handed him a box of pre-sharpened pencils.

It sounds good already, she said.

A year later, Seventh completed his novel, which he titled, in honor of his mother, *Out of the Shadows*. He placed the manuscript in a box, and presented it to Mudd for her birthday. She read it that night, declaring it the next morning the finest novel she had ever read, and predicting it would do for Cannibal-Americans what *One Hundred Years of Solitude* had done for the Mexicans, who were taking over their bodegas.

But it was not to be. Seventh's novel was rejected by every publisher who bothered to read it, and many more who didn't.

If it's fiction, it's ludicrous, one editor said, summing up the feelings of most. If it's nonfiction, it's worse.

Mudd blamed the publishers—the Jews, the Germans, the British, the Chinese.

The Chinese? Seventh asked. They own publishing houses?

They own everything, goddammit, said Mudd.

. . .

Ah, yes—the old *Antagonist-with-a-Heart-of-Gold.*

It was Seventh's most despised narrative trick. Pure cliché. Give the antagonist a little depth, a little shading.

The savage killer.

Who saves the baby.

The creepy pedophile.

Who murders the even creepier pedophile.

The narcissistic mother.

Who once stood up for her son.

The reader wonders, Well, maybe the mother was good? Maybe things aren't so black-and-white?

It was a sin he despised, and yet he had just committed it himself.

She stood up for him. Once. And maybe not even once. Maybe she was just standing up for Cannibals.

That was why he hated the device so much. It wasn't about giving the antagonist depth. It wasn't about creating a rounded character. It was about the writer patting himself on the back for his noble objectivity, for his boundless largesse, for his preternatural generosity of spirit.

Bullshit, thought Seventh.

Sometimes impartiality was just cowardice.

Sometimes even-handedness was servility.

And yet there she was in his mind's eye, his mother, his antagonist, Mudd, moving slowly down the street, burdened by her own being, head hung low as people pointed at her from their cars and frightened children cowered behind their wary parents.

Sad music.

Fade to black.

Scene.

Dick.

. . .

When Zero was a baby, First was eighteen. It was the time of his most vociferous battles with Mudd. Zero would cry to hear the yelling and fighting, the slamming doors, the shattering cups and vases. Seventh, a child himself at the time, would pull her from her high chair and rush her upstairs to his bedroom, where he would close the door tightly, lay her on the bed, and place his hands over her ears so that she couldn't hear the war waging around her.

They're just playing, Zero-Hero, he would whisper softly to her, his own tears mixing with hers. It's okay, Zero-Hero; they're just playing . . .

. . .

It was Father's idea to send Seventh away to summer camp. Seventh didn't want to go, but Father was adamant that he get out there and meet some people. People, he meant, from other communities and other backgrounds. Mudd was opposed, fearing the influence the other children and counselors might have on him, certain they would lure him away from his own community. But Father insisted, and Mudd, pregnant and tired, didn't possess the strength to argue.

Seventh hated camp. He felt isolated, different. He could find no common ground with the other campers, and lived in fear of being discovered, of the other children learning who he was and where he came from. While the other kids swam and played baseball, Seventh spent his days at the front office, begging to be sent home.

Lots of children miss home, said the camp director.

I don't miss home, said Seventh. I just hate it here.

At night, while the other kids roasted marshmallows and sang songs, Seventh went to bed, lay down, and tried to come up with a way to escape and return home. He thought about Julius, and about how long and difficult his own journey to freedom had been, and about how much courage it took for him to go forth on his own. And so, thus inspired, one night, Seventh left. He waited until his counselors were asleep, took a flashlight and what little money he had, snuck past the front office to the main road, and began to walk. He had no idea where he was going, whether he was getting farther from home or closer. But what did Julius know on that boat? What did he know when he set out for Detroit? The dark woods frightened him, but he refused to turn back. He managed to get three miles away before being spotted by a gas station attendant. The police arrived and drove him back to camp, and the camp director, embarrassed and deeming Seventh an unacceptable insurance risk, sent him home. His parents were livid.

But Julius went on a journey and you said he was a hero! Seventh cried.

Mudd clopped him on the back of the head.

How dare you compare yourself to Julius! she said, and grounded him for a month.

The punishment didn't bother Seventh in the least. He was ecstatic to be back in Brooklyn, and for the first time in weeks, he fell asleep without crying. Downstairs, though, Mudd and Father began to fight.

You made him afraid of other people, Father shouted.

He was smart to come back, Mudd replied. He knows where he belongs!

You'd be happy if he never left!

You'd be happy if he never returned!

Tenth, just a baby at the time, began to cry.

Seventh went to him, bent low over his crib, and covered his ears.

It's okay, Ten-Ten, he said. They're just playing.

And then Seventh went back to his bed, lay down, and tried to come up with a way to escape and return to camp.

. . .

Montaigne was a liberal humanist, say the liberal humanists.

Montaigne was a religious conservative, say the religious conservatives.

Montaigne was Jewish, say the Jews.

Montaigne was a firm Roman Catholic, say the Roman Catholics.

Montaigne: *When they asked Socrates where he came from he did not say From Athens, but From the world.*

. . .

Mudd hated the term *Cannibal-American.*

You think it matters what you call yourself? she said. It's what they call you that matters, and they're calling you a savage. They're calling you a headhunter.

Montaigne again: *Every moment it seems to me that I am running away from myself.*

That confession gave Seventh comfort. Everywhere around him, people were loudly proclaiming who they were. But Montaigne, dead four hundred years, was offering something different:

Maybe you didn't have to know who you were.

Maybe that was no great achievement.

Maybe it was enough—maybe it was the very beginning of wisdom itself—just to know who you weren't.

. . .

Julius was the pioneer, the brave forefather who left his own parents and the blessed Old Country behind and brought their people to the New World hoping for better lives. His fearlessness was an inspiration for all subsequent generations of Cannibal-Americans to never stop searching for a Cannibal homeland, and to never let fear hold them back. They knew him, one and all, as Julius the Brave.

His wife-sister, Julia, though, was their people's martyr, and Mudd took a special satisfaction in telling her story. No woman had ever suffered as much as Julia, said Mudd. She was slapped, kicked, chased, pummeled, and mauled; she suffered from the moment of her birth to the moment of her death, and it was said that there had been only a handful of days in all her seventy-two years when she wasn't covered in blood. On one of those days, Mudd said, Julius himself didn't recognize her. He shouted in fear to see a strange woman in his home, and the police came and, believing her to be black, beat her with their clubs until she bled. Only then did Julius realize it was Julia, and he begged the officers to cease.

Crucifixion? Mudd said. Crucifixion was a cakewalk. Julia would have killed to be crucified.

Her suffering was an inspiration for all subsequent generations of Cannibals: to never surrender, to never succumb, to never give in to oppression and hate. They knew her, one and all, as Julia the Anguished.

In her youth, though, said Mudd, she was known as Julia the Beautiful. She was the most beautiful woman who ever lived, and when she and her brother, Julius, who was the most handsome man who ever lived, arrived in the New World, all the men of all the nations desired her, and some even desired Julius (Animals, Mudd said). But Julia's heart belonged only to her people, and so she married her brother, as she desired Cannibal children and hoped that being betrothed would protect her from the lecherous desires of the men of the New World. But the covetous men of the other nations did not care that she was married, and when she would not give them what they desired, they either took it by force or destroyed it. If she wasn't raped, she was beaten; her nose was broken, her teeth knocked out; she was racked, stretched, broken on the wheel, and hung in a cage in the town square, where passersby would mock her and pelt her with stones. But such was Julia's beauty that even with half her comeliness, she was still more desirable than the most beautiful women of the other nations.

And so, Mudd said, one morning, as he was going to work, Henry Ford saw Julia in her cage, and his heart filled with desire for her. Detroit was Ford's town by then, and he immediately had Julia uncaged, and cared for by the city's finest physicians, and from the steps of his palace he forbade anyone to ever cause her harm.

Palace? Seventh asked.

Practically, said Mudd.

But the price to be paid for her rescue was steep: Ford declared Julia his own, a possession with no more freedoms or rights than one of his automobiles. If she didn't submit to his dark desires, he warned her, or spoke of them to anyone, he would fire her husband and throw the both of them into the street. It was the early days of the Great Depression, and Julia knew they could not risk being without employment. Ford gave Julius longer hours on the line so he could have more time with Julia alone, and assigned him to the most dangerous machines, hoping he might be killed and Julia would be his forever.

Here Mudd's voice would fill with emotion as she told her children the story.

Night after night he defiled her, she said. Not a single Model T rolled off the assembly line in those days that he hadn't violated her in, not a single one.

She would dab the corners of her eyes as if she had been crying.

They produced nine thousand vehicles a day, Mudd, Fourth pointed out.

Mudd nodded.

That poor woman, she sort of wept.

Such was Julia's greatness that Unclish decided to honor her memory, and so he passed a law, from now until the end of time, that it was forbidden for any Cannibal to own a Ford ever again, or to lease one, or to even buy one secondhand.

Whoever does so, he declared, is a traitor, an enemy of our people.

And worse than Jack Nicholson.

. . .

What about F-150s? the Elders asked. For they are not cars, but trucks.

Ford trucks too, said the Elder Elders, are forbidden.

What about Lincolns? the Elders asked.

Lincolns are permitted, said the Elder Elders.

But Lincoln is owned by Ford, said the Elders.

Yes, said the Elder Elders, but nobody drives Lincolns anyway.

I drive a Lincoln, said the Elders.

Then you are a fool, said the Elder Elders.

Ease up, Larry, said the Elders. We're on the same team here.

. . .

One Sunday when he was five, Seventh learned that he would live forever.

It raised some difficult questions.

He woke with a start that morning to the sound of a vacuum cleaner downstairs. He sat up, his young heart filling with joy.

Do you hear that? he asked his brothers.

Is that the vacuum? asked Fourth.

It is, said Third. Vacuum!

Guests! cheered Second.

Thank fucking Christ, muttered First.

Mudd did not keep a particularly tidy home, and so the unusual sound of vacuuming heralded something special. Vacuuming meant visitors were expected, and visitors meant Mudd would be on her best behavior—though she often insisted there was nothing wrong with her hitting and yelling (That's part of being a family, she said), she never did either in front of guests or strangers.

The boys hurried downstairs to the kitchen, where coffee was brewing—We have a coffee machine? asked First—and Mudd was busy arranging a plate of fancy pastries.

Who's coming? Seventh asked.

Just get dressed, Mudd said.

Why? asked Second.

I said get dressed! she snapped, and would have clopped him then and there if there hadn't come at just that moment a loud knocking on the front door. Mudd swore—Seventh, put away the vacuum! Put away the vacuum!—grabbed the plate of pastries, and hurried to the door, smoothing her dress and tucking a stray hair behind her ear as she went.

Unclish! Mudd said to her esteemed brother-in-law as she opened the door. Goodness, I forgot you were coming!

Any hope the boys had of a casual Sunday disappeared. Their uncle was a serious man, as humorless as he was intimidating; he had probably laughed once, long ago, but never since, and had Mudd mentioned earlier that he was coming, any of the brothers old enough to leave on their own would have done so hours ago.

I am indeed worthy of forgetting, Unclish replied with his practiced humility. It is the *important* things we shall work today to remember.

Mudd sighed at his wisdom and held a hand over her heaving bosom.

(First once told Seventh he thought Mudd had a crush on Unclish.

Oh please, said Seventh. She's married to his brother.

So? said First. Julius married his sister.

Gross, said Seventh.)

Mudd held her pastries out to Unclish.

Morning glory? she offered.

Unclish politely declined and entered the house; he walked as if carried upon the wings of seraphim, one hand tucked inside the lapel of his long black overcoat, the other gently tipping his tall silver top hat as he crossed the threshold.

The boys straightened their backs, fixed their hair, and kissed their Sunday good-bye.

Today, he said to them, you become men.

But the Giants game is on, said First.

Mudd clopped him on the head. The only giant you'll be watching is your uncle, she said.

Unclish led the boys to the living room, where he closed the blinds, drew the curtains, and handed each of the brothers a signed copy of *The Complete Guide to Field-Dressing and Processing Your Deer.* Theirs, he said, to keep and guide them for the rest of their lives.

Seventh looked at the cover, upon which a smiling hunter in a camouflage jumpsuit kneeled proudly beside a gunned-down deer.

Which one's us? Seventh asked First.

What do you mean which one's us? asked First.

Are we the hunters or are we the deer?

We're both, stupid, said First.

Gross, said Seventh.

Unclish set up before them a serious-looking metal easel, upon which he had placed a large pad. He removed his top hat and coat, laid them on the chair beside him, and class began.

Tell me, he said to the brothers, why are we here?

Because Mudd said we have to be, said First.

The other children giggled.

We are here, Unclish said tightly, because we are dying.

We are? asked Third.

It's just an expression, Second reassured him.

We are, said Unclish.

I'm dying? Third asked, beginning to panic. Sixth had died just a year earlier, and Third was still having trouble understanding what death meant, where Sixth had gone, and when he would be back.

You're not dying, said Seventh.

Then why did he say I was dying? Third asked.

First nudged Third with his elbow.

Stop asking so many questions, he said. I wanna wrap this up and watch the Giants game.

Our people have consumed America, Unclish said, his voice beginning to rise, as it often did when the chance to preach presented itself. Its values, its morals, its philosophies! And in turn we have been consumed *by* America. Today our people are disappearing. You are the last, my children. Look at what the great Cannibal Jesus achieved with only twelve apostles. He conquered the Roman Empire! He conquered the world! But it won't be easy. You must know all our laws, and you must know all our rules, for it is upon you that the future of our people rests. Today we begin to study them, and we will study them every Sunday morning until they are complete.

Every Sunday? First asked.

Every Sunday, said Unclish.

Even Super Bowl Sunday?

We begin with the first three rules of our people, said Unclish. These are the three most important rules of all, the three rules you must never forget and the three rules you must teach to your own children, so that they may teach them to their children and their children may teach them to their children. The rules are as ancient as our people, except for Rule Number Three.

What's Rule Number Three? asked Second.

Unclish pulled the cap off a thick black marker and turned to the presentation pad.

Rule Number One, he spoke as he wrote, and then, below it, in large black letters: *No Cops.*

He underlined each word twice.

No.

Cops.

If you remember nothing else, Unclish said, remember this.

He looked each brother in the eye, a look of such gravity as they had never seen.

No cops, he said. Ever.

Minority communities have always had something of a love-hate relationship with the authorities, who are supposed to protect them from oppression but who often become the source of oppression themselves. For the Can-Am community, though, the police presented an even greater threat than to other minorities—a threat to their ancient traditions, which were prohibited by the very law the police were sworn to uphold. To call the police upon the death of a Cannibal, Unclish explained, was to ensure that the Consumption, the central rite of their unique cultural heritage, could never take place. State and city regulations demanded the removal of a deceased body from the home, by a qualified remover, to be released only after examination, and then only to a registered funeral home or cemetery representative.

If that happened, Unclish explained, they were as good as dead.

Good one, said First.

But Unclish never joked, and First knew it.

Death, Unclish said, is for other people.

He turned to the window, peeked out the curtains, turned back to the Seltzer brothers, lowered his voice to a whisper, and said:

Cannibals live forever.

What? asked Second.

Cannibals, said Unclish, live forever. When we Consume our beloveds, they live on inside us. They guide us, inform us, comfort us, inspire us. They become us, and we become them. In this way, my children, the past lives on and never dies. But remember: just as Consumption assures us eternal life, burial in the ground assures our eternal death. For we are not trees, and we do not grow in dirt. The grave is an end, fit only for an animal. It is for this reason that the police must never be called. If we follow the rules, if we remain with our people, we will live forever. You will live forever, and you will live forever, and you will live forever.

Forever? asked Third.

His eyes were bright, and Seventh knew he was thinking of Sixth. Seventh was too, and he knew what Third was wondering: if Cannibals who were Consumed lived forever, and Unclish had Consumed Sixth, was Sixth alive?

Where was he?

Why hadn't he said hello?

Maybe they could go find him, thought Seventh.

Unclish turned and wrote the letters *N*, *Y*, *P*, and *D* vertically on the board.

Now Your People are Dead, he said as he completed the acronym. If you call the police, children, your mother and father, your sister and brother—your *people*—are dead. No. Cops.

The brothers fell silent, looking one to the other and at The Guides in their laps. Mudd had said it before, but to hear Unclish confirm it was something else: The future of their entire people was in their hands.

Unclish turned to a new page on the presentation pad.

Rule Number Two, he spoke as he wrote, and then, below it, in large black letters:

Commit Nothing to Paper.

He underlined the word *nothing* twice.

Our people, Unclish said, invented math. Did you know that? We invented the microscope, the telescope, the telephone. So much have we done for the world, and yet the world still treats us as savages, as beasts, as monsters. One day we will find acceptance. One day we will be free to live as our ancestors did. But until then, absolute secrecy is of the utmost importance; anything written down can and will be used against us, and so it is critical that nothing ever be written down.

What about this? First asked, holding up The Guide.

What about it? asked Unclish.

It's written down.

Except that, said Unclish.

But you just wrote that down too, said Second.

Wrote what down?

That we shouldn't write anything down.

Unclish clopped them each on the head with the back of his hand.

Stop being stupid, he said.

He flipped over yet another sheet of paper and wrote, *Rule Number Three*.

Rule Number Three, he said, is just as important as the first two rules. Maybe even more important.

And then, below it, in large black angry letters, he wrote:

JACK NICHOLSON IS A SON OF A BITCH.

He underlined the word BITCH twice.

Who's Jack Nicholson? Seventh asked.

We'll get to that next week, Unclish said.

What's a bitch? asked Third.

We'll get to that too, said Unclish.

And with that he pulled on his long black coat, put on his tall silver top hat, and left. The brothers watched him go.

Who's Jack Nicholson? Seventh asked First.

Who gives a shit? said First, turning on the television. But by then the Giants game was already long over, and the Giants had lost by seven. First was furious, and he threw his copy of The Guide to the floor and kicked it at the wall.

If *that* son of a bitch lives forever, he said of Unclish, we're *all* fucked.

. . .

The publication of *The Complete Guide to Field-Dressing and Processing Your Deer* nearly proved disastrous for the Cannibal-

American community. Even before it was published, many thought it an unnecessary risk of exposure, not to mention a flagrant violation of Rule Number Two. Unclish, though, was adamant that a book of rules and regulations was critical if their people hoped to maintain their unique cultural identity in the melting pot of America. He assured them that nothing could possibly go wrong, but the first copies appeared with a tragic typo, right on the front cover, the word *Deer* somehow having been spelled *Dear*.

The Complete Guide to Field-Dressing and Processing Your Dear caused a wave of panic across the community. The people blamed Unclish for the debacle, and for jeopardizing their people. Those who passed through Brooklyn in those days might recall seeing flyers posted around certain areas with the face of pro wrestler André the Giant, who was Cannibal, and the words RULE TWO! scrawled beneath him. Unclish decried these postings, claiming they were violations of Rule Two themselves. And so, as the day of the book release approached, Can-Ams took to their basements and attics, awaiting the pitchforks and torches once again. But it never came to pass. Booksellers, thinking the book a satire, placed it in the Humor section, where it had a reasonably successful holiday season.

Father, telling this story to Seventh, said it demonstrated his brother's hubris and need for validation.

Unclish only loved his people, he said, so that his people would love him.

Hogwash, said Mudd when Seventh asked her about it later. That was no typo. That was your uncle sticking his finger in the eye of the nation that ostracized his people! He was mocking them, laughing at them! Your uncle is a hero, Seventh.

And your father, she added, is worse than Jack Nicholson.

. . .

Eighth returned from the kitchen, wringing his hands. He was beginning to panic.

She doesn't have a Guide, he said. How can Mudd not have a Guide?

So? First asked. She doesn't have a Guide, so what?

We need it.

For what?

To know what to do.

About what?

About what? About her.

What about her?

She died at ten past noon, said Eighth.

So?

So it's almost one.

So?

So *Two to Drain*, said Eighth, *Twenty-four to Consume*. We don't have much time.

The words made Seventh shudder. He hadn't heard them in years.

Two to Drain, Twenty-four to Consume.

How many times had Unclish made them repeat that? A thousand? Ten thousand?

The Victuals, as the Cannibal funerary tradition is known, consists of four basic steps: Draining (of the blood), Purging (of the organs), Partitioning (of the corpse), and Consumption (of the meat). *Two to Drain, Twenty-four to Consume* was one of Unclish's Sunday morning maxims: Following death, one has two hours to Drain the body of blood, followed by a twenty-four-hour period in which to Consume it. After two hours, the undrained body is considered putrescent; after twenty-four hours, the eating isn't considered a true eating. Violating either of these parameters could render the Victuals an Incomplete Victuals, and instead of the deceased being blessed with eternal life, they would be condemned to eternal death.

Wait! Third suddenly called. I have one!

You have one what? asked First.

A Guide! said Third.

Where? asked Eighth.

In my room!

Jesus Christ, get it, you moron! said Eighth.

Take it easy, said Zero.

We're running out of time, Eighth said.

Time? First demanded. You're not really considering *eating* her, are you?

What do *you* want to do? asked Eighth.

Call the police, said First.

No, Tenth declared. No cops.

Fifth sided with First.

We can't eat her, guys, he said. Don't be ridiculous.

Why not? asked Eighth.

Did you see the size of her? said Fifth.

She's enormous, Fourth agreed. It will take a year. It will take ten years.

We're not supposed to eat *all* of her, said Eighth.

How much of her are we supposed to eat? Fourth asked.

One bite, said Eighth. A bite and a half, technically.

A bite and a half? asked Second. That doesn't sound right.

Again Seventh felt that bilious resentment toward Second for marrying a Jewish woman, and it made him realize that this might not ever happen again: a Cannibal family gathered together to Consume their beloved.

They were the last.

Eighth recited another of Unclish's mnemonics:

> *A bite and half*
> *and you won't need another,*
> *whether it's your father, your sister,*
> *or even your mother.*

The words stung Seventh; the old dictum was having the paradoxical effect of making him want to run screaming from the house while at the same time making him want to run upstairs, fall to his knees beside Mudd's bed, and beg her for forgiveness.

A bite and a half, said Fifth. I remember that.

Me too, said Ninth.

A bite and a half isn't too bad, said Fourth. Considering.

First got to his feet, irate.

Are you all nuts? he demanded. Have you lost your minds? Do you even hear yourselves?

How big a bite? Eleventh asked Eighth.

Yeah, said Twelfth. How big a bite? Third's bite, or Zero's bite?

Your own bite, Eighth said.

You're talking about a felony, said First. Do you realize that? A felony. That's jail time, real jail time.

What did you *think* we were going to do, First? Eighth demanded.

I thought we were going to do what everyone does when their

mothers drop dead, said First. I thought we were going to have a little booze, tell a couple of stories to make it seem like she wasn't a complete cunt, then pick a cemetery and fight over the inheritance. That's what I thought we were going to do.

I will not let you insult our mother, said Tenth.

She wasn't my mother, asshole, said First. She gave birth to me, but she was never my mother.

Tenth stood now too, fists clenched, and stepped to First. He was younger, taller, and broader than First, but First's anger was so intense that it gave even Tenth pause. The two were ready to come to blows when Third came bounding down the stairs.

Got it! he said proudly.

The siblings froze, from Zero to Twelfth, and any thoughts of fighting disappeared—for what Third held in his hand was not a copy of The Guide, but an ancient brown leather valise with a worn wooden handle and heavy golden clasps that had blackened with age.

Is that . . . is that what I think it is? asked First.

Zero, who had never seen the case before, looked to Seventh. What is it? she asked.

Third? Seventh asked. Jesus, Third, where did you get that?

Where the *fuck* did you get that? asked First.

Third set the case down on the coffee table, mistaking their shock for approval and happy to be the center of attention.

Mudd! he said proudly.

Mudd? Seventh asked. Why did Mudd have it?

She gave it to me, said Third. She said I should keep it, and remember who I'm from and who I am and who I'm not am and who I was or is.

He unclasped the latches and laid the case open. He had been using it to store his treasures: a pair of dice, some stray Monopoly money, and a few pieces of bubble gum. But below those lay an old, faded copy of The Guide.

Third stuffed a piece of gum into his pocket and pulled out The Guide. He beamed with pride and held it out for them, but all eyes were on the dreadful Knife of Redemption that he had revealed in the case beneath it. Its pointed silver blade gleamed; the sharp teeth of its serrated edge seemed hungry, ready to bite. Ancient carvings on the cheek of the blade ran from the hilt to the fang-shaped gut hook below its point. It looked deadly just lying in repose.

What the hell is *that*? asked Zero, wondering what Third was doing in possession of such a dangerous weapon.

Seventh felt a terrible dread pass over him. He hadn't seen the knife since he was a child, when Unclish had brought it to one of their Sunday morning lessons.

This, Unclish had said, holding the fierce weapon in his hand, is the Knife of Redemption. With this knife, your ancestors were Drained, they were Purged, they were Partitioned, and they were Consumed. That is why it is called the Knife of Redemption, children: because it redeems us from this finite life, from our body, and with it we are blessed with immortality.

Seventh stepped closer. The blade seemed to have tarnished with age, but as he leaned in for a closer look, he saw that what he thought was tarnish was actually dried blood.

Sixth's blood.

That was why Mudd had it.

Sixth's was the last Consumption. The tradition, Seventh recalled, was that the knife remained with the last family to use it. In that way it never stayed in one place, making it less likely to be discovered by authorities. It also reminded one and all that the Knife of Redemption didn't belong to any one person; it belonged to the people.

And that was when Seventh decided that he would do as his mother had asked.

He would honor her last wish, and he would make sure his brothers joined him.

Not because Mudd deserved it; he suspected she didn't. But because their people were a chain, as she always told him, an unbroken chain stretching back millennia, and Sixth's blood on the edge of that blade had reminded him of all the Cannibal men and women and children, generation after generation, wherever they were and whenever they lived, who had performed this sacred ritual in the face of threats, oppression, even death.

It was up to them now.

To continue the chain.

To save their people.

And that meant it was up to him.

It was one thing to leave your home and people. It was one thing to say you no longer wanted to belong to them. But it was another thing altogether to be standing at the edge of their muddy grave, the cold shovel in your hand, deciding whether to bury them or pull them out.

Mudd's Consumption might be the last Consumption.

Ever.

It had to be done, thought Seventh.

And it had to be done right.

First was having none of it. As the others stared dumbstruck at the knife, First stood and began to button his coat.

Well, team, he said, I'm out. When the old knife enters, that's my cue to leave. It's been delightful, really. Brothers, sisters, you throw a hell of a party. I'd have brought a cake, but it looks like Mudd ate them all. I mean, all the cakes, everywhere, on earth. Congratulations, family, or condolences, whichever you choose; I'm on the congratulations end of the scale, I think you know that already. So: mazel tov, salud, huzzah, hooray, and hosanna. Good riddance, Mudd, you miserable fuck. I'll spit on your grave if they ever dig one big enough.

He turned and walked out, slamming the front door behind him.

Eighth turned to Seventh, worry on his face. He can't leave, he said.

I know, said Seventh.

Meat, said Eighth.

I know, said Seventh.

Meat? asked Zero.

Meat, Eighth explained. M-E-A-T. It's an acronym. Must Eat All Together. If we don't all eat her, it's not considered a true Consumption. Seventh, he can't lea—

But Seventh was already hurrying out the door.

. . .

Our people are a chain, Mudd told Seventh.

A chain? Seventh had asked.

A chain, she said, made up of many links. And you are the next link. So if you ever decide, Hey, you know what? I don't want to be a Cannibal anymore, I just want to be myself, well, listen, that's okay.

It is?

You do you, right? said Mudd. But before you do you, do me a favor, okay?

Sure, Mudd.

Do me a favor and imagine all those links of the chain of your people, hundreds of them, thousands of them, stretching back for miles and miles and miles, more links than there are grains of sand on the beach, more links than there are drops of water in the ocean, each one a life, each one a member of your people who put his people before himself, and I want you to turn to those links, and I want you to look at them—your parents and your grandparents and your great-great-grandparents—and I want you to say, Fuck you.

Mudd? Seventh asked.

I want you to say, Kiss my ass. I want you to say, I don't care if you died for our people, I don't care if you suffered and slaved, I don't care. Because I'm too good to be a link. But remember this, Seventh: However special you think you are, a link by itself is nothing. It can't hold anything, it can't support anything, it can't protect anything. And that's what you'll be without your people:

You'll be nothing.

. . .

Each part given out during the Allocation or the Apportioning or the Assigning or the Disbursement has its own deep significance, but Seventh knew that to receive the skin of the deceased, as he had, was a particularly special honor.

The skin, Unclish once explained, is the garment we wear as we go through our lives, the coat of our physical existence, a coat marked with the many colors of our lives—with our scars and bruises, our joys and our sorrows. Here, from childhood, the red patch on your knee from when you fell off the tire swing. Here, the brown scar on your abdomen from your midlife hernia. Here, the blue bruise on your arm from when, old and frail, you slipped and fell on the icy sidewalk.

Brown-black birthmarks.

Purple-gray wounds.

To be gifted this vivid varicolored robe, Unclish said as he looked down at his own veiny skin, is to be given a whole life.

. . .

Perhaps nowhere in the world is snow more welcome than in Brooklyn. The dirty browns and dead grays disappear beneath the gathering whiteness, the grime and filth erased, magically, if only for a few hours. On school snow days, Seventh used to watch out the front window, silently cursing the people who trudged down the sidewalk, ruining the untouched snow, and the hideous plow that barreled down the street turning the cheerful white back to depressing gray, laying waste to the new world that was just beginning to form from the darkness.

Small flakes began to fall as Seventh and First stood on the sidewalk, looking up at the old brick house that had loomed so long and so large in their consciousnesses: the crumbling brick face, the loose shutters, the faded fake security sign. Seventh nodded toward the roofline, where the sagging rain gutter had separated from the house, causing the downspout to buckle.

Remember when you threatened to jump? he asked.

No.

You did.

When?

Auntie Hazel, said Seventh. After she died. I was in the living room. Suddenly I hear Mudd screaming: You get down here right now, young man, and eat your auntie!

The two brothers began to laugh.

Hazel was huge, said First. Not Mudd huge, but big.

No! Seventh shouted in his best Voice-Cracking Teenager. I'm not coming down until you say I don't have to eat her! Say it! Say it or I'll jump!

The brothers doubled over in laughter.

She weighed like two-fifty, said First. I was afraid I had to eat the whole thing.

You were right on the edge, said Seventh, your feet dangling over the side. I really thought you were going to jump.

She told me to, First laughed. Mudd. She said I better jump, because if I didn't she was going to kill me herself. I stayed up there for a *while*, man. I won too. She backed down.

Seventh shook his head.

No, she didn't, he said.

She did. She said I didn't have to eat her. You came outside and told me so yourself.

I lied, said Seventh. I told you Mudd said you didn't have to eat her. But I told Mudd you ate her.

Bullshit, said First.

Truth, said Seventh.

Ever the peacemaker, said First. That's a bad habit, brother.

I'm trying to quit.

So what'd you do with Hazel, then? Flush her?

I gave her to Third, said Seventh. I swear he could've polished her off by himself.

The wind whipped around them, scattering the last of autumn's dead brown leaves. First lifted his coat collar around his ears.

So why are you out here trying to convince me to eat Mudd? he asked. Let Third eat my share and be done with it.

Must Eat All Together, said Seventh.

I didn't eat Hazel, said First. You didn't care then—why do you care now?

Because Hazel didn't leave us a house in Brooklyn, said Seventh. You heard Mudd: If we don't do it right, we don't get the house. I could use that money. Publishing's not what it used to be.

Nothing is, said First.

He looked up at the house again.

It's a shithole, Seventh. It can't be worth enough. Not enough to eat her.

This isn't the neighborhood we grew up in, said Seventh. The market's an Apple Store. The playground's a Prada shop. The house is a shithole, yes, but it's a two-story semi-attached five-bedroom shithole in the hottest real estate market in Brooklyn.

First pulled his phone from his pocket.

Hey Siri, he said. What is the average price of a five-bedroom house near Bensonhurst, Brooklyn, New York?

Seventh smiled at the old secrecy.

Can't even tell Siri where we are, huh? he asked.

Old habits die hard, said First.

I have found what you're looking for, said Siri. The average price for a five-bedroom house in Bensonhurst, Brooklyn, is one point three million dollars.

First whistled.

That's money, said Seventh.

Divided by twelve, said First.

Still money.

But First just shook his head.

I'm sorry, Seventh. I'm not eating her, not for all the money in the world. And trust me, I could use some cash right now.

I'll eat your share, said Seventh. Just like Third with Hazel. No one will know. Just come back inside and say you're on board so they think it's legit. Eighth's a stickler for the rules.

Seventh knew that eating someone else's share was a violation of the rules of Consumption, but he hoped that as they prepared her, First would change his mind. It was either that or he was going to walk away right now anyway.

That woman was poison, said First. You shouldn't be eating her.

Maybe I'll throw her up, said Seventh.

First allowed himself a small grin.

Will that count? he asked.

I'll check with Eighth, said Seventh. You coming back in?

First looked up at the old house in front of him.

Sometimes, brother, he said, it feels like I never left.

. . .

One cold December afternoon long ago, Father took Seventh into Manhattan to see the Christmas windows at Macy's, which were filled with wondrous displays of animatronic Santas that blinked their eyes and waved their hands. All the city smelled like roasted chestnuts, and joyful shoppers filled the sidewalks, laughing and caroling, brightly wrapped gifts in their arms.

Cannibals don't celebrate a winter solstice holiday like everyone else, and Seventh always felt terribly left out of the festivities. And so later that day, as he and Father trekked back to Brooklyn, Seventh decided to invent a Cannibal winter holiday, so that Cannibal children in the future would have something to celebrate too. It would be a joyful holiday, he decided, a day of presents and treats, a day that would combine the flickering candles of Hanukkah, the glistening string lights of Christmas, and the magical fireworks of New Year's Eve. He figured since they already had a Remembrance Day to commemorate the very bad thing that had happened to their people—whatever that bad thing was and whenever that bad thing happened—his new holiday would commemorate all the days in history on which *nothing* bad happened to their people, the days on which Cannibals were not beaten, not raped, not chased out of their countries with pitchforks and torches. He named his new holiday Nothing Day.

Two weeks later, the very first Nothing Day arrived. Seventh woke early, before the rest of the family, and got to work. As quietly as he could, he wrapped their gifts—a clay pot he'd made in school for his parents, a pack of baseball cards for First, and a dictionary he'd found for a dollar at a yard sale the week before for Second. For Third, who loved cardboard boxes, he filled a large cardboard box with a bunch of smaller ones, and wrapped the whole thing with a big red bow. He piled the gifts on the coffee table, strung Christmas lights from the ceiling, found some votive candles in the kitchen cabinet—they weren't exactly Hanukkah candles, but they were close enough—and placed them around the room. The soft glow of the candles and the happy blinking colors of the string lights made him feel warm inside, and the spirit of Nothing Day filled his soul. Then, when everything was ready, he placed a frying pan on the living room floor, dropped a package of Red Devil Super Loud fire-crackers into it, and set them on fire.

BAM! BAM! BAMBAMBAMBAM!

The loud explosions made Seventh jump with joy, and when his terrified family came racing down the stairs in their bathrobes and pajamas, he held his hands overhead and cheered, Happy Nothing Day!

What the hell are you doing? Mudd yelled, her eyes wide with panic.

It's Nothing Day! Seventh said, holding her Nothing Day gift out to her. Happy Nothing Day!

Are those my good candles? she demanded.

Good candles? Seventh asked.

Those are my Remembrance Day candles! she yelled. Who said you could touch my Remembrance Day candles?

But it's Nothing Day, he said. The day when nothing bad happened to our people. We give presents, see?

Mudd slapped the gift out of his hands. Seventh could hear the pottery shatter when the box hit the floor. Then she grabbed a nearby vase, pulled out the flowers, and doused the firecrackers, sending a plume of white smoke into the air.

A day when nothing bad happened to us, she said as she stomped back upstairs to bed. That's the most ridiculous thing I've ever heard.

Father held Seventh as he wept, and said that even if Mudd didn't like Nothing Day, he did, and would celebrate it with him every year.

Then the fire alarm began to wail.

But maybe next year, buddy, he said, we'll do the fireworks outside.

. . .

It would be nice to be Siri, Seventh once said to Dr. Isaacson.

Why is that? Dr. Isaacson asked.

No family, no past. No parents, no people, no chains. No identity.

Hey Siri, are you black?

No.

Jew?

No.

Arab?

No. I'm nothing.

You mean Other?

No, I mean nothing.

I'll put you down as None.

Perfect.

Well, she is an Apple, Dr. Isaacson said.

In a predominantly Android world, said Seventh.

Lousy Androids. They control the media.

They're taking our jobs, said Seventh. Filthy animals.

She's female too, said Dr. Isaacson.

Yeah, but you can change that in her preferences, said Seventh.

So she's gender fluid, said Dr. Isaacson.

Yes, said Seventh. She's a Gender-Fluid-iOS-Based-Non-Cor-poreal-American. I'm surprised Rosenbloom hasn't published her memoir.

They don't have it easy, said Dr. Isaacson.

It's a struggle, said Seventh, and it was clear to Dr. Isaacson he wasn't referring to Siri anymore.

People like their boxes, said Dr. Isaacson. Even when they say they don't, they do. They like putting themselves in boxes, they like putting other people in boxes. They think the boxes will protect them. They think the boxes are worth protecting.

But my box, said Seventh with a shake of his head. It's killing me.

I know, said Dr. Isaacson. The good news is that boxes are fairly simple to climb out of.

Then how come so few do? he asked.

I said it was simple, said Dr. Isaacson, I didn't say it was easy.

No, no, the doctor continued. Not easy at all.

. . .

Well, said Seventh, what's it going to be?

He had gathered his siblings around the dining table, much as they had gathered earlier around their dying mother's bed. But the tension was higher now; death had come, and time was running out.

Our mother has passed on, he said to them. Now, some of us liked Mudd, and some of us didn't. Some of us loved her, some of us hated her. We've never agreed on that, and we never will. But we don't have to. All we have to agree on is what to do with her. Do we eat her, or do we bury her? Those are the only choices. Some of you may want to eat her for cultural reasons. Some of you may want to eat her for inheritance reasons—this house is worth a considerable amount of money. Some of you may hate her so much you don't want to eat her at all. Love, hate, or money, it doesn't matter. All we have to agree on is what we're going to do. And we have to agree on that right now.

He suggested they put it to a vote. All those assigned a part by Mudd for Consumption would have a say. Zero, therefore, would not.

I'll just sit here quietly horrified, she said.

Seventh adored Zero, but he really didn't need her negativity right now.

I'll go first, he said, raising his hand overhead. Consumption.

For love, hate, or money? asked Fourth.

For culture, said Seventh. Look, guys, this is it. We're the last. I'm not doing it for her; I'm doing it for everyone who came before her. And for anyone who comes after us.

Eighth agreed with Seventh. Consumption, he said.

Tenth did too. This is larger than us, he declared. This is our duty.

A heavy silence filled the small room as the undecideds looked from one to the other.

Okay, said First. I'm in.

You're in? Second asked in disbelief.

For money, no doubt, Tenth said with disgust.

Absolutely for money, said First. I earned that money.

You're sick, said Tenth.

Love would be sicker, said First.

How much money are we talking about? asked Second.

According to Siri, said First, the average price for a five-bedroom around here is one point three.

Million? said Ninth.

First nodded. Million, he said.

That's money, said Second.

Divided by twelve, Fourth pointed out.

By eleven, said Zero. Count me out.

You're in, said Seventh. If we sell the house, you'll have nowhere to live. We're counting you in.

Hey Siri, First said. What's one point three million divided by twelve?

I have found what you're looking for, said Siri. One point three million divided by twelve is one hundred eight thousand, three hundred and thirty-three.

A hundred thousand? asked Ninth. Each?

Vultures, Tenth muttered. We should be happy to eat our mother, not sitting around here counting our silver pieces.

Said the guy who got her fists, said First.

So?

So try a plate of ass, Flex, said First, then tell me you want to eat her for free.

Tenth looked as if he might leap across the table at First. Seventh quickly intervened.

You're right, Tenth, he said. You are. We should be happy to eat our mother. And some of us are. But some of us aren't, and, to be fair, that's as much Mudd's fault as anyone else's. Like I said, though, we don't have to agree on that.

He turned his attention to those who hadn't yet voted.

If we're in, he said, we all have to be in. All of us. Must Eat All Together. Anyone who wants out, say so now, and we end this right here. We call the cops, bury her, and go home.

Eleventh raised her hand. I'm in, she said.

Tenth objected. He knew that Eleventh was planning to use the money for sex reassignment surgery, a use he thought should be prohibited.

Why? Twelfth demanded

Because the Elders prohibited it, said Tenth. And because Mudd didn't approve of it, either. You disgusted her.

If I lived a life that Mudd approved of, said Eleventh, I would disgust myself.

I'm in too, said Twelfth, putting her arm around Eleventh. Dr. Emmanuel Zion. Seventy grand, but he's the best in the business.

This is wrong, said Tenth.

I'll give you his number, Twelfth said to Tenth. Who knows, maybe he can turn you into a man, too.

He is a miracle worker, said Eleventh.

Animals, said Tenth.

Fifth? asked Seventh.

Fifth bit his nails, a habit Seventh recognized from his youth. How much again? he asked.

A hundred and eight thousand, said Second.

Three hundred and thirty-three, added First.

Okay, said Fifth. In.

Second raised his hand (In, he said. Money.), and Third, happy just to raise his hand, joined in too. Fourth agreed, and so did Ninth—both of them for money too.

Then we're agreed, said Seventh, with equal parts triumph and misgiving. We do it.

Tenth couldn't contain himself any longer. You're sick, all of you, he spat as he went for the door. You're a disgrace.

He turned to look at them before leaving.

You're worse than Jack Nicholson, he said. All of you. Worse than Jack fucking Nicholson!

. . .

In 1976, Jack Nicholson was nominated for the Academy Award for Best Actor. He'd been nominated before, but never before had his victory seemed so assured as that year, and never before had the Cannibal-American community so desperately needed him to win.

To them, the 48th Academy Awards ceremony was more than just another flashy Hollywood gala. Winds of social change had been blowing across the nation, casting a bitter chill over the Cannibal-American community; their old ways and traditions were simply no match for ABBA, Farrah, and cocaine. The sixties and early seventies had decimated their community, the young generations being lost in ever-increasing numbers to the twin scourges of assimilation and intermarriage.

And so, on the evening of March 29, 1976, as Hollywood gathered for that year's Oscars ceremony at the Dorothy Chandler Pavilion in Los Angeles, Cannibal-Americans across the country gathered around their television sets, hopeful that a victory by Nicholson, who was Cannibal, would inspire a renaissance of their community; that he would stand on that world stage, look into those television cameras, and thank the Cannibal community for their support and their love and, in so doing, deliver them at last from the shadows of shame and secrecy that had hounded them across time.

Mudd was beside herself all day with anxiety and excitement, cleaning and re-cleaning that which she had already cleaned. She despised television, but this was, after all, history in the making—

Cannibal history—and she had permitted Humphrey to purchase a small black-and-white TV for just this occasion.

As the awards presentation began, the tension in the living room was palpable. Mudd tapped her foot nervously; Unclish, who had once considered a community-wide ban on television, stood beside the couch, twisting his beard and saying, Yes, yes, hmm, hmm.

Art Carney, who was not Cannibal, was greeted with thunderous applause as he made his way to the podium to present the Academy Award for Best Actor.

This year, he said, those nominated for best performance by an actor are . . .

He glanced down at the card in his hand.

Walter Matthau, he declared, in *The Sunshine Boys*!

The crowd inside the pavilion cheered, and the camera cut to the beaming Matthau seated in the audience. Carney and Matthau had appeared together in the original Broadway production of Neil Simon's *The Odd Couple* some years before, and their shared history made his nomination even sweeter, for the actors and the audience alike.

Jew, grumbled Mudd.

Jack Nicholson, Carney continued, in *One Flew Over the Cuckoo's Nest*!

Again the crowd erupted, and now Mudd cheered with them.

Nicholson, in his trademark dark sunglasses, smiled broadly. Anjelica Huston, seated beside him, clapped her hands and smiled with pride, while Matthau, in the small picture-in-picture window at the top of the screen, no longer beamed. He seemed, to Mudd, to scowl.

Look at that fat bastard, will you? said Mudd.

Who? asked Humphrey.

Matthau. He should rot in hell.

I like him, said Humphrey. He's a good actor.

They stick together, said Mudd. Hoo boy, do they stick together.

Who?

Who, Mudd said with disgust. Neil Simon, *Jew*, hires Walter Matthau, *Jew*, and now Art Carney, *Jew*, is going to give him the Oscar.

Art Carney isn't a Jew, said Humphrey. He's Catholic.

Art Carney listed the rest of the nominees, took hold of the envelope, and tore it open. Mudd grabbed Humphrey's hand in her own, squeezing it so tightly he thought his bones would crack.

And the winner is . . . , said Art Carney.

Silence fell over the audience at the pavilion.

Mudd held her breath.

Carney looked down at his card.

Jack Nicholson! he declared. In *One Flew Over the Cuckoo's Nest*!

Mudd leapt to her feet, cheering and stomping, her hands raised overhead in triumph.

Unclish cheered too, clapping his hands and slapping Humphrey on the back.

He did it! he said. Our boy really did it!

Nicholson kissed Anjelica Huston and made his way to the stage.

Is she Can? Mudd asked. I think she is. Huston, Huston—that could be Can, don't you think?

How should I know? said Humphrey.

Look at that jaw! said Mudd. That's a Can jaw if ever I saw one!

Nicholson bounded onto the stage, doing a little Ed Norton shimmy in tribute to Art Carney. The crowd went wild.

Here we go, said Mudd, shaking with excitement. Here we go.

Carney handed the gleaming trophy to Nicholson, and the two men embraced.

Did you ever think you'd see it? Mudd said. Did you ever think you'd see the day when one of our own people would be standing on that stage, accepting the Academy Award?

Jack Nicholson took his place at the podium and looked out across the auditorium.

Well, he said with his sly grin, I guess this proves there're as many nuts in the Academy as anywhere else.

The audience cheered, and Mudd joined them, laughing and slapping her knee.

He's funny, she said. I didn't know he was so funny!

But since you gave me the chance, Nicholson continued, I'm really happy to get an opportunity to thank Saul and Michael . . .

Nicholson paused.

Mudd clutched Humphrey's thigh tightly in her hand.

She didn't know who Saul or Michael were, but Nicholson seemed to be steeling himself, gathering his courage, looking for the words, preparing to reveal himself and his people to the world.

And Louise, Nicholson continued with some uncertainty.

Mudd's grip on Humphrey's thigh tightened.

Mudd . . . Humphrey said, grimacing as her fingers crushed his bones.

And Brad, Nicholson continued, and Lawrence and Bo. And all of the guys in the company, all of the feebs brigade . . .

Mudd leaned forward and searched Nicholson's eyes, waiting for him to declare who and what he was.

And to my people, she wanted him to say. *The great Cannibal people. Who have suffered, who have been shamed, who have been hidden in darkness. To you, I say, Stand up! Stand up with me and be counted! For today, something something, and tomorrow we will rule the world!*

But the moment never came.

Nicholson smiled, made some lame joke about his agent, thanked the audience, and walked off the stage.

Unclish shook his head in disgust.

I should have banned that damned box when I had the chance, he said, putting on his top hat and leaving in a huff, slamming the front door behind him as he left.

That son of a bitch! Mudd shouted.

Mudd, said Humphrey. Mudd, calm down.

Not one word! Mudd shouted. Not one word about his people, his heritage, his history! Only shame and more shame and more shame!

What do you expect him to do, Mudd? Humphrey asked.

I expected him to have a spine!

You expected Jack Nicholson to stand up at the Academy Awards in front of the whole world and tell everyone he's . . . he's . . .

Even you can't say it! she roared.

This isn't about me, Mudd!

It's about our people! Mudd shouted, and stormed out of the room.

It always seemed to take a moment for the air to return when Mudd stormed out of a room. When it did, Humphrey stood and went to the television.

Eh, he said to himself as he shut it off. So what's wrong with a little shame?

. . .

Eighth was flipping through Third's copy of The Guide, a look of utter bewilderment on his face.

What in the hell, he asked, is this?

They had agreed to Consume Mudd, but over an hour had already passed since she had died. *Drain all her oil,* Unclish had taught them, *or Momma will spoil,* and they knew they had to move fast.

Eighth had grabbed The Guide from the valise, but as he flipped through it, it was clear from the look on his face that something was terribly wrong.

What is it? Seventh asked.

What is it? Eighth said. It's porn, that's what it is.

It's what?

It's porn.

Eighth tossed The Guide to Seventh, who opened it to find a naked woman cupping her impossibly large breasts. All she was wearing was a white chef's hat. Above her, it read in large pink letters:

Hungry?

Seventh checked the cover. It was still the original cover—the camo-covered hunter, the blood-covered deer—but the pages inside had been swapped out for the pages of a pornographic magazine (*Juggs,* from the looks of it). Every page featured women with breasts the size of Chevys.

Here's the beef, read the headline on one page.

It's Whopper Time, read the next.

Seventh looked to Third, who covered his face in shame. Uh-oh, spaghetti-o, he said.

Where's the rest of it? Eighth demanded of Third. Where's the rest of it?

Don't yell at him! Zero said. He didn't know.

Our mother's up there rotting, said Eighth. Where's the rest of it?

Third began clopping himself on his head.

Don't be stupid, he chastised himself. Don't be stupid.

Seventh grabbed his arms, trying to stop him.

It's okay, he said, it's okay. You didn't do anything wrong, buddy; we all do things like that.

Third hid his face behind his hands. We do? he mumbled.

Of course, said Seventh. But right now I need you to think, Third; I need you to think really hard. Where did you put the rest of it? The Guide, Third, where'd you put it?

Third squeezed his eyes shut and held his breath. Finally he said, Oopsie.

Oopsie?

I chucked it.

You chucked it? Seventh asked.

You *asshole*, Eighth shouted.

Hey! said Zero.

Drain all her oil or Momma will spoil, said Second. Drain all her oil or Momma will spoil!

You ASSHOLE! Eighth shouted again.

He didn't know! said Zero.

Panic filled the room. Those Seltzers who loved Mudd began to worry that she wouldn't live forever; those who cared for their people began to worry that the chain was about to be broken; and those who just wanted Mudd's money were afraid they would now never receive it.

Aw fuck it, let's just do it! said First.

Do it? Eighth demanded. Do it how?

With the knife, shithead, said First. Of Redemption. Let's just take the knife, go up there, and, you know, Drain her.

Y'know, Drain her? asked Fifth. No, I don't *y'know, Drain her.* Drain her how?

How do you think? said First, and he drew a finger across his throat.

Do you know how much blood is in a woman that size? asked Eighth.

No, said First. Do you?

Gallons, said Ninth.

We'll pour it down the sink, said Fourth.

And how do you propose we get it to the sink? asked Fifth.

A hose, offered Eleventh.

She's not a keg of beer, said Tenth.

Drain all her oil or Momma will spoil, said Second. Drain all her oil or Momma will spoil—

All right! Seventh shouted. Everyone just calm down!

He slammed The Guide/*Juggs* on the coffee table.

Folks, he said, there's only one answer. We're out of time, we don't know what we're doing, and even if we did, we don't know how to do it.

He ran a hand through his hair and took a deep breath.

There's only one person who can help us, he said.

First shook his head.

Oh Jesus, he said. No. No way.

No, said Second. Uh-uh.

No, no, no, said Fourth, Fifth, and Ninth.

Eleventh and Twelfth, in unison, said: No.

Yes, said Seventh. We have no choice.

A terrible silence filled the room.

We're going to have to call Unclish, he said.

. . .

The story Mudd told them was that even before Unclish reached legal age—he was just Ishmael Seltzer back then—he was already considered by many to be the Cannibal community's spiritual leader. He was a scholar, a polymath; he knew all their rules, all their history, all their legends, and all their stories. He was a fearless leader, a captivating speaker, and a tireless organizer. By age twenty, he'd founded the University and begun raising funds for its construction. By thirty, he was a master Victualist. By the time he was forty, people came from far and wide to seek his advice on all manner of tradition, his verdict on all matters of law. By fifty, when he entered a room, people stood; when he spoke, they fell silent; and when he left, they thanked the Ancient Spirits for bringing him forth to lead them.

The Seltzer children despised him.

I bet when he dies, First said, he'll taste like shit.

I bet shit tastes better, said Second.

Where others saw a scholar, they saw a pompous phony (but for Eighth, who dreamed of becoming him, and Third, who knew no hatred in his heart). Unclish wore heavy black suits and a white silk scarf and a tall silver top hat, and he twisted his white beard and said, Yes, yes, hmm, hmm, as if lost in a thought so complex it left no neural power for ordinary speech. Though he was raised in

Brooklyn and rarely left, he spoke with a fake Harvard accent (he never attended, he claimed, because they have a Cannibal-American quota of none). The accent may have fooled adults, but to the children their father's brother sounded less like a sage and more like Thurston Howell III from *Gilligan's Island*, and they enjoyed nothing more after their Sunday morning classes than gathering in one of their bedrooms and mimicking him until they collapsed in laughter.

Oh, Lovey, Ninth would say, do be a dear and cut me a slice of Gilligan.

Of course, dear, Fifth would respond, but you simply must try a bite of the Professor.

None of this was said within earshot of Unclish, of course, for they feared him as much as they disdained him. He was a passionate ideologue who brooked no insolence and tolerated no rebellion. With his fist ever in the air, he ranted about the treachery of nations, cursed Cannibals who left the fold, and blasted the evils of America.

We have survived everything but freedom! he would fulminate from his seat at the end of the dinner table, banging the table with his fist and causing the silverware to jump. War, hatred, violence, oppression—all these combined could never do to us what Coca-Cola and Disney and Burger King have. We have lost our way! We have intermarried, we have assimilated! We have bought into the American Dream, but that dream is someone else's, and the dream they dream is a dream of our destruction!

The louder he shouted and the more agitated he became, the more Mudd adored him, and she often lamented to her children that she wished she'd married Unclish instead of his brother.

I got Garfunkel, she said.

Who's Garfunkel? Seventh asked.

Simon and Garfunkel, she said. Two Jewish fags. Simon was the talented one.

Simon and Garfunkel weren't gay, Fourth corrected her. Each one married and had children.

Mudd clopped him on the head with the back of her hand.

They were Jews, said Mudd. That's enough.

. . .

Mudd was going bad. Fast. Her extremities were beginning to swell, and beneath her dingy nightgown, her corpse had turned a dull, two-day-old roadkill gray. The nightgown caused Seventh another pang of guilt; Mudd couldn't have been more than a few Whoppers shy of five hundred pounds, and the nightgown, enormous as it was, barely fit her. It wasn't the fit, though, that caused his remorse; it was the nightgown itself: the pattern of tiny pink flowers and the once-white lace edging along the bottom.

The never-ending desire for beauty. For the *lie* of beauty. Of a beautiful ending.

An old man in the coffin in his three-piece suit. Pocket square. Silk tie.

He looks so peaceful, says the family. So alive.

Unclish stood at the foot of her bed, twisting his beard and saying, Yes, yes, hmm, hmm. He had aged too. Seventh sensed it the moment he opened the front door and saw his esteemed uncle on the front stoop, sniffing the plastic flowers Mudd had hung there.

Second, Unclish said to Seventh. These smell divine.

Seventh, said Seventh.

That's what I said, said Unclish.

Come, Unclish, he said. Mudd is upstairs.

Yes, Fifth, he said. We must hurry.

Seventh was worried. Confusing a few names or numbers was easily enough forgiven—there were twelve of them, after all, and it had been years since Unclish had seen them—but it wasn't just that. Unclish was smaller than Seventh recalled, his top hat too big, his suit too large. It seemed to Seventh that as much as Mudd had grown, Unclish had shrunk. Where once Seventh looked up at him, now he looked down. When they were younger, Unclish's eyes burned with an inextinguishable zeal; now it seemed that his fire, like the flame of a once-bright candle, had begun to flicker.

Yes, yes, said Unclish as he looked over Mudd's corpse. Hmm, hmm.

Eighth looked to Seventh and pointed at his wrist, indicating the passing time.

It's been two hours, Unclish, Seventh said. Since she died.

Since she *died*, Eighth added. Two hours.

Unclish cast Eighth a withering look. Without turning his eyes from his insolent nephew, he gently took Mudd's left big toe between his thumb and forefinger.

Two hours and eleven minutes, my child, he said to Eighth. To be exact.

He released her toe, and wiped his hands on the bedsheet.

Do you have any idea, he asked the room, what today is?

The brothers, not wanting to anger him, racked their brains.

Columbus Day? Fifth offered.

That's in October, said Fourth.

It's Washington's birthday, said Second.

Washington's birthday? asked First. You mean Presidents' Day?

Presidents' Day *is* Washington's Birthday, said Second.

It is? asked Ninth.

IT'S REMEMBRANCE DAY, YOU JACKASSES! Unclish bellowed, and suddenly, despite his diminutive size, he was the fiery leader the brothers had known and feared in their youth.

Do you children remember nothing of our traditions? he demanded. Has America finally crushed you in her insatiable jaws? Must we 'tweet' about your holidays for you to remember, you chumps, you patsies, you bootlickers? Must we pay some whore celebrity to bring it to your weak and compromised attentions? Must we print it across the backside of Kim Kardashian's yoga pants so that you might, for one brief moment, remember who you are and where you came from?

He closed his eyes and shouted to the heavens:

SHALL OUR ENTIRE PEOPLE DIE WITH YOUR BLESSED MOTHER?

The brothers, chastened, stood silent. Remembrance Day was the most sacred day of the whole Cannibal calendar; even those Cannibals who observed no other traditions observed Remembrance Day. Of course, because secrecy was so central to their survival, the precise details of the holiday have been lost to history, and nobody remembers exactly what Remembrance Day was established to remember. Something happened—of that there can be no question—and whatever it was, it was bad. It was tragic. It was the most tragic thing that ever happened, otherwise why would they remember it, even if they didn't? All that is known for certain is that somewhere (no one can remember where), on some particular day (no one can remember which), something terrible happened to their blessed ancestors (no one can remember what), and it is important that they never forget it, whatever it was and whenever it happened, and that they curse the names of those who perpetrated whatever it was that was perpetrated, whoever they were, and whatever they did. The brothers could thus be excused for forgetting, but Seventh knew he needed Unclish to conduct the Victuals, and he quickly apologized.

I'm sorry we forgot, Unclish, Seventh said. But what does Remembrance Day have to do with Mudd?

Unclish composed himself and explained that to be born on Remembrance Day was a great honor, as it was a sign from the Ancient Spirits that the child would one day devote their life to the Cannibal people. No honor was greater, in fact, except for dying on Remembrance Day, which was a sign from the Ancient Spirits that the deceased had devoted their life to the Cannibal people.

No chances, therefore, Unclish declared, could be taken with Mudd's Victuals.

They must perform it with the utmost precision and care.

We cannot do it here, he said with finality. She's far too large. There is no way to Drain her, to Purge her. The neighbors will see us coming and going, and they will alert the police if they should happen to see any blood. We cannot risk being interrupted or compromised.

Where do you propose we do it, then? asked First.

Unclish twisted his white beard a moment and said, Yes, yes, hmm, hmm.

At the University, he finally announced.

The . . . University? asked Seventh.

The Seltzers, one and all, turned white with dread.

We must go, said Unclish, to the University.

• • •

Declared the Elder Elders: It is a greater honor to die on Remembrance Day than it is to be born on Remembrance Day.

What's the difference? asked the Elders, still miffed about the whole Cannibals-Can't-Drive-a-Lincoln thing.

Because, said the Elder Elders, surely it is a greater thing to have devoted one's life to our people in actuality than it is to merely promise to devote one's life to our people.

You're really hung up on the whole greater-lesser thing, said the Elders. It's not healthy. Why can't they both be great?

One must be greater than the other, said the Elder Elders, as I am greater than you.

That's what you think, said the Elders.

That's what I know, said the Elder Elders.

And they did not speak until dinner.

• • •

Despite its grim purpose, Seventh remembered Remembrance Days with a small degree of fondness. The solemnity of the occasion meant that Mudd was more sedate and earnest than on other days; instead of yelling at the boys, she sat on the couch and wept.

It made Seventh sad to see her cry, but he preferred her melodrama to her actual drama. She lit Remembrance Day candles and placed them around the usually dark house, and a rare sense of calm glowed where otherwise rancor burned.

He scolded himself for forgetting it.

It wasn't all bad, was it? he asked himself.

The traditions, the holidays. There was some good, wasn't there?

Crabs in a bucket, Dr. Isaacson said when Seventh told him that Zero had phoned.

What about them? Seventh asked.

Dr. Isaacson explained that crab fishermen know a little trick about crabs: When they put them in a bucket on the deck of the ship, they don't have to cover them to keep them from escaping.

Why not? asked Seventh.

Because if one crab starts to get out, Dr. Isaacson said, the others always pull him back in. Halfway to freedom, to safety, to happiness, the crab's own kind will pull it back down into the depths of certain doom.

It had made sense to Seventh at the time, and he thought of it often when Mudd had phoned him over the years, but maybe now the situation was different. Because I got out of the bucket, Seventh thought. I escaped. And they're not pulling me in, I'm returning. To the bucket. To Seltzerland. To protect it, defend it, build it.

Some weeks ago, Rosenbloom had sent out a company-wide email. In the 1950s, it read, the total number of newly published English-language books with the word *identity* in the title was thirty-seven. Since 2010, more than ten thousand have appeared.

Let's get on that, people, Rosenbloom wrote.

Everyone else was climbing into their boxes, Seventh thought, writing *Keep Out* on the outside and sealing themselves up inside. Why shouldn't I?

. . .

The dream of the University, Unclish wrote in the fund-raising materials, is the result of a nightmare. The Nightmare of Acceptance.

In every other nation, he wrote, and in every other time, we have been met with resistance. With rejection. And though we struggled, and though we fought, we were, in a sense, fortunate. Because that rejection kept us together. Oppression made us stronger. But today we are drowning in the quicksand of acceptance, and the more we struggle, the further we sink.

The University, he continued, will be our savior, situated on our own land—Cannibal land!—in a beautiful wooded township of New Jersey, to which Cannibals will come from far and wide. There will be a grand main hall, an even grander library, classrooms, a Victual Center. And there will be that treasure which had eluded them for so long: pride.

As for courses, he wrote with a contrarian flourish, our distinguished professors will create a syllabus that focuses on the writings, philosophies, and history of our people. The specific courses have not yet been chosen, but here is what we *won't* be studying:

The Greeks. The Romans. The Enlightenment. The Reformation. The People's Revolution of China. The Russian Revolution. The French Revolution. The American Revolution. Shakespeare. Molière.

Tolstoy. Plato. Nietzsche. Wittgenstein. Marx. Lenin. Freud. Darwin. Galileo. The Inquisition. The Rwandan Genocide. The Holocaust. The African Slave Trade. The Irish Famine. The Starving of Ukraine.

The list continued for two pages.

The writers we *will* read, he concluded, will be *our* writers.

The history we will examine will be *our* history.

The tragedies we will remember will be *our* tragedies.

He had a Cannibal artist compose a watercolor rendering of what the University would one day look like. Mudd wept to see it: the grand, Gothic main hall, the pointed lancet windows filled with gorgeous stained glass featuring famous scenes from the Cannibalian Diaspora: Samuel handing Julius the old leather valise, Julia resisting Henry Ford, Julius fleeing Detroit. Unclish used the artwork in his fund-raising drives and gave Mudd a poster, which she hung proudly in the living room, making room for it on the wall by removing the photos of her children. Every summer the children begged to visit the University—it is true they were more interested in the Olympic-size pool than the course selection, but their interest filled Mudd with pride regardless. A visit, though, never came to be. Mudd was too large to travel, she said; the drive was long and the car unreliable; the children, she said, couldn't miss school.

Next year, she promised every year. Next year in New Jersey!

Eighth would fume to hear that their visit had once again been canceled, and he would lie on the couch, hands behind his head, staring up at the poster, dreaming of the day he would enroll and study the works of his people.

Someday I'm going to go there, he said wistfully. Mark my words, someday I'm going to go there.

Me too, said First, clopping Eighth on the head with the back of his hand. And throw a rock through those goddamned windows.

. . .

Mudd didn't like discussing Auntie Hazel, and refused to when pressed. It was only from Father, years later, that Seventh heard her story.

Hazel was Father and Unclish's younger sister, and as she watched her brother Ishmael grow in esteem, she committed herself to documenting his rise for future generations. A record. A new New Testament. A *Foxe's Book of Martyrs*, minus (hopefully) the martyr bit.

It began as a small notebook. Hazel was a stenographer by trade, and could record an hour's worth of details in a matter of minutes. The project was a direct violation of Rule Number Two, yes, but since she was writing for the sake of her people (and about him), Unclish granted her dispensation and permitted the project to continue.

Just as we learned from the lives of our forefathers, he said, so might our descendants learn from us.

She began modestly. Names. Dates. City of birth. But soon the entries grew longer. Verdicts. Rulings. No law or decision escaped her notebook, and she soon decided that no moment of the great man's life should be forgotten. Nothing was too mundane, nothing was unimportant, from what he ate for breakfast to what he wore to work to when he went to bed.

Two eggs, scrambled. No toast. IBS.

The notebooks quickly piled up. Dismayed by all she might be missing, Hazel quit her job. Posterity demanded it. Her people demanded it. She transcribed, word for word, every discussion he had—initially just concerning matters of law and tradition, but soon no words he spoke were lost to her pages.

Who am I, she decided, to decide what is worthy of posterity and what is not?

His grocery list. His laundry list. His argument with the parking officer. His discussions with the postman:

Said Unclish: I thought last pickup was at six p.m.

The postman responded: That's during the week. Today is Saturday.

Said Unclish: I know what today is, thank you very much.

Unclish became concerned—and more than a little annoyed. She was there when he showered, there when he dressed, there when he went to sleep, and there when he woke, asking what he had dreamt of that night and what he would be having for lunch. One day he woke from a nap to find her going through his dirty laundry.

Boxers, she wrote. *White. Yellow stains in front. Brown in rear.*

He grabbed the notebook from her and tore out the offending page.

Hazel, he shouted, the minutiae of my life are no more important than yours! You need to stop this!

Hazel went home and considered what he had said. Her brother was wise, wiser than any man on earth, and did not waste his breath; his every word was imbued with meaning and intent.

It didn't take her long to figure out what he meant: that rather than record the minutiae of his life, she should record the minutiae of hers. Not the life of a nobleman, but the life of a peasant, of an ordinary Cannibal in the New World. What better way to teach future generations how to live? She began immediately the next morning.

I woke. I brushed my teeth. I had a coffee. I had another coffee. I watched Kelly Ripa. I fell asleep.

She grew depressed. Her brother's activities, no matter how mundane, were filled with meaning and import. Hers, by comparison, seemed dull and uninteresting. The closer she looked, the less she saw, and what she saw she didn't like.

Bland conversations.

Petty thoughts.

Banal dreams.

Hemorrhoids.

Earwax.

Yellowing teeth.

Shat, she wrote. *Pissed. Farted.*

So what else is new?

Her depression deepened. She took to bed, only leaving her house to get food. Humphrey tried to intervene, worried for his sister's health.

What are you doing to yourself? he asked.

Looking, she said.

For what?

Something good, she said.

He confiscated her notebooks, but she wrote on the backs of books, the pages of magazines. The next day he confiscated her pens, but she cut her thighs and calves and wrote on the walls with her blood. He hurried out to the pharmacy to get bandages, but by the time he returned, she was dead on the sidewalk beneath the open window of her fourth-floor apartment.

Beside her was her notebook. As the sirens began to wail in the distance, he picked it up and read the last entry:

The End.

And then, below it:

Thank goodness.

. . .

First drove an Escalade, a large Cadillac SUV with wide double rear doors, the only one of all the siblings' vehicles that could possibly fit Mudd's corpse inside (even so, they would have to remove whatever seats could be removed, and push forward whatever seats could be pushed forward), and so it was decided he would take her with him as they drove to the University. First refused, suggesting they rent a van instead, but Unclish insisted there was no time.

We have to leave now, he said. She's already gray.

First finally acquiesced, asking only that he not have to drive with her alone; Seventh, having taxied to Brooklyn anyway, agreed to ride with him. Zero drove Third in Mudd's old Subaru; the others all drove their own cars. They would follow First, who would follow Unclish.

Carrying Mudd to the Escalade was going to require the combined strength of them all. As they headed upstairs to bring her down, Ninth approached Seventh and pulled him aside.

Listen, Ninth said quietly, I know I should have told you this sooner, okay, but to be honest, I really didn't think this was going to go this far, you know? I thought we'd bury her, for Christ's sake; I didn't think we'd actually agree to . . . this. But now, all of a sudden, Unclish is here, we're heading out to the University, and I mean . . .

What is it, Ninth?

Ninth sighed heavily. He waited for the last of the brothers to disappear up the stairs.

I'm vegan, he said to Seventh.

You're vegan.

Don't say it like that.

Since when?

I'm a veterinarian, Seventh. I don't eat animals; I never have.

You ate Auntie Hazel.

I wasn't a veterinarian then, Seventh; I was a kid. And besides, I gave my portion to Third.

It's one bite.

It's a bite and a half, said Ninth. I can't.

You can't back out, Ninth. We all agreed.

I'm not backing out, Ninth said. I'm just . . . I'm just asking you to help me.

Help you? Help you how?

Eat my share, said Ninth.

No.

Please.

Ninth, we agreed to give her a proper Consumption. If you want to throw her up afterward, that's your call.

That's still eating, Seventh.

That is not eating, that's swallowing.

That's eating. That's the definition of eating.

Seventh took out his phone. Hey Siri, he said, what is the definition of eating?

First called from upstairs.

Guys, he shouted, we need you up here!

I have found what you're looking for, said Siri. The definition of eating is to take into one's mouth and ingest.

See? said Ninth.

Hey Siri, Seventh continued, what is the definition of ingest?

I have found what you're looking for, said Siri. The definition of ingest is to take into the body by absorbing.

There, said Seventh. If you spit it up, you're not absorbing. If you're not absorbing, you're not ingesting. If you're not ingesting, you're not eating.

Ninth rubbed his chin, uncertain.

First called again:

Guys, come on! She's heavier than a goddamned piano!

Okay, Ninth said to Seventh as he headed for the stairs, fine. But *no absorbing*.

The other nice thing about being Siri, thought Seventh as he trudged upstairs after his brother, is that she doesn't have siblings. No brothers. No sisters. No nothing.

Thanksgiving?

Empty table.

Christmas?

House to herself.

Grandparents' Day?

What's a grandparent?

No wonder she's so goddamned chipper.

. . .

May any people Consume the deceased, asked the Elders, or only Cannibals?

Only Cannibals may Consume the deceased, said the Elder Elders.

And may any Cannibals Consume the deceased, asked the Elders, or only family?

Only family may Consume the deceased, said the Elder Elders.

But what if one of the family has married out? asked the Elders. May the daughter-in-law, if she is not Cannibal, Consume the deceased?

No, said the Elder Elders.

But is not a daughter-in-law family? asked the Elders.

Yes, said the Elder Elders.

Then why may she not Consume? asked the Elders.

Because only humans may Consume the deceased, said the Elder Elders. And non-Cannibals are subhuman.

Jesus, dude, said the Elders.

. . .

Tenth climbed onto Mudd's bed and lifted her by her shoulders, while Third took her legs.

Wouldn't it just be easier to chop her up first and then bring her down? First asked. You know, like movers, with a bed? They don't bring the whole damned thing down in one piece.

We do not *chop her up*, Unclish said. We Drain, then we Purge, then we Partition, then we Consume.

It took the combined effort of every member of the Seltzer family to extricate their dead mother from her house. They had to remove the bedroom door from its hinges, and the railing from the staircase, and the storm door from the entryway, but eventually they got her outside and into the back of First's SUV.

And behold, the Seltzers went forth.

Unclish had First open all the windows, to keep the body cold and buy them some time before beginning the Victuals, and he reminded them all to drive with an abundance of caution, obeying speed limits and traffic signs so as not to get stopped by the police. As it turned out, his concerns about speeding were misplaced. Commuters fleeing the approaching winter storm weren't waiting for rush hour to head home, and traffic on the Garden State Parkway was heavy. Mudd was bloated, blue, and starting to stink.

This is nice, said Seventh of the vehicle, trying to distract First from the stench filling his car. Escalade, huh? What do these go for?

With the corpse or without? said First. I'm taking a cleaning fee off the top of the money, just so you know. This is my only ride.

Not that it's any of my business, said Seventh, but why does a guy in an Escalade need money so badly?

It's a leftover, First said of the truck. The last one.

Last what?

The last Can-Am Limo, said First, and he began to explain:

After leaving home at eighteen, First took a job driving for Tel-Aviv Car Service in Queens. It was run by Jews who assumed, given First's dark but ambiguous features, he was Israeli.

You from Israel? they asked.

Of course.

Which part?

Y'know, First had said. The main part. With the Dome.

Jerusalem?

Bingo.

He was hired on the spot. He liked the job, but resented the percentages the company took. First had grown up listening to Mudd condemn then-President Ronald Reagan for not acknowledging his Cannibal heritage. (On the plus side, though, he called his wife Mommy, which Mudd thought spoke well of him.) First, though, admired Reagan—not because he was Can-Am, and not because of the whole Mommy thing, but because Reagan ushered in what came to be known as the Greed Is Good decade. Here at last was a view of America that First could embrace:

Every man for himself.

Make a buck, keep a buck, and to hell with everyone else.

First had been told the story of Julius in the melting pot a thousand times. Mudd told him the It-Was version, Father told him the Was-It version, but First had his own capitalist version: Whatever happened that day in Detroit, whether Julius wanted to get into that pot or not, the one person First knew for sure wasn't in the pot was Henry Ford.

Because Henry Ford owned the damned pot.

And he owned the suckers in it.

With that in mind, First decided to start his own car service, with his own cars and his own drivers. He was a determined young man, and soon Can-Am Limo had a fleet of vehicles operating in all five boroughs. Aside from the occasional *Fuck Canadians* he found scratched on the cars, it was a heady, successful time.

America, he thought with a smile. Was it not worth it?

He had contracts with dozens of corporate clients, and moved into a sleek renovated loft in Lower Manhattan. Then, on 9/11, it all went dark. In the wake of the World Trade Center attacks, his clients began to suspect that First, given his dark but ambiguous features, was Muslim . . . and therefore a terrorist.

Are you crazy? he said to them. I'm Israeli. I'm from Tel A-fucking-viv.

I thought you said you were from Jerusalem.

I was born in Jerusalem. But I moved to Tel Aviv . . .

No amount of denial could convince them, and so he did the only thing he could to assert his loyalty to the United States: He bought a case of tiny American flags, and covered his fleet in them. He put tiny American flags on the windshields, tiny American flags on the passenger windows, tiny American flags on the bumpers; he even put tiny American flags inside the car, attached to the fold-down cup holder and the backs of the headrests, desperate to prove his unwavering patriotism. But it was no use; actual Muslims, also trying to prove their loyalty, did the same thing with their cars and stores, so that the tiny American flags on First's cars made him seem even more Muslim than he had seemed before.

One by one his clients switched to other, non-al-Qaedian car services. Soon he had nothing left but one last Escalade and a case of two thousand tiny American flags. He sat in his office, ready to give up, ready to return home as Mudd always said he would, 'with your tail between your legs.' But as he boxed up the leftover flags, he noticed something. There, etched on the side of the tiny wooden flagpoles, were the words *Made in China.*

Even in his misery, the irony of this made First laugh; as an American who had been run out of business by other Americans who thought he was un-American, it gave him a particular joy to see American flags made by the nation's largest economic competitor, sold to Americans expressing their support for America while actually supporting a Chinese company that probably made flags for every country in the world.

And it gave First an idea.

A quick search revealed that the Chinese company that made the American flags was named All-American Flags Incorporated, and it had, via a combination of shoddy manufacturing, cheap materials, and underpaid labor, put out of business a US-based flag company called American Flags Incorporated. The Chinese had simply added the word *All* to the name, undercut their stateside competitor by 50 percent, and priced them out of business. Their strategy had worked, but that was ten years ago; America, First knew, was now a very different place, full of knee-jerk nationalism and the reactionary xenophobia that comes with it.

Why not profit off the very same tribalism that had bankrupted him in the first place?

The following day, First opened All-All-American Incorporated, making cheap American knockoffs of cheap Chinese knockoffs of American products. He simply ordered the parts in bulk from China, assembled them in his garage with underpaid Muslim workers who had, like him, been laid off in the wake of 9/11, and stamped them with the All-All-American Incorporated logo. *Proudly Knocked Off in the United States of America* was emblazoned on every item they sold.

And they sold thousands.

He didn't need to be cheaper than the Chinese company; he only needed to match their price. Nationalism and paranoia did the rest.

The money rolled in, and First expanded. AAAI made American knockoffs of Chinese knockoff cell phones, American knockoffs of Chinese knockoff children's toys, American knockoffs of Chinese knockoff watches, American knockoffs of Chinese knockoff laptops. They had a great few years, and First made more money than he ever imagined. But once again, fate was against him, and the Great Recession hit. It gave the Chinese the opportunity they were looking for. Fear of Others now took a back seat to Fear of Financial Ruin; Americans were less worried about being blown up than they were about going under. The hatred of all things foreign was replaced by a love for all things cheap, and the Chinese seized the opportunity, opening a new company called All-All-All-American Incorporated, which specialized, as the packaging proudly declared, in *Chinese Knockoffs of the American Knockoffs of Cheap Chinese Knockoffs You Love, at the Cheap Chinese Prices You Need.*

First couldn't compete. It wasn't long before the orders dried up and he had to fire his staff, who were now suing him, claiming they were being fired simply for being Muslim.

But I *am* Muslim, First said to his attorney.

I thought you were black, said his attorney, who, because he now thought First was Muslim, stopped returning his calls.

And that was the end of that.

This Escalade, First said to Seventh, is all I have left. That's why I need her money. I hate taking it, but I need it.

You should write a book, said Seventh. *The Absolutely True Story of a Part-Time-Muslim-Israeli-Limo-Driving-Corporate-Cannibal-American.* It'll be a bestseller, trust me.

First sighed.

I thought I was leaving this Cannibal shit behind, he said.

It's one bite, said Seventh. A bite and a half.

No, said First, I mean back then—when I left, when I was eighteen. I packed my bags and walked out the door, thinking I'd find that mysterious, wonderful creature called an American. Open-minded, accepting, like Julius found on that boat, remember? But I didn't. You know what I found? Cannibals. Everywhere. Not Cannibals like us, but cannibals. Male cannibals in suits and ties, female cannibals power-dressed in tailored skirts and shoulder pads, cannibals in corner offices driving Porsches. And they consume, brother; they consume. They consume cars and clothes and houses, they consume and consume and consume, and yet they stay hungry, these cannibals. Stark raving mad hungry, even when their bellies are full. Just eating, eating, eating. And so you watch that, and you think, Shit, I better eat too. I better eat before all the food gets eaten up. So you start eating too, and you realize that now you have the hunger, that bottomless hunger that never leaves. And so you eat and you eat and you eat, but all that eating, that takes a lot of energy, you know? Stalking, killing, dragging it all back to the cave. That's a young man's game. You get older, you can't do it anymore, and you begin to wonder if it was worth it. You've been eating your whole damned life and you're still hungry. And let me tell you, that's when it's over—that's when you're done. Because with these cannibals, if you're not hungry, if you're not one of the eaters—the eaters who don't even know why they're eating anymore—then you're one of the eaten. I'm almost forty, and let me tell you, Seventh—I'm meat. I'm lunch. I'm done. The colors of America aren't red, white, and blue, brother; they're green and gold. Maybe I should have just stayed with the Cannibals I knew. At least they ate for a reason, you know.

Seventh looked out at the sea of gleaming automobiles around them.

I know, he said.

· · ·

Julia kept the indignities she suffered at the hands of Henry Ford a secret, concerned what Julius might do to Ford if he knew. Without explaining why, she begged Julius for them to leave Detroit, to return to New York. She cried, she yelled, but he refused—the pay at the Ford plant was just too good.

It was then, Mudd told her children, that Julia knew she would have to save herself, even if it cost them their income, even if it cost them their home and their future. She could not allow herself, as a Cannibal woman, to be defiled any longer. And so, one Friday night, after work had stopped for the weekend, Ford grabbed Julia as he always did, and dragged her to his office.

At last, he said, undoing his pants. We have all night.

Julia trembled with fear. As he tore at her clothes and buried his face between her breasts, she reached for the letter opener on his desk. Murder would mean the end of her freedom, but it would mean the end of the bastard Ford too. But as she did, she noticed, on the wall behind his desk, a framed photograph of Adolf Hitler.

All night? she said. Oh, I couldn't possibly.

Your fool husband is busy cleaning toilets! said Ford as he groped and pulled at her. Don't be concerned with him.

Oh, it's not him, she said. It's just that it's Shabbos.

It's what?

It's Shabbos, said Julia. The Sabbath.

Ford zipped up his pants.

You're . . . Jewish? he asked.

Yes, she said. You can still rape me, of course, but I'm afraid I do have to be home before sundown.

Ford went pale.

You're a . . . Jew? he asked, the word itself like dirt in his mouth.

You didn't know? Julia asked.

No, I didn't know! shouted Henry Ford. I thought you were a fucking Indian!

Julius never learned why he and Julia were chased out of the Ford factory that night, or why their belongings were set aflame, or why their windows were shattered, or why swastikas were painted on the front door of their home.

The fools must think we're Nazis, said Julius as they fled.

With nowhere else to go, they returned to Brooklyn. There Julius fell into a deep depression, and he cursed America and he cursed fate, and every morning and every night, Julius apologized to Julia for getting fired, and he promised that he had cleaned the toilets that night the best he could, and he swore he wasn't a Nazi and that he didn't even know what National Socialism was.

Julia kissed him, and told him that she knew it wasn't his fault, and that she loved him no matter what, and they held each other close, and nine months later, Julia gave birth to a beautiful boy they named John.

Because, said Julia, in this nation of Johns and Jims and Jacks, I want him to belong.

Because, muttered Julius when she was out of earshot, this world is a toilet.

And because it will never be cleaned.

. . .

Carol lay on the examination table as the technician conducted her ultrasound. Everything seemed fine, said the tech, but they wouldn't be able to tell the baby's sex via sonogram for several more weeks, after the fetus was well out of what was known as the Indifferent Stage.

It gets that from me, joked Seventh.

Before we become male or female, the nurse explained, we are simply a person. Not male, not female, not rich, not poor, not Democrat, not Republican. We possess what is referred to as an indifferent gonad, which will eventually become either testes or ovaries.

An indifferent gonad, said Carol. Sounds nice.

It does, the nurse laughed. Around the eighth week or so, the indifference ends. And that's when we become one thing or the other.

Enjoy it, kid, Seventh thought. *Existence will never be this simple again.*

He lay in bed that night with his head on Carol's belly, trying to listen to their child's heartbeat.

Can you imagine? he said. For one brief, wonderful moment, we are not one thing or another. We are everything and we're nothing.

Maybe that's what heaven is, suggested Carol. A place of eternal indifference. And maybe that's all life is—a constant striving to get back to the indifference we had when we were just forming.

So the indifferent go to heaven? said Seventh.

Yup, said Carol. Hell is for the people who think they're unique.

Seventh kissed her belly and then they discussed names. They wanted something positive, something hopeful.

How about Adam? said Seventh. Because he's our first.

Too biblical, said Carol. How about August, because that's when he's due.

Too Roman, said Seventh. Phoenix, because he will rise from the ashes.

Sage, said Carol, because she will be wise.

Gilligan, said Seventh, because he's marooned.

Marooned?

On earth, said Seventh. Waiting to be rescued.

Scotch, she said, because he's going to need it.

Ice, said Seventh, because it will reduce her swelling.

Gauze, said Carol, because it will stop her bleeding.

Target, said Seventh, because let's be honest . . .

Rum and Coke, said Carol, if they're twins.

Black and Blue, said Seventh.

Pitchfork and Torch, said Carol.

Seventh got up and poured himself a glass of wine.

I got it, he said, holding up the bottle. Riesling.

Riesling? That's a name?

Reese, said Seventh. It's hopeful.

That she'll be sweet? asked Carol.

Seventh climbed back into bed and she rested her head on his chest.

That she'll go with everything, said Seventh.

Carol laughed. That laugh, that laugh . . .

. . .

Mudd wept when Seventh married Carol, because Carol wasn't Cannibal.

But I'm happy, Mudd, he said.

Someday you'll realize there are more important things in this world than your own happiness.

Like *your* happiness?

Like your people, Mudd said.

Carol, meanwhile, was telling him the opposite.

Chains, chains, chains, she said. What a lovely ornament you'll make, Seventh, dangling there at the end of your chains.

So angry did Seventh become at Mudd that it was one of the few times in his life that he lashed out at her, and the only time he caused her to cry.

And exactly what will my misery achieve for our people, Mudd? What has *your* misery done for our people?

Mudd glared at him.

I stayed, she said. I put my people over my own selfish happiness.

Seventh felt the dam of anger within him break.

You and the mangy dog can argue about who stays better, he said. I'm leaving.

Her eyes filled with tears, but Seventh steeled himself and walked out, just as he'd watched his brothers do before him.

He wouldn't see her again until the day she died.

. . .

At last Unclish exited the highway, and the others followed. Down one road and then another he turned, the suburban streets soon giving way to more rural, wooded landscapes. The low-canopied roads twisted and turned on themselves, the houses growing more sparse as the woods grew more dense, until finally Unclish slowed and turned onto a narrow, potholed dirt road. A hundred feet farther down the road, Unclish at last pulled to a stop in front of a pair of tall, forbidding iron gates that hung off their rusted hinges, secured together by a long padlocked chain.

DANGER, read a rusted sign that hung from the chain. KEEP OUT.

Unclish dug some keys out of his pocket and unlatched the padlock, and the chain fell to the ground. The gates were heavy, cold, and had frozen to the icy ground; even the combined efforts of Tenth and Third could only open them wide enough for them to squeeze through one by one.

We'll all leave the cars here, Unclish said. It isn't far.

The Seltzers followed Unclish down the overgrown drive, past deep thickets and dense underbrush, ducking beneath the heavy pine tree branches that hung low to the ground. At last they came around a bend in the road, where they discovered, rising up before them, an ancient, abandoned Gothic building. It seemed, with its flying buttresses and elaborate spires, as if some ancient ruin from twelfth-century Europe had somehow made its way across the Atlantic to the woods of New Jersey, where it had been left to rot and decay. What wasn't covered in ivy and moss was covered in garish graffiti.

What the hell, asked First, is that?

Unclish looked up to it as if at the gates of heaven, and held his arms out to his sides. We have arrived, he said.

We have? asked First.

Where? asked Seventh.

Behold, said Unclish, the University.

This? Second asked. *This* is the University?

You have got to be kidding me, said First.

Eighth stared in disbelief at the Eden he had dreamed of as a child. It bore only the faintest resemblance to the poster in Mudd's living room.

What . . . what happened to it? he asked.

As our people crumbled, Unclish said with a heavy heart, so did the dream of a university. The older generations urged their children to attend, but the melting that began so long ago in Henry Ford's pot had taken its toll. They chose Yale and Harvard over their own people's university. They didn't want to know about our past, about our suffering, about our pain. All they wanted to know was what percentage of our graduates went on to law school. They wanted to know what kind of Greek life we would provide. Greek life, can you imagine? Like the Greeks who enslaved our ancestors? Like the Greeks who raped our women? Greek life? Greek life was dedicated to our death!

His voice rose and echoed through the cold empty woods.

Not a single student enrolled, he continued. Not a single class was taught. I thought this would be our beginning; I didn't know our end had already arrived. But it will serve our purposes today, my children. Your mother's Consumption will be the University's first Consumption. And, perhaps, its last.

They made their way up the crumbling stone steps. Seventh offered Unclish his hand, but Unclish waved him off. He stepped to the tall front doors, carved of a heavy wood, to which a large yellow sticker had been affixed: CONDEMNED—ENTRY PROHIBITED.

Unclish tore the warning off and threw it to the ground.

We have been condemned by far greater enemies, he said, than the board of health.

He pressed the doors open, and the loud creak of the ancient door hinges filled the lobby, a tall cathedral space of such wondrous beauty, even in disrepair, that it made Zero gasp as she stepped inside.

Oh my, she whispered. Oh my, my, my.

The light was dim through the shattered stained-glass windows, but even in that spare light, the grandeur of the room was overwhelming. For Seventh, it was agonizing. The ruined beauty of this condemned place seemed to condemn him in turn, its ruin his own fault. Cigarette butts, beer cans, and discarded hypodermic needles lay strewn about the floor, each one another witness in his prosecution.

Seventh tried the light switches.

Nothing.

Unclish stepped carefully across the buckled marble floor, over the deep green moss that had grown along the grout lines and the black puddles of rainwater that had formed between them, to face the tall graffiti-covered wall at the back of the room.

Kill the fags.

Kill the Jews.

Fuck this.

Fuck that.

He removed his top hat, as one might upon entering a temple.

This, he said, was to be a marvelous fresco. Floor to ceiling. Wall to wall. Painted by our people's most skilled artists. A landscape of the Old Country, with grapes the size of apples, apples the size of grapefruits, and grapefruits the size of a Chevy.

Grapefruits, huh? said First, kicking aside a discarded condom. Father said the Old Country was a toilet.

Your father was a toilet, Unclish snapped.

Maybe I can write this trip off as research, Fourth said to Seventh as he examined the spray-painted messages of hate. *Xenophobic Patterns in Pre-Genocidal America*.

And then Fourth disappeared.

And then Second disappeared.

And then First disappeared.

Seventh couldn't see them. He couldn't hear them. All he could hear were the excited students pressing past him, laughing, cheering, calling to one another after the long summer break, hurrying to class on the first day of the semester.

One calls to the other, asks how his break was.

Good, good! the friend calls back. Catch you later!

Proud young women laugh as they walk by, tossing their dark Cannibal locks as they go, eyeing him, giggling, hurrying off.

Two professors rush across the great room, dog-eared copies of the bestselling *Out of the Shadows* in their hands.

Did you like it? one asks.

I loved it, says the other.

(It's about time, the *Times* had raved.)

. . .

Getting Mudd's corpse into the University was going to be even more of a struggle than getting her out of her house. They didn't have stairs and doors to contend with this time, but it was a much farther distance, over rocky terrain, with no way to know when a cop might drive by.

As the brothers prepared to move her, Tenth approached Seventh and pulled him aside.

I don't like this, he said, hands on his hips.

Like what?

This, he said. This place, this town.

You have another university you want to use? asked Seventh.

I stopped for gas down the road, said Tenth. Got a bad feeling.

From what?

From the locals.

What kind of a feeling?

A bad feeling.

Did they say something? Seventh asked.

They didn't have to, said Tenth. They were giving me looks.

What kind of looks?

Looks, said Tenth.

Seventh knew the looks; they all knew the looks. It was nothing overt, nothing big. It wasn't a You're a Fucking Cannibal Look, the way it wasn't necessarily a You're a Dirty Jew Look, or a You're a Scary Black Guy Look.

It was the You're Not Me Look.

When Seventh returned from school the day Mudd scared off Oscar Kowalski, she sat him down in the kitchen and asked him what he had learned from the experience.

To fight back? he offered.

Yes, said Mudd. But also this: that it doesn't matter how much you want to belong, it doesn't matter how much you want to be one of them. Because it doesn't matter how you see yourself—they will see you the way they want to see you.

But they don't know what I am, said Seventh.

It doesn't matter, said Mudd. They know what you aren't—you aren't them. And that's all that matters.

A pickup truck slowed as it passed by, its brake lights bloodred in the darkening woods.

Seventh turned to watch it.

Could be slowing for a squirrel, he thought.

It's probably slowing for a squirrel.

.   .   .

They're not looking at us, Father would say whenever Seventh thought they were being looked at. Malls, streets, restaurants. Everywhere Seventh looked, he saw himself being watched.

They are, Seventh would say.

Who? Father would ask.

Those guys, Seventh would say. Over there.

Why would they be looking at you?

It looks like they're looking at me.

It only looks like they're looking at you because you already think they're looking at you, said Father. If you didn't think they were looking at you, it wouldn't look like they were looking at you.

But Seventh knew a You're Not Me Look when he saw it.

It is not enough to withdraw from the mob, wrote Montaigne, *not enough to go to another place. We have to withdraw from such attributes of the mob as are within us.*

Sure thing, Monty, thought Seventh. But it's the mobs outside us that are carrying baseball bats.

• • •

The pickup slowed to a stop. Seventh's heart beat wildly in his chest. He didn't want to get caught—Mudd's corpse was still waiting in First's truck—but there was a part of him, small but raging, that wanted a fight. That wanted to defend his people. Against the blood-thirsty haters. Against the crazed mobs of gunmen.

What was it, thought Seventh, about crazed mobs of gunmen and pickup trucks? Crazed mobs of gunmen love pickup trucks. If you just got rid of pickup trucks, you could get rid of half the violence in the world. Look at photos of war zones around the world and you'll see pickup trucks loaded with crazed mobs of gunmen. They can't get enough of them. Buy a pickup truck and leave it alone for ten minutes; when you come back, the bed will be filled with a crazed mob of gunmen, flags waving, guns at the ready. Somali flags, ISIS flags, Confederate flags. Vans are for serial killers. But pickups are for crazed mobs of gunmen.

Ford. The Choice of Crazed Mobs Since 1914.

Tenth took a step toward the truck. Seventh did the same.

The driver gunned the engine and peeled away.

• • •

> *Leave him to rot*
> *in a roadside ditch.*
> *Jack Nicholson*
> *is a son of a bitch.*

Rigor mortis was beginning to set in. As even the youngest Cannibal knows, chemical changes in the body cause the muscles to contract four to six hours after death; further chemical changes prevent those muscles from softening. The Victuals must begin before rigor mortis makes the body unworkable.

> *Be quick like a rabbit,*
> *not slow like a tortoise.*
> *There's only four hours*
> *before rigor mortis.*

By the time they extricated Mudd from First's truck, carried her down the driveway, and laid her down inside the main hall, her face was fixed and frozen, her fingers and toes already stiff.

Quickly, Unclish called upon seeing her corpse, or it will be too late!

Seventh, fetch the chain from the front gate! Third, bring the Knife of Redemption from the car! Make haste, children, haste!

> *Don't let her get stiff,*
> *don't ignore her lividity.*
> *Only you can prevent*
> *postmortem rigidity.*

Like whispers from an ancient grave, the old dicta were returning. As diligently as Unclish had worked to drill them into his head, Seventh had worked since then to forget them. And he had. Now, though, he could hear them, a grim ghostly chorus—himself, his brothers, and Unclish, gathered in Mudd's living room on Sunday mornings—reciting them aloud in unison.

Don't blow a fuse,
or turn to booze.
We got the blues
because of the Jews.

That one was probably Mudd's.

Seventh and Third hurried to the cars as Unclish had commanded, Seventh watching for pickups as they went. Third seemed practically giddy, and Seventh wondered if he understood what they were about to do, or even that their mother was dead.

You okay, big man? he asked.

Yup! said Third.

Listen, buddy, you know Mudd's . . . Mudd's dead, right?

Third nodded with excitement. Guess what? he said, a child with a secret he could no longer contain.

What?

Soon I'll be Sixth!

Soon you'll be Sixth?

Soon I'll be Sixth.

How will you be Sixth?

Because Mudd is Sixth.

Mudd is Sixth?

Because Mudd ate Sixth.

Right, said Seventh. So now she's Sixth. And when you eat Mudd, you'll be Sixth.

Yup, he said. And I'll be Mudd too.

You will, said Seventh.

I'll be everyone and everyone will be me.

Not a bad deal, said Seventh.

Third smiled as he pulled the old valise from Second's car. Not a bad deal, he said.

They returned to the lobby with the chain and the Knife of Redemption, and everyone got to work. Unclish handed Tenth the chain, directing him up the stairs to the balcony above the colonnade. From there, Tenth was to toss one end of the chain over one of the buttresses high overhead; Fourth, waiting below, would grab the end once it made it over. It took a few tries, Tenth cursing and gathering up the chain between each attempt, but at last the end of the chain arced over a thick buttress near the center of the dome and Fourth caught it. Unclish called Third over and, to test the strength of the buttress, had him grab the ends of the chain and lift his feet off the ground.

Whee! giggled Third.

Seventh braced for the building to collapse, but the buttress held. Unclish worked quickly; he was suddenly a young man again, his hands a blur as he secured the chain to Mudd's lower legs, looping it around her calves and ankles in such a way that when he was done, the more one pulled on it, the tighter it became.

Now! he directed the brothers. Pull! Pull!

Tenth and Third took hold of the free end of the chain and began to pull so as to raise Mudd into the air. But even with their combined strength, they were barely able to lift her legs off the floor.

Everyone! Unclish shouted.

First through Fifth hurried over; Seventh through Tenth grabbed hold; Eleventh and Twelfth kicked off their shoes and with Zero grabbed the end of the chain.

On three, called Tenth.

The siblings pulled. They groaned, they shouted, they swore.

C'mon, you fat fuck, First grunted.

Slowly, inch by inch, chain link by chain link, Mudd began to rise into the air. Harder and harder they pulled, and higher and higher she rose—legs first, then hips, then torso, until at last her head was all that remained touching the floor. With a final shout, the siblings yanked with all their might, and Mudd lifted into the air, swinging gently back and forth. Unclish shouted at them to keep pulling—Higher, higher! he called—until her head was a full three feet off the ground, whereupon Unclish commanded them to wrap the end of the chain around a nearby column and secure it with the padlock. The siblings did as they were told, muscles straining to keep her elevated until the click of the padlock released them. They let go, and turned around, and there hung their mother before them, an inverted five-hundred-pound Christ, arms outstretched, awaiting the resurrection only her sons could deliver.

Unclish dragged an empty trash can beneath her, and raised the Knife of Redemption overhead.

May you be Drained, he called out, as your ancestors were Drained before you!

And with a flick of the ancient knife, Unclish slit Mudd's throat.

. . .

Hey, sweetheart, Seventh said. Are you ready for the talent show?

Reese's voice was impossibly small through the phone.

I guess, she said.

You're going to do great, said Seventh.

Are you coming? Reese asked.

Seventh glanced back at the corpse of his mother hanging behind him, her blood steadily draining, drip, drip, drip, into the old trash can Unclish had placed beneath her.

Well, honey, he said, I kinda got my hands full here . . .

But Dad, said Reese, I need you to be here.

I'll be there, sweetheart, said Seventh, I promise. I'll just miss the beginning, that's all, but you go on at the end. I'll be there, trust me, I will.

It was ten past five. The show started at eight, and Reese didn't go on until the end. He figured that would be around nine or so, which gave him four hours to get the Victuals done, have a bite and a half of Mudd, and get back to the city. Tight, but not impossible.

Promise? Reese asked.

Promise.

Fuck, thought Seventh as he put away his phone.

Maybe First had a point. Maybe they should just chop her up and get it over with.

You need to go into town, Unclish said, a thin sheen of sweat on his brow.

Town? Seventh asked. Now? Why?

Why? Unclish snapped. Look at her! The Knife of Redemption is not sufficient for American bodies such as this. It has served us well, but it was crafted centuries ago, with Old Country corpses in mind, not these grotesque New World forms. My God, a lifetime of Cornucopiacation in the Old Country could never have produced a behemoth such as this.

First overheard them.

We're not going into town, he said. We're getting this done, now, and we're going home. I have a Leatherman in my truck; it can cut through a goddamned soda can.

We need a hacksaw, Unclish said, not some pocket knife. And trash bags, paper plates, ice, a cooler, a grill . . .

A grill? First asked.

We need to cook her, said Unclish, or have you forgotten even that part of the ceremony?

Unclish, said Eighth, it's been hours . . .

The cold has given us some extra time, said Unclish. She will not be the best meat we ever had, but our people have eaten worse.

He closed his eyes and recited:

> *Though she smells like hot garbage*
> *and industrial waste,*
> *remember: She's your mother!*
> *And season to taste.*

You want us to buy a *grill*, said First. Are you out of your mind? Is there some medication you forgot to take this morning?

You have a better idea? Unclish asked.

Yeah, said First. A much better idea. We go into the woods, find some logs and branches, start a fire, and throw her ass on it.

An open fire will attract police, Unclish said. Open fires are forbidden.

I don't remember that rule, said First. You're making this up as you go along.

You don't remember anything, said Unclish. *Open Fire, Cops Inquire.*

I don't remember that, either, said Eighth.

For First to question Unclish wasn't unusual, but Eighth raising objections concerned Seventh. If Eighth was having doubts, the rest of them would soon, too.

I'll go, said Seventh. It will take two minutes.

It won't take two minutes, said First, it's a goddamned half hour in each direction.

Just go, said Ninth, his own exasperation beginning to show. She has to Drain anyway.

Give me the keys, Seventh said to First.

I'll come, said Zero, looking at Mudd's corpse. I gotta get out of here.

No, said First, heading for the door. I'll drive. If I can make it from Manhattan to JFK in thirty minutes flat, I can get our asses back here before six.

Light snow had begun falling; the storm was getting closer. Seventh, riding shotgun, gripped the dash with both hands, watching the snowflakes dancing out of the Escalade's way at the last moment; you couldn't hit them if you tried to, which is what it seemed First was doing, gunning the engine through the yellow lights and flooring it around bends.

Take it easy, would you? said Seventh.

I knew that old fuck would complicate things, First shouted. I knew it.

Crashing won't get us home any quicker, said Seventh.

That was fucked up, said Zero, shaken by the Draining. That was extremely fucked up. He practically chopped her head off. Did you know he was going to cut her head off?

It's tradition, said Seventh.

It's tradition? asked Zero. That's your answer?

Yes, that's my answer.

What if the tradition was shooting her in the face? Zero asked.

Then I would have done it myself, First said as he gassed the Escalade around another corner.

I'll never understand the fascination we humans have with tradition, Zero said. So some fool in the past wore this hat, or ate this food, or fought this war, or died on this cross. So? So we wear the hats that they wore and we eat the foods they ate and we wear little crosses around our necks, never stopping to consider that these ancient people we emulate were utterly ignorant of even the most basic knowledge of our world. The average third grader today knows more than they did. No fault of their own, but they also believed the world was flat, that there was nothing morally wrong with people owning other people, that Earth was six thousand years old, and that God tossed it together in under a week. We even decide who to *hate* based on these ancient fools. *Two hundred years ago, your fool ancestors did this to my fool ancestors, so now fuck you.* Idiots. People two hundred years ago were assholes, all the time, to everyone. What's that got to do with us? We should be assholes because they were assholes? It's like they tell you day one of your driving lessons: Don't drive in the rearview mirror. Worry about what's ahead of you. But that's not what we do, is it? Look at Unclish. This is our sage? This is our wise man? The man has lived his entire life looking in the rearview mirror, walking backwards through life. What did this one say five hundred years ago, what did that one say? What did he do, what did she do? Hell, if it was just five hundred years ago it wouldn't be so bad. But it's not. Because the know-nothings we're emulating from five hundred years ago were emulating other know-nothings from five hundred years before them, who were emulating some know-nothings from five hundred years before them. We are literally stuck in the past.

Seventh found himself growing annoyed with Zero, though he couldn't say why. He didn't disagree with her, but the more she went on, the more he wanted to contradict her, question her, tear her arguments apart.

College students, he thought.

Had the ride gone on any longer he might have engaged her, but they were approaching town, and a familiar anxiety descended upon Seventh as they did, one that intensified the closer they came. It was a discomfiting feeling he hadn't experienced in years, and at last he placed it: It was the feeling he used to have when he was a young boy, and Mudd would drive through a black community. As soon as they entered 'the black area,' as she called it, Mudd would drop her hand from the steering wheel and press the button that locked the car doors.

Ka-chunk.

Animals, she would mutter.

First pulled to a stop outside the hardware store, where a CLOSED sign hung in the window.

Do these rednecks ever do any work, he said, or do they just spend all day fucking their sisters?

Nice, said Zero. Mudd would be proud of you.

First time for everything, he replied.

It's the weather, said Seventh. Snow's coming.

They drove around town for a while, and indeed everything was closed. With nowhere else to go, Seventh suggested they try the gas station; the convenience mart might have something they could use.

Evening, said the attendant as they entered. Can I help you folks?

The You're Not Me Look. Seventh could see it despite the attendant's bullshit smile.

We were just at the hardware store, Seventh said.

They close early, the attendant said.

Genius, thought Seventh.

We're having a barbecue, Zero said. Just need a few bits.

Strange night for a barbecue, said the attendant. Cookin' up something special, are ya?

We need trash bags, Seventh said. A cooler, flashlights, that sort of thing.

Hmm, said the attendant. There's some houseware-type things in the back. Might find a cooler there.

Seventh watched the attendant leer at Zero as she walked to the back of the store.

And a grill, Seventh said, stepping into his sight line.

A grill? asked the attendant. Like a barbecue grill?

A little one, said Seventh. Like a hibachi.

Hi-what?

Hibachi, said Seventh.

What's a hibachi?

A little grill, said Seventh.

The attendant frowned and scratched his head.

That a Japanese thing? he asked.

Seventh wasn't sure, and his own ignorance interfered with the pleasure he was taking in the attendant's confusion. It only made him angrier.

Yes, he said. It's a Japanese thing.

I'll google it.

Don't google it.

I don't think we have any little Japanese grills, said the attendant. We got soy sauce, if you want that.

Zero returned with a small cooler, inside which she carried trash bags, flashlights, paper plates, plastic cutlery, and a bag of ice.

The attendant smiled to see her.

Did y'find the soy sauce? he asked.

We need a saw, said Seventh.

Soy sauce? asked Zero.

A saw? the attendant asked. Like an electric saw?

A handsaw, said Seventh.

The attendant shook his head.

Nah, 'fraid not, he said. That's more a hardware store—type thing. They open at eight in the a.m., if you're still needing it then. Tell 'em Jimmy sent you; they'll hook you up.

Marvelous, said First when they got back in the car, slamming the door behind him. No saw, no grill. Now what?

We tried, said Seventh. Unclish will understand. We'll have to make do with the knife we have, and build a fire in the woods.

A pickup truck pulled in and stopped at the gas pump behind them. Seventh watched them in the side mirror.

He was nice, said Zero. The attendant, I mean.

First started the engine and put the car in gear. Seventh pressed the auto-lock on his side.

Ka-chunk.

Animals, thought Seventh.

. . .

Mudd revered Julius the Brave, and she wept for Julia the Anguished. But of all the stories Mudd told, none thrilled her as much
as the story of their son, John. Fearless, defiant, unyielding, John was
a man possessed of great physical strength and tremendous pride in
his people.

They knew him, one and all, Mudd said, as John the Strong.

Mudd's eyes lit up with pride as she told of his many conquests
and battles; here at last, she said, was a Cannibal who wouldn't
take it anymore. Instead of being raped, he raped. Instead of being
a victim, he victimized. Instead of looking down the barrel of a
gun, cowering, hands raised overhead, John held the gun, finger on
the trigger, demanding what was his.

And a few things that weren't, she said with a wink.

John, she said, grew up in a filthy tenement in Brooklyn, hungry,
cold, and sick. From his mother, he heard tales of abuse at the hands
of Henry Ford. From his father, he heard tales of backbreaking
labor, only to be chased from Detroit with little more than the shirt
on his back. John listened to his parents' stories, and vowed that the
same fate would never befall him or any other Cannibal again. He
was going to deliver his people from the shadows, release them, like
Moses, who was Cannibal, from bondage. He set about studying
martial arts, boxing, and wrestling, performing push-ups and sit-
ups by the thousands. By seven years of age, it was said, he was so
strong that he assisted in the Victuals, holding the corpses of family
and friends upside down by their ankles for hours as they Drained.
When he was nine, Mudd said, he competed in an international

martial arts tournament, where he defeated not just the competitors but also the evil master, who had a prosthetic hand made of knives and a room full of mirrors in which he hid.

That's *Enter the Dragon*, said First.

Mudd clopped him on the head with the back of her hand.

Where do you think they got it from? she said.

At twelve, by mutual agreement, John left school and took to working for a notorious Mafia boss. Though he rose quickly up the ranks, John was dissatisfied. Why should a Cannibal lower himself to work for an Italian? But the Mafia boss was a vicious man who did not take kindly to the idea of his protégé leaving. He threatened John, and said he never wanted to hear of it again. John could think of no way out, and was about to resign himself to his fate—and he might have if his mother, Julia, hadn't passed away a few weeks later. As he sat beside her corpse, watching her Drain, he recalled the way she had fought Henry Ford, and this inspired John to fight for his own freedom. And so, the following night, he invited the crime boss over for dinner.

What's the occasion? asked the boss as he sat down to eat.

My mother died, said John.

I'm sure she was a good woman, the boss said respectfully.

John came to the table, a plate full of meat in one hand, Julia's severed head in the other.

Good? said John. She was delicious.

The boss fled from John's house, and not only did he never threaten John again, he made him boss over all the Brooklyn families.

And you, Mudd said to Seventh, you're afraid of some dumb Polack.

. . .

Asked the Elders: Was it wrong for John the Strong to invite the crime boss over to Consume his mother? For only Cannibals may Consume the deceased.

No, said the Elder Elders. Because he did not invite him over to Consume his mother; he invited him over to fool him.

But how could he know that his ruse would be successful? asked the Elders.

Ah, said the Elder Elders. Because even the dumbest Cannibal is smarter than the smartest Italian.

Thou painteth with a wide brush, said the Elders.

Only a fool, said the Elder Elders, would paint with a thin one.

Like an Italian? asked the Elders.

Like an Italian, said the Elder Elders.

. . .

Of all her children, Mudd expected Third to be her John the Strong. Third the Valiant, they would call him someday, Third the Indomitable. But hints of future disappointment appeared early. She wanted Third to be aloof, but he was friendly. She wanted him to be wary, but he was trusting. Even as a young boy, he waved to strangers on the street, smiling widely and saying hi to everyone he passed.

Why, hello! the strangers said.

They were nice! said Third.

Mudd clopped him on the head.

Don't be stupid, she said.

The larger he grew, the more of a disappointment he became, and Mudd shook her head to see the wide shoulders and powerful arms he would never use to smite their enemies. She tried to make Third see the light, or rather the dark, by placing him in dangerous situations—taking him to high-crime areas at night, leaving him outside public high schools when they let out—and hoping he would experience enough brutality that he would learn the need for vigilance. But while Third's size provoked a fair number of comments, his quick smile and boundless trust turned any would-be aggressors into fast friends. From gang members to mobsters, Third was beloved.

How long will Someone punish me? Mudd sighed.

Mudd's disappointment with Third rankled Zero, who had been a disappointment to Mudd since the moment she was born. And so the more Mudd criticized Third for his lack of vigilance, the more Zero praised him for his amiability. It wasn't as if Zero's relationship with Mudd could grow any worse. As she got older, Zero, rejected by Mudd, rejected Mudd in turn. She rejected Mudd's traditions, she rejected her people, and she rejected her bigotry, making no secret of her belief that all people, Cannibal or non-Cannibal, had equal capacity for good and evil. Mudd usually ignored Zero, but this degree of willful naivete she could not abide.

That optimism's gonna bite you in the ass one day, little girl, Mudd said.

Zero laughed. You're the biggest optimist I know, Mudd. What could be more optimistic than bigotry? Than believing that only black people are criminals, that only Jews are greedy, that only Muslims are violent. No, I'm a pessimist, Mudd. I believe we're all criminals, we're all greedy, we're all violent, none less so than any other.

Not Cannibals, said Mudd, wagging her enormous finger in Zero's face. We're different.

But Zero was not Humphrey, and Mudd did not frighten her. She slapped Mudd's hand away.

Spare me, she said. I love this notion that defending your people is somehow noble. Tribal superiority is easy, Mudd; we're wired for it. It's like a stone taking credit for falling down a hill. It would be something for a stone to roll up a hill; for that they could be praised. I'm trying to roll up the hill, Mudd; you're just rolling down.

Now it was Mudd's turn to laugh.

And even a rock, she said to Zero, would say you're a damned fool.

. . .

It was getting dark when they returned to the University. The main hall was cold and gray, and the Seltzers sat around the room, shivering, checking their phones, trying not to look at Mudd's corpse, whose shadow now fell long across the lobby floor. It was a ghoulish scene, but somehow Seventh felt a sense of relief as he entered the main hall and pulled the heavy door shut behind him.

I'm home, he thought.

Unclish, said Seventh, we need to talk.

He explained that the hardware store had been closed, and though the gas station had some basic supplies, they weren't sufficient. The fact was, without a grill or anywhere to buy one, and without being permitted to build a fire, they would not be able to cook the meat at the University. He suggested they Purge Mudd now, and then, using the Knife of Redemption—and perhaps a little more elbow grease than usual—Partition her. They could then pack the meat in the cooler, head back to Brooklyn, and cook it—her—there.

Seventh's motives weren't entirely selfless; if they left the University immediately, and traffic into the city wasn't too terrible, he might still make Reese's show.

Let's get going, he said.

I agree, said First.

Unclish shook his head.

Impossible, he said.

Unclish, we have no choice, said Seventh.

She's already Draining, Unclish pointed out.

So?

So *Two to Drain, Twenty-four to Purge*, said Unclish. We can't Purge her until tomorrow.

Two to Drain, Twenty-four to Consume, Seventh corrected him.

Twenty-four to *Consume?* asked Unclish. That's preposterous. How could you Consume in just twenty-four hours? You need to Drain for twenty-four hours. Then you Purge. Then, following that, you Partition and Consume.

First stepped forward, incredulous.

You expect us to stay here for twenty-four hours while that fat bitch drip-dries? he said.

That's not what you taught us, Unclish, Eighth insisted. You taught us *Two to Drain, Twenty-four to Consume*.

Don't tell me what I taught you, Unclish snapped.

I'm not hanging out here for twenty-four hours, said Second. No way.

Unclish, said Seventh, we can't stay here overnight—

Why not?

My daughter . . . , said Seventh, and he immediately regretted it. What about her?

She . . . she has a school performance . . .

Seventh knew what was coming.

Oh, a school performance! Unclish said. I'm sorry, I didn't realize. Does she play the viola? Does she do a little song and dance? Well, then, by all means, let's violate thousands of years of tradition! Let's interrupt the Victuals of a saint, on Remembrance Day, so you can go watch your fool daughter do a handstand!

She doesn't do handstands, Seventh said.

She folds herself in half, he thought.

She ties herself in knots.

She forces herself into boxes.

She's her father's daughter.

This is ridiculous, said First. I'm not going to stay in this hellhole overnight because Uncle Dementia here can't remember the goddamned rules. Who died and made this decrepit asshole boss, anyway?

Your mother, said Unclish.

Our mother what, old man? asked First.

Your mother, said Unclish, made me the executor of her will. And a sizable will it is. She sold her house, two months ago, in case you didn't know, with the specific direction that until I am satisfied that the Victuals have been completed in the correct and traditional manner, no monies from the sale of the house will be released to anyone.

She sold the house? Seventh asked.

Unclish nodded.

When? asked Seventh.

How much? asked First.

Sale conditional upon her demise, of course, Unclish continued, a condition that has obviously been met.

She sold it? asked Seventh. Why?

Because she knew some of you would only perform the Victuals if there was money to be had, Unclish explained. I told her she was wrong; I told her you were good children, that you knew this might be our people's last Consumption, and that you wouldn't need to be bribed to perform our most sacred tradition. Clearly, I was mistaken.

I've got no shame about doing this for the money, said First. I'd be a lot more ashamed if I was doing it out of love.

She knew you would say that, said Unclish. She also knew that you would want to cut corners—throw her ass on the fire, as you in fact suggested. I disagreed, fool that I am. I said that given this could very well be the last Consumption ever, surely her children would desire to perform it in the strictest manner possible. I was wrong about that too. In fact, First, she predicted it would be you, specifically, who would chafe at the particulars. And so yes, children, your mother made me, as your eldest brother has phrased it, boss. Consume her in the proper manner, and you will receive your monies. She will Drain overnight. In the morning, you will return to the hardware store for supplies, and then we will Purge and Partition her. In the evening, we will have the Consumption. That is all. Now let's get some sleep; tomorrow will be a busy day.

The Seltzers were dumbstruck, and for a moment nobody spoke.

What'd she get for it? First at last demanded.

For what? Unclish asked.

The house.

For God's sake, First, said Tenth, have you no shame? The woman is dead, her body is hanging not five feet away—

I want to know, demanded First, his voice reverberating through the main hall.

I want to know too, said Ninth. I'm in this for the money; most of us are. If she sold it for nothing, I think we should know.

Why would she sell it for nothing? Tenth asked. Just to screw us?

Yes, said Second. Just to screw us. To make us eat her, and then discover that she sold it for a dollar. That doesn't sound like Mudd to you?

Sounds like Mudd to me, said Fifth.

You people are hideous, said Tenth. The woman whose corpse hangs before you happens to be your—

Five two, Unclish said.

The brothers paused their bickering.

What? asked Second.

Five two? asked First.

Five two, said Unclish.

Five two what? asked Fourth.

Five million two hundred thousand, said Unclish.

Five *million*? asked Second.

Unclish nodded. Two hundred thousand, he said.

Bullshit, First scoffed. He's lying, trying to get us to do his bidding. Who'd pay five million for that Whopper-grease-covered shithole?

A holding company of some kind, said Unclish. They bought the houses on either side too. Knocking all three down, ironically enough, to put up a Whole Foods. Organic meat, no antibiotics, that sort of thing. I assume by the looks on your faces that we are agreed, then: We stay the night and finish tomorrow. Either that, or we leave our fortunes, along with your mother and our history, and go watch Seventh's daughter play the clarinet.

First pulled his phone from his pocket.

Hey Siri, he demanded. What's five million two hundred thousand divided by twelve?

Never have a dozen people focused so intently on an iPhone.

I have found what you're looking for, said Siri. Five million two hundred thousand divided by twelve is four hundred thirty-three thousand, three hundred and thirty-three.

First looked up from his phone.

That's nearly half of a fucking *million*, he said.

Apiece, said Second.

First smiled and nodded. Apiece, he said.

Now the others began to smile too.

Some laughed, in relief, or disbelief, or both. Second hugged First, Eleventh hugged Twelfth, and Third hugged Fifth, simply because everyone else was hugging, which made the others laugh and cheer.

I take it we're staying, said Unclish.

We're staying, said First. We're staying, we're staying, we're motherfucking staying.

Your enthusiasm, said Unclish as he walked away, is heart-warming.

. . .

Gonna be a late one, Seventh texted Carol. *Rosenbloom meeting. Not sure I'm going to make the show.*

Reese would be hurt, no doubt, and experience more anxiety about performing without him there, but it was half a million dollars, for God's sake. That would be far more important for her in the long run than her father being at a talent show.

He watched the dots on his screen, waiting for the response he knew was coming.

It wasn't going to be pretty.

Why don't you be a man for once? she was going to say. Why do you always let him push you around? You gotta stand up for yourself, Seventh! He's not going to respect you until you do. I would be like, no, uh-uh, sorry, Mister Rosenfuck. I'm *going* to my daughter's show. He leaves early Friday for his Sabbath shit, Seventh, why can't you take off for your daughter's talent show? It's bullshit, Seventh. You *need* to stand up to him. You *need* to be a *man*.

He loved Carol, but he was beginning to tire of her macho Latina *Oh-no-you-di-int* bullshit. He wondered what life might have been like with a Can-Am woman. There would be struggles, sure, but at least they would understand each other, at least they would relate.

Of course, his Can-Am wife would text back. *Reese will be disappointed, but she'll get over it.*

It's a lot of money, he would respond.

It isn't about the money, she would send back. *This is about our people. This is about our unique cultural heritage.*

The dots stopped.

No response from Carol. No anger, no condemnation. Just silence. The most dreaded response of all.

Fuck, thought Seventh.

He was really getting tired of her Latina bullshit.

. . .

Mudd reveled in her children's failures, and she would phone Seventh to gleefully report their bad news. Their defeats proved she had been correct—correct when she said they should never have left, correct when she said they would be sorry. And so Seventh already knew why his siblings needed money. He knew that First's business had failed, even if he hadn't known what the business was or why it had closed, and he knew that Second hated his marketing job and would love to quit, but was at the same time afraid he was going to be fired.

He ran from our Consumptions, Mudd had chortled, and now all day he bows to consumers. That's the Spirit of the Ancients at work.

He knew Fourth's teaching job relied on the publication of his books, and he knew Mudd thought it ironic that Fourth's books on the history of mankind were not read by any significant portion of mankind.

Maybe he should have written about our people instead of their people, she said.

He knew Fifth's psychiatric practice was struggling, and he knew Mudd had told Fifth that it would.

People don't want to be fixed, she said. They want other people to be fixed, to be turned into them.

She never spoke of Eighth's failures, nor of Tenth's, since these were the sons who hadn't left her; rather, she crowed about their successes, about Eighth's finishing law school and Tenth's finishing the New York City Marathon. Ninth successfully completed his veterinary training, but even that Mudd found a way to scorn. Veterinary medicine doesn't pay what human medicine does, and Ninth was having a difficult time making ends meet. This Mudd attributed, like everything else, to his traitorous homosexuality.

Maybe if he wasn't an animal himself, she said, he wouldn't have to work on them.

And though she never mentioned Eleventh and Twelfth by name, Seventh knew that they had long desired to transition, and he knew that they couldn't afford it, and he knew it was to them Mudd was referring when she wept into the phone about how at least in the Old Country, men used to be men.

It's the government, she said. The deep state. They're putting estrogens in the water, did you know that? In the bottled water. To weaken us, Seventh, to subdue our people. They're running around drinking girl juice; it's no wonder they want to wear panties.

Her rejection of Eleventh and Twelfth infuriated Seventh, perhaps because he, too, felt trapped like they were in a box not of his choosing. At least the twins knew who they wanted to become; Seventh didn't even know that much.

What about me, Mudd? he asked. I edit other people's books all day when I really want to write my own. Is my failure as sweet to you as the others'?

But you tried, Seventh, she said. You wrote a book about us. About our people.

An unpublished book, said Seventh.

It's not your fault, she comforted him. The Cannibal market's too small for the Jews to make a profit.

I thought it was the Chinese, said Seventh.

It's everyone, goddammit, said Mudd.

. . .

Unclish liked to compare the history of their people to a movie. An epic, he said, with a running time of ten thousand years. Each of us walks on screen, stays the briefest of moments, then leaves.

And you dare to say you know what the movie is about? he scoffed. To say, moreover, that the movie is about *you*? That you, in your split-second scene, are the protagonist of a millennia-long narrative filled with tens of thousands of characters in dozens of nations?

Remember, said Unclish: the only reason you matter at all is because of all who came before you, and all who will come after.

This, many years later, was what Dr. Isaacson would refer to as the Temptation of Grand Narrative. We are born, he said to Seventh, we stay the briefest of moments, and we leave. Faced with such staggering insignificance, we seek to attach ourselves to some larger story—our people, our nation, our religion. We call this pride, said Dr. Isaacson, but it is really just a form of low self-esteem. The ultimate effect, in fact, is to make ourselves less important, our purpose, goals, and dreams smaller and more irrelevant.

We are enough, said Dr. Isaacson. You are enough. Live your life, free of earlier chapters. Your own chapter—nasty, brutish, and short—is as grand and glorious a narrative as any thousand-year epic that came before you.

With night beginning to fall, Unclish sent Seventh and Second to look for beds. The east wing, he said, was where the dormitories were located; there might be some old mattresses there they could use.

The University—what had been built or what was left of it—was laid out in the shape of a T, the main hall being the stem off of which branched the arms of the east and west wings. Seventh led the way down the trash-strewn hallways of the east wing, pausing to peer now and then into the dark dorm rooms as one might pass through a graveyard, wondering about the students who might have lived there.

What if they come back? asked Second.

Who?

Whoever was here, said Second. Whoever left those needles, those condoms. They could be gang members, Seventh; they could be crack whores. They could be dangerous.

Crack whores aren't dangerous.

How do you know?

Because they're on crack.

They could be gang members, Seventh. This isn't a joke. I have kids; you have kids.

This is ours, said Seventh.

So?

So we'll defend it.

Bullshit, said Second. If they come back, I'm out of here, I'm just telling you that. You want to catch a bullet over a derelict building, you go ahead. It's not my building.

It *is* your building, Seventh snapped. It's all of our building.

Not mine.

Because you're Jewish?

No, Seventh, because I'm not an asshole. I fight with Miriam all the time about this. Our son Josh turns eighteen next year, you know what she wants him to do? She wants him to join the Israeli army. The Israeli fucking army. Said she wants him to fight for his country. I said, His country? We're from Westchester. The *North*-east, not the *Middle* East.

It's her homeland, said Seventh. She wants to defend it.

That's what she says, said Second. She says Israel is our homeland. She says we have to defend our country. I'm like, Country? What is this *country* shit? Are we still playing this game? Haven't we as a species moved on from that yet? What is a country? Tell me, Seventh. What is a homeland? It's fiction, brother, dangerous fiction. Country is a line in the sand, made by a terrified monkey who had the bad luck to develop an awareness of his own mortality. So Og thinks, Fuck me, this is scary, this whole existence thing. I could die! Now, maybe it is scary, maybe it isn't. But what does he do? He makes it worse. You know how? The little fuck makes a *country*. Asshole. He thinks, *If I have a country, I'll be safe*. And so Og grabs a stick and he draws that line in the sand, and he says, This is my country, from that birch tree to that big outcropping, to the bluff beside the meadow. That's my country. And guess what? He feels safer. He has a country, goddammit. If only he had some fireworks to celebrate. But here's the thing—he's not actually any safer. In fact, he's less safe, Seventh. Because a second monkey, Zog, just down the road, he's developed an awareness of his own mortality too. It's a virus, this awareness. It's spreading, like herpes. So Zog sees Og's country, and thinks, Hey, I need a country too. This is bullshit. And so he grabs a stick and he draws a line in the sand. He says, This is my country, from that oak tree to that stream, to that field of sunflowers at the edge of the val-ley. Og sees this and he says, Hey, man, what gives? I want the field of sunflowers. And Zog says, Yeah, well, who the fuck said you could have the birch tree? Now they're fighting. Now they're using those sticks to bash each other over their little monkey heads. Do you see how it works, Seventh? Because they were afraid of getting bashed over their heads, they're now getting bashed over their heads. Assholes. Now they have to defend their countries, like Miriam wants Josh to defend Israel, and you want me to defend this derelict crack house. Sorry, brother. Not gonna happen.

Seventh stopped as he passed a garbage-strewn dorm room with a pile of old mattresses stacked against the wall; they were filthy and mildewed, but they would get them through the night.

What young student, Seventh wondered as he righted the overturned desk, might have lived here, studied here? What posters might he or she have taped to the wall? Of singers, of actors, of Unclish?

You know those photos they take of Earth from outer space? Second continued. Show me a single nation on that photo. Show me a border. There isn't one. There's land and there's water. That's it. Nations are fictions, and I don't die for fictions.

You have enemies, said Seventh, nudging the garbage into a small pile with his shoe, whether you have a country or not.

Enemies? said Second. Please. Who? Where? They change every fucking day. Sixty years ago they said Russians were the enemy. Now Republicans say Russians are our friends, and Democrats and Muslims are the enemy. Democrats say Russians and Republicans are our enemy and Muslims are our friends. Miriam used to be afraid of black people. When we met, she would lock the car doors when we drove through the Bronx, just like Mudd used to, remember? Thirteen years later, you know who performed at Josh's bar mitzvah? Jay-Z, I shit you not. She says Jews and blacks share a common goal, says we both understand being hated. Pre-Trump she feared black people. Post-Trump she's afraid of white people. Now she locks the door when we drive through Scarsdale.

But Second had disappeared.

Seventh couldn't hear him.

He is sitting at his desk, headphones over his ears, working on a paper. Biology. Math. History.

Cannibal history.

A fellow student pops his head in the door—a Can-Am from Florida, or Michigan or Los Angeles—and taps him on the shoulder.

Party down the hall, Sev, he says. You coming? Julia's gonna be there.

Julia's the young Can-Am beauty who made eyes at him in the main hall, the one who will one day tell him to skip the talent show because Mudd's Consumption is more important. But Seventh looks up at the poster of the Old Country taped above the desk.

No, he says.

He has work to do.

For his people.

. . .

Father told a very different John the Strong story than Mudd did.

John, Father said, was a no-good thug.

John, Father said, grew up in a filthy tenement in Brooklyn, hungry, cold, and sick. From his mother, he heard tales of abuse at the hands of Henry Ford. From his father, he heard tales of back-breaking labor, only to be chased from the factory with little more than the shirt on his back.

That much Mudd and Father agreed on. But where Mudd's John was a noble freedom fighter for his people, Father's John was a violent sociopath who used his identity to excuse his actions and fool his parents. When he got caught bullying a classmate, he told his parents it was because the other boy—half his size—had been bullying him for being Can-Am.

I'm sorry, Mother and Father, he said. But I won't let our people be pushed around.

They beamed.

When he got caught stealing the answers for his eighth-grade math test from the teacher's drawer, he said it was because his people suffered an unfair disadvantage.

The tests are rigged against our people, he said.

They beamed.

When he and the local Mob boss were caught selling stolen cigarettes out of the back of a stolen tractor trailer, he said it was because his people needed cigarettes.

Which people? asked his father, who was beginning to suspect something was amiss. Cannibals or Italians?

All my people, said John.

He ran drug rings, prostitution rings, gambling rings. He was a mobster, said Father, plain and simple.

Oh please, Mudd later said when Seventh questioned her about it. When white people do it, it's investing. When our people do it, it's a crime.

The only other part of the John story Mudd and Father agreed on was that he died in a hail of gunfire. But they differed strongly on the reason why.

They shot him, said Mudd, because they couldn't stand to see a strong Cannibal male.

They shot him, said Father, because he murdered two police officers while committing armed robbery.

As tempting as it was to believe Mudd's version, Father was John's son.

When he hit me, said Father, he said it was because our people needed discipline. When he slapped my mother, he said it was because he held Cannibal women to a higher standard. When he left us, he said it was to fight on our people's behalf. He wasn't a hero, Seventh. He was an asshole.

Mudd saw no contradiction.

He was an asshole, she said. But he was *our* asshole.

. . .

After helping drag the mattresses to the lobby, Seventh decided to explore the west wing. It was dark now, and he aimed the narrow beam of his flashlight down the long central hallway, past rows of what he assumed were administrative offices of some kind: file cabinets, lamps, and swastikas.

Swastikas, everywhere swastikas: spray-painted on walls, doors, windows.

Forget about the crackheads, thought Seventh. Either there were a ton of Nazis in New Jersey, or swastikas were just really easy to spray-paint.

Maybe people weren't as hateful as graffiti tended to suggest.

Maybe they were just shitty artists.

Farther down the hall he passed what must have been the University's library. It was a large, grand room, its arched windows bricked over, its walls lined with empty bookshelves.

An ending, he wondered, the books stolen or removed? Or a stalled beginning, the books still on their way?

The library is filled with students, but they hardly make a sound, focused as they are on their studies. They sit in rapt silence at long oak tables, their laptops and coffee at the ready. And there is Julia, her dark, Cannibal blue-black hair glistening in the soft sunlight, her Cannibal skin that impossibly alluring ambiguous tone; it is not, as Seventh once thought, a nonspecific color, but rather a blending of every color, which makes it the most beautiful color of all, the color of many, the color all humankind had been blending on its palette since time began.

She glances over her delicate shoulder at him, tucks her hair behind her ear, and smiles.

He holds a finger up to his mouth—Shh!—and she smiles.

Seventh continued down the hall, at the far end of which he noticed a pair of ornate wooden doors, not unlike the front door of the main hall itself. But something seemed odd about them to him, something off, and as he drew closer, he realized that by all appearances, the doors hadn't been touched—not vandalized, not graffitied, not even opened—in years, perhaps not even since the building had been built.

Seventh reached out, took hold of the gleaming bronze handles, and pulled. The rest of the doors in the building had either fallen off their hinges or squealed loudly when opened, but these doors were silent, new. Slowly, warily, Seventh stepped inside what was the most magnificent theater he had ever seen. By virtue of his profession, he had led something of a cultured life—readings, stage plays, symphonies, film premieres—but he had never, in all those years, seen a theater as achingly gorgeous as this. Proscenium style, it contained the same high arched ceilings and tall windows as the main hall, but the theater was as undisturbed as its ancient doors had been: no graffiti, no trash, no needles. Even the dust that had settled everywhere else in the University, it seemed, dared not settle here. Rows of red theater seats led down to the wide wooden stage, where it seemed as if the show was ready to go on. Stage lights hung from the rafters, tall speakers lined the stage walls, a podium stood at center stage, the microphone still in its stand. And though he knew that the seats waited in vain for an audience that would never come, Seventh could hear the laughter and applause that would have filled the room, see the couples in their finest evening wear, air-kissing one another after the show and walking out, arm in arm, having experienced in the great Cannibal story they saw there that which other peoples long had:

I belong.

Seventh made his way down the aisle, climbed the small stairs to the wooden stage, the floorboards creaking beneath him, and took his place at the podium.

He looked out at the crowd.

A full house.

Men, women, children.

Ladies and gentlemen, he called out. Cannibals. Good evening. And welcome, at long last, more than one hundred years after Julius Seltzer first came to this country with little more than the shirt on his back . . . to the Ishmael Seltzer Cannibal-American Theater.

And the crowd goes wild.

. . .

It was Montaigne's disdain for certainty that drew Seventh to him. His adamant *un*certainty—about his opinions, about the world, about his own self. His willingness to be wrong, to enthusiastically not know. You can keep your rock stars and political revolutionaries. Self-doubt was real rebellion. Even when Montaigne made changes to his essays, he only added to them, never deleted; he wanted his readers to see his malleability; the changes were the point, not the conclusions. He contradicted himself, changed his mind, ever open, ever searching.

I like the words we use to soften and moderate the presumptuous character of our arguments, he wrote. *Perchance, To some extent, Some, It is said, I think, and others like them.*

But now, as he lay on a filthy mattress in the crumbling lobby of his people's university, Seventh wanted certainty.

Am I this or that?

Am I last or first?

Am I hero or villain?

Something felt right about this place, Seventh thought. Despite the trash and the disrepair, the cold and the dark, something felt right and warm. Lying there, surrounded by his family, all of them coming together to perform this ancient ritual, Seventh closed his eyes and smiled, enjoying that which he never thought he would:

The warm safety, the comfort, like a hug, of the box he had so long been desperate to escape.

· · ·

Side dishes are a problem. Appetizers are tricky, too, but few subjects in all Cannibal law are as debated as those governing sides. Early Cannibals held that the body must be Consumed alone, with no other food whatsoever. To include a side dish, they said, would be to suggest that this was merely a meal like any other, for sustenance and survival, rather than a sacred transubstantiation ritual and the gifting of eternal life to our beloveds. Extreme as this position was, there are still those today who hold that side dishes are strictly prohibited, that to serve one is an insult to the deceased, to their people, and to their history as well.

Not even a salad? the Elders asked.

Not even a salad, said the Elder Elders.

What about a garnish? asked the Elders.

Garnishes, said the Elder Elders, are a tool of our oppressors who wish to trick us into eating that which is not our tradition.

Trick us? the Elders asked.

Do they not cut their radishes to look like flowers? the Elder Elders said. And their carrots like springs, and their cucumbers like roses?

Indeed, said the Elders. But what about some bread? For dinner rolls look only like dinner rolls.

You want a dinner roll, said the Elder Elders, have a dinner roll.

But traditions are mutable, no matter how much comfort we take in their supposed permanence. And so, after Julius had Drained, Purged, and Partitioned his beloved Julia, he sat at the dining table he had shared with her for so many years, looked down at the plate before him, nothing upon it but a meager slice of meat, and wept. Julia, after all, had lived through terrible suffering. She had been so defiled and beaten in her youth that by her middle years, she had been robbed of her beauty itself; her ugliness reduced the number of assaults, but the anguish of beatings was replaced by the deprivations of the Great Depression. Pain had been her constant companion in youth, hunger ever after. Nobody suffered more than

Cannibals, and no Cannibal suffered more than Julia. And so, Julius decided there could be no greater insult to Julia than the empty plate that had haunted her throughout her life. He stood from the table, went to the kitchen, and brought back with him some slices of apple, which had been her favorite fruit, and some peanut butter, which she liked to spread on the apples, and a handful of short-bread cookies, which were her favorite dessert, and he consumed them with her as one.

For many years after, that was the accepted tradition. No Consumption was considered complete without a few slices of apple, some peanut butter, and a handful of shortbread cookies. To do any less, it was said, was an insult to the deceased, their people, and their history.

By the time Julius himself died some years later, his son, John, was already a notorious criminal/hero, with a large house, two cars, and a mattress full of cash. Having watched his father Consume his mother with nothing but some apples and cookies, John decided to make Julius's Consumption a lavish feast, the most opulent, sumptuous feast ever held, for any and all Cannibal-Americans who wished to come (those who didn't would answer to him).

The feast lasted three days and three nights. In addition to the two plates piled high with the meat of his father, there were two platters from every animal on earth: cows and chickens and deer and bears and bison and rabbits; there were tables full of sausage, potatoes, pasta, salads, cheese, wine, liquor, and desserts. People would speak of Julius's Consumption for years to come. As a result, what was once an austere tradition now became for many a lavish, catered affair, held at the finest clubs and ballrooms in the world. Even to this day there are those who insist that no Consumption is complete without a band and a caterer. To do any less, they say, is an insult to the deceased, their people, and their history.

Not everyone approved of this change, of course, most notably John's own son Ishmael, later Unclish, who lamented what had become of their sacred tradition.

We have not just Consumed my grandfather, Unclish said regarding John's Consumption of Julius, we have been consumed by Consumption itself.

And so, when some years later the police eventually killed John in the act of robbing a bank/reclaiming his people's money, Unclish Consumed him, as his grandfather had his grandmother, with some simple fruit and a nice piece of cake. Some years later Unclish became the spiritual leader of their people, and decreed that the only food permitted at Consumptions beyond the deceased themselves and some apples would be a single side dish (the favorite side dish of the deceased), a one-cup serving (not rounded), with no beverages (water is permitted—still, not sparkling) except maybe a cup of coffee (hot, not iced), with a nice piece of cake afterward (single layer, no filling, no pies). To do any more than that, Unclish proclaimed, would be an insult to the deceased, their people, and their history.

. . .

Early the next morning, Unclish roused Seventh, frost on his old man breath, saying, It is time for you to go to town, and to acquire for us a handsaw.

Seventh wiped the sleep from his eyes and nodded.

Okay, he said.

And a grill.

Got it.

And some fries.

Fries?

With ketchup, said Unclish, as according to Third, fries with ketchup was Mudd's favorite side dish.

Seventh pulled on his coat and hat, woke First, and they headed into town.

The first thing I'm gonna buy when my inheritance check clears? First said. A Ford. I don't even want one, I don't even care what model it is. Just to fuck her. What do you think?

Zero sat in the back, happy for any excuse to get out of the University.

I think you're petty, she said.

Perfect, said First as he pulled into the hardware store lot. I was going for petty.

It being winter, the choice of grills was slim. Seventh chose the least expensive charcoal model he could find; he didn't want to go cheap on Mudd's Consumption, but he figured they were only going to use it once, and he doubted anyone was going to want to take it home.

We'll take this one, he said to the salesman. And a bag of charcoal.

What're you grilling? the salesman asked. If you don't mind my asking.

Seventh felt his unease return. Why did this redneck give a damn what they were grilling?

I mind, said Seventh.

Meat, said First, covering for Seventh's surliness. Shit ton of it, too.

Good hunting around here, the salesman said. Caught something big, did ya?

My man, said First, with a beast this size, it's more like she caught us.

The salesman chuckled knowingly.

I hear ya, he said. But I'm afraid you're making a mistake.

Are we? Seventh asked. And how is that?

There are two types of people in this world, the salesman began. You got your charcoal people and you got your gas people. Charcoal people hate gas people, and gas people hate charcoal people. Been that way since the day the good Lord created us, I suppose, and there's no talkin' to one if you're hailin' from the other. I was at a cookout over at the park this summer, guy showed up with a gas grill, damn near started a war. Folks around town still not talking to each other over it. Now me, I'm a charcoal man myself, but I don't judge the gas people. Some of my best friends are gas people, I mean that. My wife's gas; hell, my kids are gas. Fact is, though, if you're looking for flavor, you can't beat briquettes, there's just no two ways about it. But I will say this: if you got something big, and you're looking for fast and easy—and I say this as a dyed-in-the-wool charcoal man—go with gas.

Fast, said First. We definitely want fast.

The salesman led them to a large stainless-steel floor model, a leftover from the previous season. It was fully loaded: two side burners, a warmer, electric rotisserie, and a full set of grill tools. Triple the grill area of the charcoal model, he said, and he'd throw in the propane tank as well, since it wasn't exactly grilling season.

We also need a knife, said Seventh.

Ten-inch okay? asked the salesman.

Not for the animal we're cutting up, said First.

I got a twenty-two-incher, said the salesman, but that's mostly for trees and branches.

We'll take it, said First.

Must be some beast you boys caught, said the salesman.

Yup, said First. A real mother.

. . .

It was ten a.m. by the time they pulled up at the Burger King drive-through and ordered a dozen fries. First asked for ketchup—A shitload, he said—and they headed back to the University.

First had stuck Seventh with the bill for the fries, as he had with the bill for the grill.

What do you care? he had said. You're about to be rich, brother.

About to be rich wasn't the same as being rich, and the mention of money caused Seventh's stomach to tighten; he still owed Rosenbloom a manuscript. He pulled his phone from his pocket.

Found an MS I'm liking, he texted Rosenbloom. *Gonna stay home today and try to plow through it.*

Great, Rosenbloom responded. *Is it the One-Legged-Pakistani-British-American-Fiscal-Conservative-Social-Democrat-Transgender-Polygamist one? I thought that one showed promise.*

No, responded Seventh. *A new one. Just came in.*

He paused.

Cannibal-Americans, he typed.

He stared at the words a moment. He liked the way they looked. Proud. Defiant. Out from shadows. And though Seventh knew it was forbidden to reveal that one was Cannibal, he wasn't technically revealing *he* was Cannibal, was he?

What would John do?

John would hit Send.

Seventh hit Send.

He watched the dots on the screen, waiting, as he imagined Mudd had waited for Jack Nicholson that night at the Academy Awards. For validation. For permission.

To what?

To exist.

Hilarious, Rosenbloom responded.

Then he added a /s, so Seventh would know he was being sarcastic.

Lousy Sherwood, thought Seventh.

Fuck, First suddenly said. Cop.

Seventh checked his mirror. The patrol car was close, trailing them. His pulse began to quicken.

How long's he been there? he asked.

Just noticed him, said First. Fuck. Fuck.

Okay, okay, said Seventh. Just keep going.

Where?

Anywhere. Just not home.

Home? First asked.

The University, said Seventh.

The police lights came on.

Fuck, said First. He's pulling us over. I have to pull over.

What's the big deal? said Zero.

This truck smells like a corpse, said First as he came to a stop. That's the big deal.

It smells like French fries, said Zero.

It smells like French fries and a corpse, said First.

We didn't do anything wrong, said Zero.

Like cops give a fuck, said First.

Not all cops are evil, said Zero.

Just most, said First.

The police officer stepped out of his cruiser and approached them slowly, hand on his holster as he examined the barbecue grill sticking out the open rear window.

Morning, officer, First said too cheerfully. Everything okay?

The officer bent over to get a look at him, then at Seventh in the passenger seat. He wore mirrored sunglasses, despite the heavy gray storm clouds that blotted out the sky, and his sharp-brimmed police hat perched atop his military-style shaved head as if even it were afraid to touch him.

License and registration, he said flatly.

Are you black?

No.

Jew?

No.

Arab?

No.

First handed the officer his papers.

Date of birth? the officer asked him.

Why do you need his date of birth? Seventh asked.

The police officer looked across at Seventh, his face stone. Again First stepped in to cover for Seventh's aggression.

He wants to know if it's my birthday, First said to Seventh with a laugh. Get off his back, brother; he'll probably get me a better gift than you will.

He turned to the officer, told him his birth date, and said, Don't send me flowers, though, people will talk.

The officer checked the license and smiled as he handed it back to First.

I'll keep it a simple card, he said.

Something funny, said First. I don't like the mushy ones.

I was behind you coming out of town, the officer said. Saw the grill sticking out your rear window.

Oh, said First. Yeah. Sorry—we went with the big one, had to leave the rear window open to fit it.

Nice-looking unit, said the officer. I'm a charcoal man myself. Still, I couldn't bear to watch a nice new grill like that flying around and getting banged up as you came around those corners. I got some rope in the cruiser.

First watched him walk back to his patrol car.

What the fuck's gotten into you? he asked Seventh.

He's an asshole, Seventh muttered.

He's trying to help, said Zero.

The officer returned a moment later with some rope and began securing it to the rear bumper.

Phew, he said as he worked. Something die in here?

Skunk, First called back to him. Hit one last night on our way up.

Skunk? he said. This time of year?

Zero turned to face him.

I was driving, she said. He came right at me.

The officer, getting his first good look at her, lowered his sunglasses.

Well, he said with a smile, can't say I blame him.

Zero smiled back.

The officer tied the knot tight, and tucked the ends in so they wouldn't trail behind as they drove.

White vinegar, he said.

White vinegar? Zero asked.

Little secret of mine, he said. Put it in a garden sprayer, spray the underside of the vehicle, gets rid of that skunk smell in a jiffy.

White vinegar, said Zero. I never heard of that. Thanks. We'll try that.

First waved as the officer drove away, then pulled back onto the road.

That was nice of him, said Zero. You see, Seventh? Sometimes you have to trust people.

You're twenty years old, said Seventh.

The pickup truck from yesterday drove by the other way.

So? asked Zero.

So shut the fuck up, said Seventh.

. . .

In the city, Unclish explained, Purging would have been simpler.

Nobody notices a bag of human organs in Brooklyn, he said. You drop the lungs in one dumpster, the colon in another; no one'll see and won't care if they do. What's one more colon in Bushwick? You could leave a uterus on the sidewalk in Brownsville and nobody would even stop to look at it. There's the stench, sure, but there are others.

But in New Jersey, he continued, it wasn't so easy.

In the suburbs, he said, people notice when you put things in their garbage. And they don't like it. That's America's vaunted capitalism for you: Nobody minds if you're so hungry you have to eat *out* of their trash, but try putting something *in* their trash, and they raise holy hell.

The only option in a rural area was to leave the innards in the woods, but coyotes were rare these days; you were pretty much counting on hawks and raccoons to eat the organs, and with entrails the size of Mudd's, that would take far too long and risk discovery.

We'll have to take it with us, he said.

It? asked First.

The innards, said Unclish.

With us?

We'll bag them, said Unclish, bring them back to the city. We can ditch it in the Bronx.

Plenty of animals there, said Tenth.

Unclish lifted the Knife of Redemption, closed his eyes, and held it aloft.

And now, he called, it is time to Purge.

He instructed Tenth to slide the blood-filled trash can out from beneath Mudd's corpse, being careful not to spill a single drop. The Ancients, he explained, believed that once the body was properly Consumed, the blood would turn to wine, signaling a successful Consumption, and so it was customary to divide the blood among the family members, for them to enjoy once the Victuals were complete.

Enjoy? asked Zero. Who *are* we?

Unclish placed the tip of the Knife of Redemption at the center of Mudd's pubic bone, closed his eyes, and, in a loud voice that filled the great hall, called out:

May the organs that once sustained you now be set free!

The entire process took just three cuts and two minutes. It

unsettled Seventh to see how quickly a human body could be emptied of its vital organs, how quickly we can be disassembled, how quickly we fall apart. He stared at the pile of glistening viscera on the floor below Mudd's hollowed carcass. It looked to him as if God had tripped on his way from the parts room to the workshop, and all the Mudd parts he was carrying had fallen to the ground.

Fuck, God muttered.

Five-second rule, said his assistant, kneeling to pick them up. You're good.

Seventh volunteered for the grim task of bagging Mudd's entrails; nobody else would, he knew, and he was feeling the desire to do something more than just watch. He wanted to take part. Fourth, Fifth, and Ninth, being men of science and thus more accustomed to viscera than the rest, offered to help.

I'll be honest, said Ninth as they worked, I was kind of surprised she *had* a heart.

It was the uterus that surprised me, said Fourth.

Enough, Seventh snapped.

Carol was still not returning his texts, and he had half a mind to phone her, to tell her exactly who he was and what was going on. Rosenbloom meanwhile couldn't even conceive of his people's story as anything less than a joke. Cops pulling them over, pickup trucks shadowing them all over town. Was it too much for his own brothers to treat their people's most important ritual with some goddamned respect?

It's remarkable, Ninth said of the entrails at his feet. The machinery of man and animal is so similar. Given the high estimations we have of ourselves, you'd expect to open a dog or a rat and find a completely different design, something totally foreign to our own. But you don't. With minor variations, we're pretty much the same.

Fourth agreed. Between humans, he said, the deviations are even smaller. We're practically identical, and yet we thoroughly despise one another. On the first day of class I tell my students: Picture a battlefield, a war, 9/11. Then strip away everything external— clothes, badges, weapons—strip everyone right down to their bare bones, and the tragic becomes hideously comic: a bunch of lanky, clanky skeletons, identical in every possible way, indistinguishable from one another, bashing each other over the head with sticks and claiming superiority. Assholes, Nature is telling us, you're all the goddamned same.

But Seventh disagreed.

What if she's telling us the opposite? he said.

The opposite? asked Fourth.

The opposite, said Seventh. What if Nature made our bodies the same to show us that the body itself doesn't matter—that what matters is the mind. That in form—in bones and structure—we are similar, and thus form is insignificant. What makes us who we are is not form but content—the mind, the self—and in that way we *are* different. Not better, not worse. Just . . . different.

But we *aren't* different, said Fifth. Everything we know about the mind points to similarities, not differences. Gay, straight, black, white, Western, Eastern, ancient, modern—our emotional wiring is the same. We desire the same things, need the same things, fear the same things.

Seventh was growing frustrated with what Mudd used to call her sons' liberal vanity.

They don't think something because they think it, she insisted. They think it because they want others to think they think it.

But look at the story, Seventh said to his brothers. You can't argue with the story. We started in Africa and we moved apart, moved away from each other. To be alone, to be with our own.

But that's *not* the story, said Fourth, with an arrogant tone that made Seventh want to slap him. That's only the first few chapters. We're at the midpoint, furthest away from where we started but getting closer every day to the resolution, to the ending—and that ending is unity, oneness. We're not moving away from each other; in fact, we're moving toward each other, mixing, becoming one. *That's* the direction of human life, Seventh; that's where things are going. My kids don't see color—

Oh bullshit! Seventh said with such anger that it startled them all. Yes, they do. Yes, they fucking do; we all do. Zebras see lions, no matter how progressive those zebras claim to be, and lions kill zebras. Zebra lives don't matter, not to lions, and if zebras could laugh, they would every time a lion got shot in the ass by a poacher. Black people care about black lives, white people care about white lives. That's just the way of the world. And *nobody* gives a damn about *our* lives.

He tied the bag tightly and walked away.

You're starting to sound like Mudd, Fourth called after him.

Somebody has to, thought Seventh.

. . .

Has the blood from a Victual ever turned into wine? the Elders asked.

No, said the Elder Elders.

Then why do we continue to divide the blood among us? the Elders asked.

So that our tradition will not be lost, said the Elder Elders, and our people will stay true.

So that which is false will make us true? asked the Elders.

Bingo, said the Elder Elders.

. . .

They decided to set up the barbecue on the flagstone patio out back; the joints were overgrown with weeds and the stones were crumbling, but there was a small area that was still mostly flat, and most important, they wouldn't be seen from the road.

Seventh had just finished connecting the gas when Second approached.

Can we talk a sec? Second asked.

I have to prep the grill, said Seventh.

I . . . I should have mentioned this sooner, said Second, I know. But to be honest, I mean, I didn't think this was going to go this far, you know? I thought we'd drive here, talk about Mudd a bit, laugh, cry, realize this whole idea was crazy, and head back, and that'd be the end of it.

And?

And here we are.

So?

Second sighed heavily and stuck his hands into his pockets.

I'm kosher, he said.

You're what?

I'm kosher.

You're kosher?

I can't do it. I can't eat her. I'm Jewish.

You're not Jewish, Second.

I am.

You married a Jew; that doesn't make you Jewish.

I converted, said Second. Circumcised, the whole deal. I'm a Jew.

I don't care, said Seventh.

What?

I don't care. I don't care if you're Abraham, I don't care if you're Moses, I don't care if you're Jesus fucking Christ. You're eating her.

I can't.

You ate Auntie Hazel.

I wasn't a Jew then, Seventh; I was a kid. And I gave my portion to Third.

It's one bite, said Seventh, trying his best not to lose his temper. Throw it up after; that's what Ninth is doing. Nobody will know.

It can't pass my lips, said Second. I'm not even supposed to be in the same house with it. It's a violation of my covenant with God. I'm sorry, I just can't do it.

Where's your hat?

You mean my yarmulke? Not all Jews wear yarmulkes.

Isn't that a part of your covenant with God?

We live in a bigoted society, Seventh, and I found that identifying myself outwardly as a Jew, by wearing a yarmulke, had a deleterious effect on my career. Our people have suffered this kind of hatred for centuries.

Which people?

Both.

Second, you're eating that fucking meat.

I'm not.

Yes, you fucking are. Because as I see it, you only have two choices. You either eat that bite of meat, one measly bite of meat, and trust that your God will give you a pass on this one, or you go back inside and tell First and all the rest that you're screwing them each out of half a million dollars because of your covenant with God—which, by the way, isn't much of a covenant since you can violate it for your own fucking career advancement.

Second glared at him, but could summon no real retort.

So that's it, huh? he said. It's just about the money for you?

It's not about the money. It's about our people.

Fuck you, Seventh, said Second, turning on his heel and walking away. Since when do you give a shit about our fucking people?

Thought Seventh:

Good question.

. . .

The Ancients, Unclish explained, in their great and inestimable wisdom, devised the Victuals with more than a single purpose. On the surface level, the four-step process was designed to prepare the corpse for Consumption, to make it ready to be Consumed. But on a second, perhaps more important level, the process was designed to prepare the family themselves. To make them ready to Consume.

He stood beside what remained of Mudd's suspended corpse, and the siblings gathered around him.

When our beloveds die, he said, it is only natural to see them in death as we once saw them in life: as bodies, as people, as physical beings. It is revolting to imagine ever Consuming them. And so the first thing the Ancients instructed us to do is to hang them up, as one might a deer or a cow, and Drain the blood from them. Physically, this is the easiest step, but emotionally, it is the most difficult, for not only does the deceased still resemble the person for whom we grieve, but it is also the moment when we first begin to see that they, and we, are just bodies, vessels. That we can be filled, and we can be drained; that we are a machine like any other. Then we move on to Purging, in which both we and the deceased go one step further in our transition; namely, we remove the vital organs. The engine, the carburetor, the filter. We discard that which gave us life, and when we are done, we realize that we are but an empty shell—a chassis, a frame. We come then to the third step, the Partitioning, as we ourselves are about to perform, the final step before the Consumption. The actual butchering. Here we Partition the body into cuts of beef; we remove the skin; we separate—the chuck from the rib, the flank from the round. But we also in some ways Partition ourselves— from the dead, from our beloveds. They are no longer the physical beings they once were, and our connection to them, physically and spiritually, is severed. This is grieving with a purpose—it is not mere sorrow; it is grieving so that we may move on. There will still be a hole in our souls, but that will be filled, soon, during the Consumption.

And with that, Unclish began to skin their mother.

The Seltzers immediately turned away. Some closed their eyes. Some covered their ears, not wanting to even hear what was transpiring behind their backs and be tempted to picture it.

It took Unclish's practiced hand less than ten minutes to skin and Partition their mother. When the brothers turned back around, the chain from which she once hung now dangled empty from the ceiling. Beneath it, on the floor, Unclish had laid out the various cuts of meat that used to be their mother.

Indeed, as the Ancients had predicted, for the first time since her heart stopped and her spirit departed her form, Seventh truly felt his mother had passed away.

Dr. Isaacson never missed a single session; snow, ice, attacks on the World Trade Center, he was always there. There was only one time he canceled his appointments—the day his own mother died. Seventh recalled seeing him a few days after the funeral.

God willing by you, Dr. Isaacson had joked.

He didn't hope for anyone's death, of course, but he believed that once Mudd had passed on, Seventh's world would open up, and that most of his negative feelings would disappear with her.

But that was not what happened. For Seventh to look up at the chain was to look up and see the chain of their people of which Mudd had always spoken—empty, ended, and covered in blood.

What was one person's happiness compared to a thousand years of tradition?

He saw, suddenly, rising up around him, the black walls of Henry Ford's melting pot. All around him stood his people, pressed together, unable to move, to escape; the fire below had been lit, and they all cried out in pain; and he went to them, and he comforted them, saying, Worry not, for our chain will never be broken.

Not good, said Unclish.

Not good? asked Seventh.

Unclish stood beside him, hands on his hips, looking over the cuts of meat.

Not good, said Unclish.

What's not good? asked First.

The color, said Unclish. Of the meat.

What should have been a deep red, Unclish explained, had in places turned a dull gray; in others, worse yet, it had become a repulsive swamp-like green.

Is it okay? Seventh asked. To eat?

Unclish twisted his beard.

Of course, he said at last. It's fine.

Will it make us sick? Seventh asked. I mean if it's bad . . . ?

I've had worse, said Unclish, and a deep sadness washed over him. Seventh regretted asking. He knew that Unclish was thinking about his own father, John the Strong, whose spoiled meat, Mudd told them, all forty pounds of it, Unclish had Consumed on his own.

And you, she had said, are complaining about eating a little Auntie Hazel.

. . .

According to Father's telling, John the Strong at the time of his death was wanted in seventeen states, for crimes ranging from extortion and racketeering to assault with a deadly weapon.

You know who else was wanted at the time of his death? Mudd said to her sons. Jesus Christ, that's who.

Jesus didn't assault anyone with a deadly weapon, said Fourth. He preached peace and understanding.

Mudd clopped him on the head with the back of her hand.

Don't you believe those liberals, she said, making Christ out to be John goddamned Lennon. Jesus was a fighter. He was a warrior. You know how I know? Because they killed him, that's how. They kill anyone who fights back.

Her voice shook with rage as she told the most painful part of the John the Strong story: his terrible desecration at the hands of the police.

They took his poor, bullet-riddled body to the morgue, she said. To examine him, they said. To find a cause of death. Five times they shot him, point-blank in the face, and they want to know a cause of death!

You said he was shot nine times, said Fourth. In the chest.

Mudd clopped him on the head with the back of her hand.

What part of hail of gunfire didn't you understand? she demanded. They took him to the morgue because they wanted him to spoil! They wanted him to rot! They wanted to make it impossible for your uncle to Consume him. But they didn't know your Unclish, oh no! He had the strength of John, the bravery of Julius, and the fortitude of Julia, all in one! And so your uncle went to the morgue, and there he stayed, day and night, for two whole days, until they released his father's body to him. And he brought him here, to this very house, and even though it was already days after his death, and even though his disfigured corpse was already decaying and putrid, Unclish Drained him, and then he Purged him, and then he Partitioned him. And after that, children, yes: he Consumed him. Tainted piece after tainted piece he Consumed his father, until he was so violently sick the following day that he was rushed to the hospital. They thought he wouldn't survive, but they knew him not! The doctor heard what your uncle had done, that he had eaten all that meat even as he knew it was rancid, even as he knew it could kill him.

Did you lose a bet? the doctor asked him.

No, your uncle replied, a gentle smile on his face. I won a war.

. . .

Is it permissible to eat rancid meat? the Elders asked.

It is not just permissible, said the Elder Elders, it is often obligatory.

But is it not forbidden to willfully take one's life? asked the Elders. How then may one willfully Consume toxic meat?

He who will not die for his people, said the Elders, does not deserve to live.

Yowza, said the Elders.

. . .

Cannibals over the years have proffered various theories as to why the stench of a cooking mother is as revolting as it is, but there has never been a definitive explanation. The cause could not be as simple as age—i.e., that the malodorousness of mothers is the result of their advanced years—since the stench of young mothers is as unbearable as that of elderly ones (even if they are quite delicious).

Some suggested, in less progressive times than ours, that their fetidness might be connected to their appearance; that is, that the ugly ones smell worse than the attractive ones. But simple observation put that theory to lie, as many an enchanting mother has been placed upon the pyre, her resultant stench vile enough to send her own children running for higher ground.

At the turn of the century, Unclish, who had performed more Victuals in his time than any other before him, proposed a more spiritual notion. Young children, he pointed out, produce almost no scent at all; you could be standing right beside the grill and not even know one was in there. Perhaps, he suggested, the terrible smell of mothers was the smell of guilt, of self-interest, of narcissism—of sin, really—being burned from the body. That would explain, too, why the young have almost no smell at all, for they are without fault.

The Can-Am Twitter world exploded. Women were outraged at this suggestion and many called for his censure.

Because we all know men are so pure, wrote one, expressing the feelings of many. *#Bullshit.*

Unclish's denials and claims of context fell on deaf ears. Ultimately, he was forced to go on social media and apologize for his remarks. In a post that was sent out to however many Cannibals remained in the world, he assured one and all that male or female, young or old, nobody was more sinful than he was, and nobody had more evil to be burned away.

No mother, he wrote in closing, *laid upon the fire will ever smell as putrid as me.*

. . .

At last, the grill reached five hundred degrees, and Unclish went out to the patio and began to cook.

The stench was immediate, familiar to those who have spent time in war zones where the smell of burning tires mixes with that of open sewage drains. Everyone escaped inside, but Seventh remained, watching Unclish work. Now and then Unclish would take a piece of meat off the grill, cut a small bit off, place it in his mouth, shake his head, and place it back on the grill. Seventh shuddered to think that the meat he was eating was his mother, but the small elderly man in the silver top hat moved with such grace and purposefulness, flipping, tasting, turning, that his revulsion was replaced with awe. He pictured Unclish doing this for John the Strong, John the Strong doing this for Julius the Brave, Julius the Brave doing this for Julia the Anguished.

Unclish? he asked. Were the windows in the library always bricked over? I mean, were they originally glass and then sealed up, or were they always brick and never glass?

They were always brick, said Unclish.

So that outsiders could not see in? he asked.

So that insiders could not see out, said Unclish.

But a well-rounded education means knowing about the world around us, said Seventh.

And did you have one of these well-rounded educations? asked Unclish.

Yes.

And do you know the world around us?

Yes, said Seventh.

So tell me, Fifth: How exactly has that helped your people?

Unclish turned back to the grill.

I'm Seventh, said Seventh.

That's what I said, said Unclish.

He lifted the last of the meat from the grill, closed the top, and turned off the gas. He looked exhausted, his eyes red from the smoke, his skin ghostly and pale.

We are ready, he said.

. . .

The University's dining room, as derelict as the rest of the structure, was enormous but somehow still elegant, befitting a culture such as theirs in which eating played such a central role. The deep red carpet, now pitted and spotted with moss, matched the deep red curtains that framed the tall windows; dozens of deep red chairs were stacked in the corner. Only two dinner tables remained of the many that must have once filled the room, but they would be enough. The brothers dragged the tables to the center of the room and arranged them end to end. Seventh placed chairs on either side, with one at the head for Unclish and one at the foot for Zero.

She's not supposed to sit with us, First said to Seventh, worried that Unclish would seize on any violation of the rules to withhold their inheritance. She isn't part of the Consumption.

She's part of the family, said Seventh.

Isn't that punishment enough? asked First.

Seventh wanted Zero to see it. The last Cannibal-American woman should at least witness the last Consumption.

Zero, for her part, had no interest in witnessing any of it, and would have skipped the whole grisly affair altogether, but she refused to leave Third's side.

Fourth and Fifth draped an old soiled tablecloth over the tables, Ninth set the table with the paper plates and plastic cutlery, and Eleventh and Twelfth propped up the flashlights to provide light.

So exactly how does this work? Eleventh asked Seventh as they prepped the table.

Yeah, asked Twelfth. How, exactly?

I don't know, said Seventh.

Who goes first? asked Second. Because I'm not going first.

I'm not going first, said First.

We should all go together, said Eighth.

That seems fair, Fifth agreed. Must Eat All Together—we should just agree to eat it all together.

One bite, said First. We can do this.

And a half, said Ninth.

Third was already sitting at the table, fork and knife in hand, napkin tucked into his shirt collar, like a child waiting for a snack.

I'm going to be Mudd! he said.

Zero smiled as best she could. You are, she said.

And Sixth! he said.

Very soon, she said.

Unclish entered. In one hand he held a plate of reheated ketchup-covered French fries; in the other, a metal tray piled high with medium-rare Mudd.

Jesus, muttered Second. Jesus, Jesus, Jesus.

With great reverence, Unclish laid the trays on the table.

Here we go, said First, beginning to hyperventilate. Here we motherfucking go.

Eleventh took Twelfth's hand.

We can do this, said Eleventh.

We can *do* this, said Twelfth.

Tenth breathed forcefully in and out, as if trying to psych himself up for a heavy lift.

Unclish looked even wearier to Seventh now than he had earlier on the patio. He watched as Unclish sank onto his seat in that slow, deliberate manner of the elderly, as if he was made of glass, as if sitting too quickly might cause his bones to shatter, his body to break into a thousand pieces. He hadn't moved this gingerly earlier, and Seventh was concerned, but then it had been a long day of cooking and preparing, and Unclish was no longer a young man. Even for a seasoned Victualist, the work was long and taxing.

Unclish twisted his beard a moment.

Yes, yes, he said, hmm, hmm.

And so we come at last to the Consumption, he said. The final step of the Victuals. We have Drained, we have Purged, and we have Partitioned. We have grieved for the physical being we once knew, and we have come, via the first three steps, to accept that she is gone. But there remains within us still a lacking. A longing, inside.

He winced with pain.

Unclish? asked Seventh.

To heal this longing, Unclish continued, is the true purpose of the Consumption. For in Consuming our beloveds, not only are we giving them eternal life, providing them with a physical body so that they may live for eternity, but we are also, by taking them inside us, filling the hole in our souls that was left when they passed. And now, plates.

The brothers took their plates and formed a line by his side. One by one they stepped forward, and he placed upon their plates a small serving of fries, and beside it he did place their appointed meat.

They returned in silence to their seats.

Fourth looked down at the thick slice of tongue on his plate.

Guys, he said, I can't do this.

It's just meat, said First.

It's not meat, said Fourth. It's Mom.

Ninth, looking wan, looked up from his plate of leg and glanced at Eleventh. She was pale, sickly.

What is that? he asked.

Uterus, she said.

Hoo boy, said Fifth, looking down at the reddish-brown chunk of heart on his plate. Hooooo boy.

We can do this, said Twelfth.

I don't know, said Eleventh.

Dr. Zion, said Twelfth. Remember Zion.

Eleventh took her sister's hand. Zion, she said.

It was customary, in instances such as this when the Victualist is not assigned a specific cut of meat by the deceased, for him to eat from whatever remaining, unassigned part he desired. Unclish had chosen Mudd's liver, because, he said, like a liver, Mudd had spent her life cleansing the toxins of America from her people.

He cut a small piece from the pink-brown meat on his plate, stabbed it with his fork, and held it aloft.

Cannibals live forever, said Unclish, but with such darkness and remorse that Seventh looked up from his plate.

But because of you *bastards*, Unclish continued, his voice filling with bitter contempt, Mudd will not live on.

The Selzers were confused.

Unclish, Seventh asked, are you okay?

None of us will live on! Unclish shouted. Not Mudd, not me, not you!

I knew it, said First. I knew he'd pull some eleventh-hour bull-shit.

Did we do something wrong, Unclish? asked Tenth.

We followed all the steps, said Second.

But Unclish ignored them.

It was only a few years ago, he continued, that we celebrated the one hundredth anniversary of the day our forefather Julius was melted by that bastard Henry Ford. I came to visit your mother that day, did you know that? We sat on the patio out back of the house. One hundred years ago, I said to her, our story began. She wept, your mother; she wept and said, Yes, but how long before it ends?

He slammed the table with his fist.

You at this table were our last hope! From you, a new nation of Cannibals would emerge! You were going to go forth, find Cannibal wives, have Cannibal children, and bring unto the world a new generation of our people!

He pressed himself up to a standing position, his thin arms trembling with the effort.

Unclish, Seventh began. Be careful—

BUT YOU DID NOT! Unclish shouted, his eyes wide and red with fury. You went your own way! You pursued your own dreams, your own happiness, your own 'freedom'! And now, because no new generations will come from you, there will be no one left to Consume you. You have achieved nothing but mortality. You have ensured your own destruction, and the destruction of your people. YOU WILL NOT LIVE ON! AND MUDD WILL NOT LIVE ON! AND OUR PEOPLE WILL NOT LIVE ON!

Unclish, said Seventh, take it easy . . .

Third, confused, turned to Zero.

Mudd won't live on? he asked.

Zero didn't know what to say. She was torn between concern for Third and worry for Unclish, who had broken out in a sweat.

Mudd will live in me! Third shouted at Unclish. I am Mudd! Mudd is me!

Unclish, exhausted now and unable to stand, lowered himself back to his seat.

For the moment, he said to Third, his voice a whisper. For a few years, yes. She will live on. But if there is no one to Consume you, she will die when you die.

Mudd will live, Third insisted. Sixth will live!

Unclish had no strength to debate him, and simply said to all, Begin.

Seventh reached for his fork and knife. He took a deep breath, and cut a small, bite-and-a-half-size piece off the skin on his plate.

The others did the same.

Unclish? asked Seventh. Is there any order? Should we go in some order?

But Unclish, who was now holding his head in his hands, didn't respond.

Seventh looked at the flap of skin on his fork. It was soft, its edges crispy, like the skin of barbecued chicken, but a dark, dismal gray in color. He tried to convince himself it *was* chicken, but it didn't work.

It was Mudd.

Which skin was it? he wondered. Was it from the breast that weaned him? The hand that struck him? Was it from the arm he longed for so many years would hug him?

He had turned away too quickly.

From her, from their people.

Mudd had been right. He had jumped into the pot Julius had been forced into. Maybe he had been too eager to leave; maybe they all had. And for what? Like First had said, to become meat himself?

Maybe I should have just stayed with the cannibals I knew. At least they ate for a reason . . .

Seventh lifted his fork to his lips.

The meat quivered, stank.

What a fool he had been! A hundred years after Julius, and here he was—still trying to melt. Still believing there was something left to melt into.

Melting, Rosenbloom liked to say, is so two centuries ago.

Ex uno multi, he said. Out of one, many. Many peoples, many walls, many identities, many one-foot-by-one-foot warring nations, living side by side but miles apart, prepping for war, the War of a Thousand Nations, the Battle of Everyone, the Great Hyphenate Holocaust.

And while everyone else was running to claim their square, here stood Seventh, alone, like a fool, wondering where all the melters went.

Henry Ford, after all, Mister Melting Pot, was a Nazi. Not Nazi as in bad person—a *Nazi* Nazi. He received medals from the Nazi Party. They read his books. He was Hitler's hero, and Hitler was his.

Melting Pots, ovens.

Tomato, to-mah-to.

Note to self: when a Nazi builds a giant pot and lights a fire under it, do *not* climb in.

He closed his eyes and placed Mudd into his mouth, and his lips closed around her, and behold he was filled—with Mudd, and with all those she had Consumed, and with all those they had Consumed and with all those they had Consumed before them, with Julius and with Julia, with all those who had been beaten and with all those who had been raped, with those who had been imprisoned and those who had been enslaved, and the taste was awful, the most awful he had ever tasted, for it tasted of their blood and their tears, of their hopes and their dreams, of their pain and their sorrow.

And Seventh swallowed.

And they became him.

And he became them.

And Seventh wept.

. . .

Seventh hated Grandparents' Day, the day the school opened its gates and classrooms and allowed the students' proud grandmothers and grandfathers to come see what their bright-eyed offspring were learning. He hated most school functions, but Grandparents' Day was particularly difficult.

Dad, Reese asked him last Grandparents' Day. How come I never met your mom?

Well, Seventh had said, she passed away.

I mean when she was alive, said Reese.

She died before you were born, said Seventh.

Oh. How come Mom never met her?

Well, said Seventh, my mother lived far away. In her homeland.

Where's her homeland?

Brazil, said Seventh, choosing an exotic-sounding nation in hopes it would dissuade Reese from asking to visit.

I thought Mom said you were from Guatemala, said Reese.

My father is from Guatemala, said Seventh. My mother is Brazilian.

I thought you said she was Dominican, said Reese.

She was Dominican, said Seventh. Dominican-Brazilian.

So what am I? asked Reese.

Seventh smiled, picked her up on his lap, and hugged her tightly.

You're you, sweetness. That's all that matters.

. . .

Ninth began to choke. His face turned deep red, and he pressed his hand over his mouth.

Don't, First warned him.

But Ninth shook his head, turning an even darker shade of red.

Oh God, he groaned, his face a mask of revulsion. He stood and stumbled backward from the dinner table, knocking his chair over as he did.

Oh God, he said again. Oh God . . .

But it was too late. Whether for vegan reasons, emotional reasons, or some combination of the two, Ninth's body utterly rejected his bite and a half; he grimaced, doubled over, and roared, and the meat he had pushed himself to swallow was ejected from his mouth with such force that all watched in shock as it sailed upward through the air, arcing high above their heads before peaking, cresting, and returning with a sickening splat to the center of the table.

For a brief moment, nobody spoke. Nobody moved.

That, Ninth gasped as he tried to catch his breath, counts.

And all hell broke loose.

That does *not* count, said Second, who had just violated his covenant with God by swallowing a bite and a half of Mudd's foot.

It counts!

How the fuck does that count?

That counts, said Ninth. I ate it, that fucking counts—

That does not count, said Second. Seventh, does that count?

Of course it counts! said First, whose only concern was that they had technically eaten what they were technically required to, and could finally get paid.

Unclish, that counts, Ninth said, appealing to his authority. That counts, right? Unclish?

Unclish, though, was in his own agony. He pressed himself up from his chair, hands at his throat. He seemed to be having trouble breathing.

Unclish? asked Seventh. Unclish, you okay?

Unclish winced, buckled over in pain. His top hat fell to the floor, and he followed after it, landing on top of it with a terrible crunch.

Unclish! cried Seventh. He and his siblings rushed to his side— all but Ninth, whose body was still violently rejecting his mother, and Third, who sat in his seat at the now-empty table, staring blankly into the middle distance as he shoveled piece after piece of his dead mother into his mouth.

Mudd will live, he said to no one as he chewed. Sixth will live. Julius will live. Everyone will live . . .

. . .

The brothers helped Unclish to the main hall and laid him gently down on his mattress. He was conscious but in terrible pain, cold sweat on his brow as he clutched at his stomach. They gathered around him, much as they had just one day earlier around Mudd.

Fifth suspected some sort of food poisoning, but Unclish hadn't eaten Mudd's meat, he said, and even if he had, the symptoms wouldn't appear that quickly.

He was eating earlier, said Seventh.

The meat? Eighth asked.

Seventh nodded. As he was cooking it, he said.

It's probably that, then, said Fifth. The meat.

So we're all going to get sick now? Eleventh asked.

It was possible, Fifth said. But Unclish was old, and the elderly were more vulnerable to these sorts of things, their bodies less able to cope.

We should get him to a hospital, said Fifth. He needs a hospital.

Unclish lay on his side in the fetal position, eyes closed. Ninth knelt beside him.

I ate that meat, Unclish, you saw me, I *ate* that shit. I put it in my mouth and I swallowed. That's eating, Unclish, that counts.

That is bullshit, Second began to argue. Soon all the Seltzers were shouting and objecting, pushing and shoving. Eighth and Tenth agreed with Second, Fourth and Fifth agreed with Ninth,

Eleventh and Twelfth worked with Zero to calm Third, who was shouting at Seventh, who was trying to keep Tenth from attacking Ninth. An all-out brawl was only averted when a loud metallic banging caused them all to stop and turn to find First, bashing the lid of the trash can with the Knife of Redemption.

Brothers, sisters, he said calmly when he had their attention. It. Counts. You put it in your mouth, Ninth. You swallowed. You ate. We all did. We're done, folks. We're done. With this, with Mudd, with all of it.

He tossed the knife onto the floor, where it clattered and clanged like the final bell of a prize fight.

We're done, he said.

His pronouncement took a moment to sink in. As it did, the expressions on his siblings' faces reminded Seventh of hostages upon being released after months of captivity: the leery skepticism as they emerge from their cells, the bewilderment that soon becomes belief, the hugging, the crying. This is what the Seltzers experienced now too; some had been prisoners of Mudd, some had been prisoners of their pasts. But whether they celebrated now because they wanted to Consume Mudd and actually had, or hadn't wanted to and were elated that it was over, celebrate they did. Some laughed, some cried, some cried while they laughed.

Seventh watched them, and he decided.

He would tell them.

He would tell Reese.

He would tell Carol.

Who he was.

Who they were.

He would tell them their story, and their story would live on.

Now, gang, said First, let's get the *fuck* out of here.

Fourth offered to take Unclish to the ER on his way back to the city. He would have preferred to take him to a hospital back in New York City, but Fifth thought Unclish needed immediate attention, and the local hospital would suffice.

Second and Eighth agreed to take on the gruesome job of spilling their mother's blood in the woods, and Ninth agreed to take the bag of organs with him and dispose of them at his veterinary office, where nobody would notice them amid the rest of the biomedical waste they put out every day. They were about to get to work when Unclish's voice, weak but firm in the darkening lobby, called out:

Must . . . finish, said Unclish.

The siblings turned, surprised to find him conscious. Seventh knelt beside him and took his hand.

It's okay, Unclish, said Seventh. Try to rest. We're going to get you to a hospital. Fourth will take you.

Must finish, he repeated.

We finished, said Seventh.

It's done, said First.

Unclish shook his head. No . . .

Unclish, Ninth said, don't start with me. I swallowed my bite; we all agreed that was eating.

We all had our bites, Unclish, said Seventh.

Finish . . . , Unclish said.

We all took our bites, Unclish, said Seventh, and then you passed out. Do you remember? We ate and then you passed out. You're sick, Unclish, we're going to get you to a hospital.

Bites? Unclish asked, raising himself up to a sitting position. What bites?

Of Mudd, said Eighth. Bites of Mudd. Just like you taught us, Unclish: *A bite and half and you won't need another, whether it's your father, your sister, or even your mother.*

Unclish winced with pain, shook his head.

I never taught you such a thing! said Unclish.

When we were little, said Eighth. In the basement. *A bite and half and you won't need another . . .*

It's half and a bite, you jackass! Unclish barked. *Eat half and a bite and you won't need another,* he shouted, *whether it's your father, your sister, or even your mother.* Not a bite and a half!

Half and a bite? asked First. What the hell are you talking about?

Half, said Unclish.

Half of what?

Of her, said Unclish. And a bite.

Half of *Mudd*? Second asked.

You want us to eat *half* of her? First asked. What are you, nuts?

That is *not* what you taught us, said Eighth. That is *not* what you taught us.

Half of *Mudd*? asked Eleventh. Unclish, she weighed five hundred pounds. You expect us to eat two hundred and fifty pounds of her?

Divided by twelve, said Unclish.

First yanked his phone from his pocket.

Hey Siri, he demanded, what's two hundred and fifty divided by twelve?

I have found what you're looking for, said Siri. Two hundred and fifty divided by twelve is twenty point eight three three three.

Twenty pounds, said First. Of meat. Each. Fuck off, no way.

Unclish's face contorted with pain. Sweat ran down his face, and yet he shivered with cold.

The Elders asked, Unclish said weakly, how much must we Consume? A majority, said the Elder Elders. . . . What is a majority? asked the Elders. . . . Half of the deceased and a bite, said the Elder Elders. . . . Half and a bite . . . *Eat half and a bite and you won't need another, whether it's your father, your sister, or even your mother.*

Unclish, said Seventh, the meat . . . the meat is bad. We can't eat it. Everyone's sick, Unclish—you, me, all of us. The meat is bad.

Unclish grasped Seventh by the lapel of his coat.

If we only ate when the meat was perfect, he groaned, we would never eat at all.

Seventh looked up at First, who was beside himself with anger. He pointed his finger at Unclish and was about to rant and rave— Now listen! he began—when a terrible knocking came from the front door.

BAM BAM BAM!

Everyone froze.

Who the hell is that? whispered Tenth.

The knocking came again, loud and insistent.

BAM! BAM BAM!

It's that fucking cop, whispered First. I bet it's that fucking asshole cop.

The pickup, said Seventh. It's the guys from the pickup.

I told you I didn't like this damned town, Tenth barked at him. I told you!

Shh! hissed Seventh. Quiet!

Another knock.

Open up! the person at the door shouted. I know you're in there!
OPEN UP!

. . .

Love thy neighbor as you love thyself, Father often told Seventh, for
as Mudd worked to make the children proud and fearful, he worked
to make them kind and self-aware.

For all the trouble the Bible has caused in this world, he said,
and it's caused a lot, it's worth it for that one line. That one line can
save us all.

Because then we'll all love each other? Seventh asked.

Father shook his head. He didn't interpret that precept as others
did, as a mere reminder to love your neighbor *as much* as you love
yourself. That was what religious leaders took from it, he said, because they were too foolish and arrogant to see the real admonition:
to love your neighbor *as* you're loving yourself.

As, as in *when*.

When you're loving yourself, remember to love thy neighbor.

Because the moment we begin to love ourselves, Father said to
Seventh, is the moment we begin to hate others.

. . .

The tradition the Seltzer children hated most was Loud Insistent
Knocking Upon the Doors in the Middle of the Night. Loud Insistent Knocking Upon the Doors in the Middle of the Night, observed
every Remembrance Day, was meant to commemorate the loud

insistent knocks upon doors in the middle of the night that so plagued Cannibal history. The entire history of the Cannibal people, Unclish said, could be told as a series of loud insistent knocks upon doors in the middle of the night.

They knocked on our doors in the middle of the night in the Old Country, he said, and they knocked on our doors in the middle of the night in the New World. They knocked on our doors in the middle of the night in Detroit, and they knocked on our doors in the middle of the night in Brooklyn. Whatever happened on Remembrance Day, wherever it happened, I assure you, it began with loud insistent knocks upon doors in the middle of the night. When Ford came for Julia, he knocked loudly and insistently on her door in the middle of the night. When the police came to inform me of my father's death, they knocked loudly and insistently on my door in the middle of the night. They come with pitchforks, they come with torches, they come with guns, and they come with badges. And when they come, children, they knock, loudly and insistently, on our doors in the middle of the night.

To commemorate this horror, it was a Remembrance Day tradition that all night long, Cannibals were to creep up to one another's homes, bang loudly and insistently on the front door, and run away. It gave the children a terrible fright, as it was intended to, rousing them from sleep and making them run screaming for their parents' room. Complicating the matter, however, was the fact that every Cannibal had a different idea of when Remembrance Day was. Some said it was summer and some said winter, some said March and some said September, the result being that all year long, without warning and without cause, at any time of any night, someone would creep up to their door and begin pounding on it, loudly and insistently, in the middle of the night. It left the children extremely anxious.

Good, said Unclish. You should be.

And so that night, as Seventh went to answer the University front door, he was filled with rage. Because it wasn't just a loud, insistent knock on the door. It was yet *another* loud, insistent knock on yet *another* Cannibal door.

And he was tired of them.

And they call us savages, he heard Mudd say, as clearly as if she was standing beside him.

He took a deep breath and pulled open the door, his jaw clenched, his face stone. He expected police, pickup trucks, pitchforks, torches.

What he found was a small, tight, middle-aged woman, arms crossed angrily over her chest, a nasty scowl on her pinched little face.

What are you doing here? she demanded, peering past him to get a look into the main hall. Who are you?

Sometimes you had to fight asshole with asshole.

What are *you* doing here? Seventh demanded, his fury boiling over. Who the hell are *you*?

You need to leave, she said.

No, *you* need to leave.

What are you up to in there, burning tires? she asked. It stinks. I can smell it all the way to my house. You're not supposed to be here.

You're not supposed to be here! Seventh shouted.

He enjoyed watching her flinch, enjoyed seeing her fear. She became everyone who ever tormented his people, every damned Sherwood, every Oscar fucking Kowalski.

This is our property, he said. Ours, you hear!

First came up behind him and put a hand on his shoulder, hoping to take over, hoping to settle things down. But Seventh pushed him away.

Even this, he thought. *Even this they won't let us have; even this they have to take from us: a derelict building in the woods, and even this they want for their own.*

You're wrong, he heard Mudd whisper in his ear. They don't want it. They just don't want us to have it, you see? They just don't want us to have it. Get in the pot or get out—do you see now? Do you see?

This building is abandoned, the woman said, trying again to peer past him. What are you doing in there?

Seventh wanted to smash her face. He wanted to grab the Knife of Redemption and cut her bitter little head off, let her rot on the ground where she stood, unburied, uneaten, unredeemed.

We're Cannibals, he said. We're here to eat our dead mother.

The woman's face fell and she took a delicious step backward.

Jesus Christ, Seventh heard First mutter behind him. Seventh, what are you doing?

It's been a hard day for us, Seventh said to her, what with all the gutting and trimming. But she's all cooked now, so you'll have to excuse me. It's dinnertime.

You're sick, she said, pulling her coat tightly around her and taking another step back. Sick!

No, no, said Seventh, my *uncle's* sick. Bit of a stomach thing, I'm afraid. She sat out a bit too long. The organic meat lasts longer, I find, don't you? He'll be okay, not to worry, but it does mean we'll each have to eat more of old Mom than we were expecting.

I'm calling the police.

Oh, don't leave, Seventh begged. We'd love to have you for dessert.

Mudd laughed.

You're a sick, sick man, she said as she hurried down the stairs. Love thy neighbor—did you ever hear that? Love thy neighbor!

I will, thought Seventh as he slammed the door.

As soon as they love me.

.   .   .

And then there was *Miraculous Births*, the most irritating trope of the Not-So-Great Something-American Novel. It was an ancient narrative technique, employed by storytellers as far back as the writers of the Old Testament. Pregnant geriatrics, virgin births— from Isaac to Jesus, so many founders of so many movements were born so miraculously that it seemed no one back then was born naturally at all. Miracles as plot devices have fallen out of favor in recent centuries, though, so today's writers of myth and identity use *Valiant Births* instead—births during wartime, births under foreign occupation, births on rafts. It would seem the miracle of ordinary birth just isn't miracle enough for some writers; ordinary births, they suggest, are for ordinary people. First, Mudd told Seventh, was born with his fist in the air.

Fist-first he came out, she said. Angry then and angry now.

It was an agonizing delivery, she said. Because his arm was raised as he emerged, his shoulder became stuck on her pelvic bone. The doctors tried to bend his arm at the elbow, but he was too angry, too strong. They tried every which way to twist and turn him, but he fought those attempts too. In the end, they had to cut Mudd's perineum in order to get him out, a painful procedure from which she never fully healed.

And he's been a pain in my ass ever since, she said.

Second's birth was more routine, but tragically, the nurse who swaddled him was an overweight Jewish woman named Lipschitz, whom Second mistook for his mother. He buried his face in her cleavage, and screamed when they tried to pull him away.

And he's been chasing those damned Sherwoods ever since, Mudd said.

Third's was a tale more gruesome than the others, for Third, she said, emerged from her womb the size of most young boys when they emerge from middle school. She went into labor early in September, and Third didn't fully emerge until late October. By the time his delivery was complete, she was plundered, her secret garden defoliated, and Humphrey never again showed any sexual interest in her. Third didn't understand what sexual interest was (or the larger marital strife Mudd was blaming him for), but he wept to hear the story of his birth, and promised Mudd he would never hurt her again.

Fourth emerged speaking in full sentences, capable, before the amniotic fluid was even wiped from his face, of reading and writing at the university level. The nurse clipped his umbilical cord, swaddled him, and took him in her arms, and Fourth, glancing at her name tag, said, as clear as a bell: My dear Nurse Wilson, whatever have I done to you to deserve your dragging me into this fetid cesspool of existence? If you would be kind enough to return me to the womb from which I emerged, I shall be indebted to you forever.

The nurse, a gentle British woman, passed the infant to the obstetrician and promptly passed out, breaking her arm as she fell to the floor. She took a month off, decided nursing was too stressful, and took up pottery.

Sued me for her broken arm, too, said Mudd. Limey bitch.

Fifth's birth was unexceptional, but the future psychiatrist's first words were *I'm sorry*. He was twelve months old at the time, and Mudd was holding him in her lap, giving him his bottle, when the nipple slipped from his lips and warm white milk spurted across her blouse. Though he had never spoken a word before, he looked up at her, apologized, and wondered aloud if the white milk dripping down her cleavage suggested he subconsciously wanted to have sex with her. Mudd clopped him on the head.

Don't be stupid, she said.

Sixth, of course, was born perfect. He arrived on the exact day the doctors predicted he would, at the exact time Mudd hoped he would, without a hint of pain or difficulty. There was no blood, no yelling, no fists in the air. Immediately after he was born, Mudd said, as the midwife laid him down to clean him off, he took the towel from her hand, gently cleaned Mudd's crotch, and thanked her for bearing him so selflessly the past nine months. The nurses wept to see such a loving child, and agreed that he was better than any of the ones who came before.

Eighth emerged carrying a dog-eared copy of The Guide, and though Mudd spent a few sleepless months recovering from the paper cuts it caused on her most sensitive regions, she was never more proud.

How did a book get into your uterus? First asked.

Don't be stupid, she said. It wasn't a hardcover.

Ninth was born fearful, a trait Mudd attributed to his latent homosexuality. The midwife pulled and pulled, but Ninth refused to come out.

Now he comes out, she sighed, when he later revealed his sexual preference for men. I should have left the son of a bitch in.

Tenth was born a man, covered in muscle and pubic hair, a Can-Am tattoo on his shoulder, and a five o'clock shadow. He flexed on his way out and nearly split her perineum again. Eleventh and Twelfth were born fighting, each one pulling the other by the ankle in order to be first to enter the world. Mudd claimed this was because anyone would be excited to be born Cannibal, who were the best people in all the world. Eleventh and Twelfth, for their parts, claimed they were not trying to get out, but rather to stay in: They sensed they were in the wrong bodies, and suspected that perhaps they had not yet been fully cooked.

Zero's birth Mudd couldn't recall.

But Seventh's, she said, was the most miraculous of all. For when Seventh was born, Mudd died.

You died? young Seventh asked.

Died, she said. During childbirth.

Her heart had stopped, she said, and she ceased breathing. The doctors and nurses shouted their shouts, and they rang their alarms, and they placed an oxygen mask on her, all to no avail.

But you, she said to Seventh, you wouldn't let me die.

And so Seventh, Mudd said, after delivering himself unassisted from her womb and severing his own umbilical cord, climbed up her belly, pulled the oxygen mask from her face, placed his mouth upon hers, and began to perform mouth-to-mouth. Mudd coughed, sputtered, and began to breathe.

You saved me then, she said when she told him the tale. And one day, I know, you'll save us all.

Each child was told a different version of their births; in each version, the child being told the tale was the hero, the one with promise, the one with abilities and gifts while the others caused Mudd nothing but pain and sorrow. And that was why Seventh hated the *Miraculous Births* trope. Because it was fiction, but wasn't just fiction. It was prologue. It was fate. It was chapter one of the narrative she had condemned him to. It was the foundation of the prison into which he was born. It was the lie that bound him to her altar.

This is your story, she said.

This is what you will become.

This is who hates you and this is who you will hate.

The End.

Of choice, of freedom, of will, of possibility.

The.

Fucking.

End.

. . .

Or maybe it was this, Seventh wondered:

Maybe the Ancients, in their great and inestimable wisdom, devised the Victuals with more than just two purposes in mind. Not just to prepare the body to be Consumed, and not just to prepare the family to be Consumers, but to coax the mourners, one step at a time, into committing something they never would have committed before.

To move you toward the unthinkable, the unimaginable, the grotesque.

And so they began with requiring a thing to be done that wasn't a Doing at all—it was a Not Doing: Don't call the police. Simple. No knives, no blood, no guts. Just don't do that which you think you should. That's where it begins. That's how they get you started. Not with action, but with inaction. With mere acquiescence. From there, my child, is it really such a big step to Draining? If you're not calling the police, you should keep her in good condition, shouldn't you? Keep her from bloating, keep her from bursting? No major decisions here yet—no picking side dishes or deciding between propane and charcoal. Just simple maintenance, is all. Just hang her up and Drain her—it's the least you can do. While you think about it. While you ponder it. While you discuss it. Suddenly, without doing much of anything, really, we're up to Purging. And while you never would have considered such a thing two steps earlier, now it seems almost . . . reasonable. It's not that much different from Draining, after all; the organs can foul her, spread bacteria. You don't *want* to Purge her— you're not some sort of hideous *cannibal*—but you really should finish what you started. And so you do. One cut, *zip*, and it's over. She's Purged. And there she is, no longer a she at all, no longer human— just a slab of meat you might see at the butcher. And just like that, it's time to Partition. Now, if someone had suggested three steps ago you could Partition your mother, you'd have thought them mad. But is this really your mother? It doesn't look like your mother; it doesn't smell like your mother; it doesn't bake you cookies like your mother or tell you it's going to be okay like your mother. Is cutting this thing, this meat, really such a big deal? It's meat—what else are you going to do with it? Does the butcher think twice? Hell, you've bought meat at the grocery store that looked just like this. And so you do. You cut it up. Flanks, tenderloins, ribs. It's a party. And of course, now we come to eating. No! Never! you said when asked. The horror! But here you are, at a grill, with meat, and it doesn't seem so unreasonable. You've eaten flesh before; you probably ate flesh this morning. You ate bacon from the back of a pig, you scrambled an unborn chicken. Take a bite, the Ancients urge. It's just one bite. You can eat a bite of a cow, of a chicken, of a turkey, but you can't eat this? And so you do. You take a bite of your mother. You've done the unthinkable, the unimaginable.

What, then, Seventh now argued to his brothers, is the difference if we eat one bite or a hundred bites, a hundred bites or a thousand bites? Bite and a half or half and a bite—so what? We've already eaten one bite, haven't we? We've already broken laws, we've already gotten blood on our hands. Why not, then, Consume however much Unclish tells us to?

No, said First. No way.

The brothers gathered at the front door, out of earshot of their uncle, to discuss the issue of their eating the required half and a bite of Mudd.

It's the rule, said Seventh. You heard Unclish. We ate one bite of her already, what's a few more?

A few more? said Ninth. It's twenty pounds, Seventh—each. That's a thousand bites. That's ten thousand bites.

I didn't sign up for eating half, said Fourth. I have high cholesterol as it is; I'm not eating twenty pounds of meat.

Rotten meat, Fifth added. Seriously rotten.

Not all of it is rotten, said Seventh. We can find enough of it that's okay, enough that isn't spoiled.

We have to get out of here, said First. If that neighbor calls the cops, if they show up, we are going to jail, kids. And not just for a night. This is felony shit, folks. *Brooklyn family kill and cook mother, story at eleven.*

We didn't kill her, said Seventh.

I'm sure they'll mention that.

He's sick, Eighth said to Seventh, regarding Unclish. I supported this in the beginning, more than anyone, but come on, Seventh: He can barely remember our names, let alone the rules. And the rule is a bite and a half, I'm sure of it. We're going to sit here and eat half that woman, only to have him wake up an hour later and say we have to eat the whole damned thing.

Okay, said Seventh, fine. Let's do this, okay? Let's sit him up, get some fluids in him, and ask him again. Clearly and succinctly. Once and for all. Whatever he says, goes.

If he says done, we're done, said First.

Yes, said Seventh.

Deal, said Second.

Deal, said Ninth.

No deal, Zero called out.

She was kneeling beside Unclish, holding his hand in hers.

Why not? asked First.

Because he's dead, said Zero.

. . .

If the deceased has no offspring, declared the Elder Elders, it is incumbent upon their nephews and nieces to Consume them as they would their own parents. Anyone who does not is considered wicked in the eyes of our people.

Let me ask you something, said the Elders.

What?

Why, asked the Elders, if there's only one of each of us, are we referred to as plural?

Because, said the Elder Elders, it is more important that we are respected than it is that we tell the truth.

Well, then let me ask you another question, said the Elders.

Shoot.

Why am I called the Elders and you're called the Elder Elders?

Because I'm older than you, said the Elder Elders.

Exactly, said the Elders. Which means you're closer to the start of the story, chronologically speaking—our story, I mean, the Cannibal story. The story begins at the beginning, does it not? Day one. In the beginning. Once upon a time there was a man, and he ate his brother. That's the start, right?

You are most wise.

So if that, back then, was the beginning, I'm actually 'older' than you—in respect to the beginning. Further away, you see, closer to the end. I am the product of more Cannibal wisdom.

I don't follow, said the Elder Elders.

Take the Ancients, said the Elders. Someone came before the Ancients, did they not?

The Ancient Ancients, said the Elder Elders.

Right, said the Elders. Except wrong. The people before the Ancients were closer to the beginning of the story than the Ancients. So as far as the beginning of the story goes, they're *less* ancient than the Ancients. They're only more ancient to us, standing here now. But why tell the story from us, from our place in time? Why label everything in relation to where we stand today? We're just the most recent chapter. The story isn't about us, so why are we telling it as if we're who mattered?

So what are you saying? asked the Elder Elders. That we don't matter?

I'm saying that perhaps we don't matter as much as others.

The Elder Elders clopped the Elders on the back of his head.

Don't be stupid, he said.

• • •

They would be coming, Seventh knew. The neighbors, the police, the mobs. Any minute. Mobs are all the rage these days, after all. Seventh could hear the businessmen in his head, the investors, the Rosenblooms, the CEOs.

Forget digital, they were saying, the real growth is in riots.

Buy now, the *Wall Street Journal* would advise. *American Truncheon. Taser Incorporated. International Gauze.*

Hernandez Town wasn't going to take shit from Abdullahville anymore, Abdullahville was sick and tired of Rosenbloom Village, and if Hernandez Town thought Rosenbloom Village was going to sit by while they inseminated their way to a political majority, they had another thing coming.

Seventh thought they should do it.

Do what? asked First.

The Victuals, said Seventh. On Unclish.

Oh, for fuck's sake, said First.

We're the only ones left, said Seventh. You want to just leave him here?

Yes, said First. I want to just leave him here.

Is that the way our people end? asked Seventh. Is this what becomes of us?

Us? asked First. What is this us shit? Suddenly there's an us? There is no us, okay? There's only a dozen guilt-ridden siblings with mild food poisoning in a collapsing building in tax foreclosure with the body of their dead uncle. There is no larger significance to this; this is not some historical moment. Zero was right—if someone a hundred years from now tells this story and gives a damn what we did or didn't do, then *they're* the assholes, the same way we're assholes giving a damn about what people a hundred years ago did. This doesn't matter, Seventh, don't you get that? The sun will rise tomorrow just as it did today, maybe the better for the loss of one more fool the night before, one less tribe, one less story. This is how things end, Seventh, and everything ends. And if we stick around here much longer, it's going to end in jail.

It doesn't have to end, said Seventh. The chain. The links . . .

Yeah, well, said First, I don't know about the rest of you, but I'm tired of being in chains.

He pulled his coat on and began to button it.

Bring him to the hospital, he said of Unclish. He ate some bad meat. Oh fuck, he's dead? Damn. Boo-hoo. The end. At last, hallelujah, the motherfucking end.

What about the money? Second asked First. We still get the money, right?

Unclish is dead, said First. We're the executors of the will now. The money's ours, whether we eat her, bury her, turn her into jerky, or leave her here to rot.

It's not about the money, Seventh insisted. It's about the chain; it's about what's right.

Money *is* right, goddammit! First shouted. Right is compensation, brothers. Right is damages. You smash my car, you pay me. You break my arm, you pay me. YOU FUCK MY LIFE, YOU PAY ME. We did the math, me and Siri—*my* math. One shrink session, three hundred a pop, every week for twenty-seven years. Four hundred and twenty-one thousand, two hundred dollars. That's what it cost me to start over, to begin again. To erase her, to get to the blank page I started with. That's what she owes me, four hundred and twenty-one thousand, two hundred dollars, right around the amount we'll each get from the sale of that miserable house, destined for demolition, which I for one will be watching from the sidewalk across the street, in a comfortable lounge chair with an ice-cold beer. And as for that chain, little brother? There are two types of people on it. One, a miserable fuck, yelling, Stay. And another, even more miserable, wishing he had run.

And then First turned, opened the door, and walked away.

Again.

The cold wind blew in blustering flakes of snow. At last it was beginning to fall in earnest. If only it could cover the world, thought Seventh. If only it could cover the past and the present and future; if only it would snow so long and so deep that it would cover up all mankind.

Second followed First out the door.

Where are they going? asked Third, who was sitting beside Un-clish. He hadn't spoken since the Consumption.

Home, Fourth said, as he too headed for the door. We all are.

Not finished, said Third.

We're finished, said Fourth as he walked out. We're finished.

Not finished! Third called after him.

Zero patted Third's shoulder. It's okay, she said. It's okay.

Seventh looked around at the remaining brothers.

Anyone else? he asked.

Fifth stepped forward. I'm sorry, Seventh, he said, and he shook his head to hear himself utter yet another apology. I'm sorry and I'm sorry and I'm sorry; that's all I ever said to that woman. I thought Consuming her would finally alleviate my guilt, once and for all, and maybe it has. But now I just feel a coward.

Being a good son isn't cowardice, said Seventh. Being a good Cannibal isn't cowardice. It's bravery.

I had a patient, said Fifth, a young man with the usual dysfunctional family afflictions—depression, anxiety, low self-esteem— who nevertheless prided himself on being a good son. He took care of his aging father, feeding him, changing him, even going to church with him and praying with him. Parishioners shed tears to see it, and the priest often spoke of him in his sermons, comparing his devotion to his father to the way Jesus devoted his own life to his Father in Heaven. Eventually the father died, and the young man sank into a deep and dark depression. That was when he came to see me. The darkness he felt was more severe than one normally associated with simple grief. He was utterly broken. Eventually, many months later, we traced the cause of his melancholy back to a single moment in the hospital, a day or so before his father passed away. He had been at the hospital, standing beside his father's bed, straightening the items on the nightstand, when his father, in the midst of a feverish dream, suddenly lifted his arm up—and the young man jumped back in fear.

His father, you see, had been a son of a bitch. Abusive, violent, prone to fits of rage. All of which the son excused, tolerated, dismissed. He was a good son to a bad man. And even with his father wasted away, tubes running in and out of him, not even strong enough to breathe on his own, the son, who could kill him now with one blow, still feared him. He still cowered when his father raised his hand. That was the source of his depression. While others praised his devotion, he knew it was really just fear. He didn't have the courage to be a bad son. To walk away. To leave his broken family and find a new one, to turn his back on *that* man and join the larger family of Man. I advised him to move on, before it was too late. I advise you to do the same.

And he walked out too.

And then there were seven, thought Seventh.

Not including Zero-Hero.

Who, he knew, didn't count.

. . .

It is opening night, and Cannibals from across the country have come to the University to see the premiere of the award-winning two-act Cannibal play, *Melting Point*, adapted from the bestselling *Out of the Shadows*, in the very first Cannibal theater in the very first Cannibal university. Expectations are high as the curtain rises, and the crowd gasps in horror to see before them the heinous Melting Pot of Henry Ford, thirty feet tall, black and terrible and all-consuming. A young woman runs onstage—tattered dress, unkempt hair, bare feet—looks out at the audience, and calls, Julius! Julius, come quick!

Julius runs onstage, carrying an ancient leather valise. A dozen other tired, hungry immigrants follow him.

Look! Julia cries, pointing over the heads of the audience.

Is that . . . ? one of the immigrants asks.

The Statue of Liberty, Julia says. The New World!

The immigrants cheer and dance and sing, but Julius, troubled, clutches his valise and steps away.

God help us, he whispers.

The New World, though, is nothing if not enticing, and as the first act proceeds, Julius begins to fall for its gleaming charms. After a heartwarming scene of Julia and Julius taking their first ride in a Ford Model T—If only Father could see this magical carriage! Julia shrieks—they set out for the promised land of Detroit. Julius and Julia are excited, but the audience grows anxious, knowing what's coming. Henry Ford appears, eliciting howls of rage from the audience, kissing Julia's hand as he welcomes the two to Detroit. But there is more outrage to come, for as act 1 draws to a close, the Melting Pot creeps, ghostlike, to center stage, spewing smoke. A sign descends from the rafter, announcing that it is Americanization Day. Julius enters, and climbs the ladder to the pot's edge.

The crowd holds its breath.

Julius turns back to Julia and smiles.

America, he calls out to her. Was it not worth it?

He holds his arms wide, closes his eyes, and falls into the pot.

Curtain.

The crowd during intermission is afire with indignation. Is this what we paid to see? they demand. This assimilationist Was-It retelling of history? This cheap propaganda for the New World? Some demand their money back; some leave in a huff, swearing to never return.

The curtain rises on act 2, the audience ready to hiss and boo and let the company know what they think of them. But there, onstage, is Julia, in the back of a Ford Model T, being violated by Henry Ford. She screams, begs for mercy, but Ford tears at her, slaps her. By the end of act 2, Julia has been beaten beyond recognition, Julius is a shadow of his former self, and they are chased from Detroit by the very same immigrants who cheered with them in the play's opening scene.

Julius collapses. Julia holds him in her arms as the mob draws around them.

America, Julius says. It was *not* worth it.

And Julius dies.

Curtain.

The crowd erupts. Encore! they shout. Encore!

The door to the empty theater opened.

Seventh? Eighth called. You in here?

You missed a hell of a show, said Seventh.

Eighth made his way down the aisle and sat beside Seventh, who knew what his brother was going to say before he spoke a single word.

You're leaving, said Seventh.

Eighth nodded. I am, he said.

Seventh had thought Eighth would be the last to go. Even Tenth, he thought, would leave before Eighth.

Picture a candelabra, said Seventh.

I have, said Eighth.

There are three candles, Seventh said. Red, white, blue. They're burning. They're on fire. Does the red one help the blue one? Does the blue one give a damn about the white one? No. What's white ever done for blue? Fuck white, says red. Fuck blue, says white. Fuck red, says blue.

Candles are assholes, said Eighth.

Seventh nodded.

They are, he said.

They've always been assholes, said Eighth. And who can blame them? They're born, they burn, they die. Bad way to go, too, lighting your head on fire. Candles have it rough. Red, white, blue—they're all pretty fucked.

You'd think they'd come together, said Seventh. In their times of trouble.

Are we still talking about candles?

Help me, said Seventh. With Unclish. I can't do him alone.

But Eighth shook his head.

This used to mean something to me, he said. This place, these rules. These stories. I felt I was part of something, preserving something. But now I think, Whose rules? Whose stories? Unclish's? Julius's? Mudd's? Father's? I've been holding on to this bullshit identity as if it was a ship in a storm that could keep me from drowning. But it was just a plank of old driftwood, Seventh; it only dragged me farther out to sea. I'm done.

Would you eat me? Seventh asked.

Eat you?

If I died. Would you eat me?

Half and a bite? asked Eighth.

Bite and a half, said Seventh.

Eighth shook his head.

And condemn you to eternal life? he said. I don't like you, Seventh, but I don't *hate* you.

Good, said Seventh. Just checking.

They hugged, and Seventh couldn't remember the last brother he ever hugged, or if he ever had.

. . .

Third lay down in the back seat of Zero's car, curled into the fetal position, and fell asleep. It was late afternoon, and traffic back to the city was light. Zero drove in silence, checking on Third in the rearview mirror every now and then.

He asked me to make a baby with him, said Zero.

Third?

She nodded.

When?

After Unclish died, she said. He wanted to make sure Mudd lived.

Does he even know how to make a baby?

It was more like he was asking me for help, she said. Like there were some directions somewhere. Two cups water, three cups flour, that sort of thing.

What did you tell him?

I told him I'd have to go shopping.

They smiled. By Seventh's feet sat the old leather valise. He texted Rosenbloom.

Just finished a manuscript, he wrote.

Good? Rosenbloom asked.

Great, replied Seventh.

What's it about?

It's about this family, Seventh replied, *and how the death of their matriarch causes them to reconsider their dreams of assimilation in a nation that won't accept them.*

That's what they're all about, wrote Rosenbloom.

This one's about Cannibal-Americans, wrote Seventh.

There was a long pause.

As I Lay Frying? wrote Rosenbloom.

And then: *This Is Where I Eat You?*

And then, after a much longer pause: *I pay you good money, Seventh. And it isn't to jerk me around.*

I'm going to have to put him somewhere, said Zero. Third, I mean. A home, something. A care center.

Seventh agreed.

Mudd should have done that a long time ago, he said.

Maybe he'll be happy now, she said. It's over, we're all gone. There's nobody left to defend. Isn't it wonderful? No need to be a warrior. He can just be Third, I can just be me, you can just be you.

Whoever the hell that is, said Seventh.

The snow fell heavy now on the highway. Traffic slowed as they grew closer to Manhattan, and came to a standstill in the middle of the George Washington Bridge. Zero pointed to a small sign on the suspension cable that read NEW YORK. There was another one, facing the other way, that read NEW JERSEY. Somewhere below them, or far above, was the invisible border between the two states, whose residents had about as much love for one another as gas people have for charcoal.

What a bunch of assholes, she said.

Who?

People, she said. I'm from here, you're from there. Rah rah, bang bang, kill kill. That's not just my opinion, either—that people are assholes. It's a fact, did you know that? A biological fact.

That people are assholes?

Yes, she said. Fourth told me. When we got back from buying the grill, remember? After I said the cop was decent and you told me to shut the fuck up?

Sorry.

I was pissed off, said Zero, and he was trying to cheer me up. I said, Jesus Christ, are *all* people assholes? And he said, Yes. They are. From birth. He said that in the womb, we start out as a tiny little group of cells—a blastula, he called it. The cells burst, and form an opening. In some creatures, that opening becomes the mouth. In others it becomes an anus.

An anus?

An asshole, said Zero. That's the first organ to form; everything else comes after that. And so all creatures are either Mouth Firsts or Asshole Firsts. Guess which type humans are. We're assholes, Seventh, from day one. Every one of us. Gandhi was an asshole, Stalin was an asshole, Jesus was an asshole. Take everything else away— class, education, race, religion, appearance, rank—and essentially, we're all just a bunch of assholes. It literally explains everything— Mudd, Unclish, you, me, religion, war, politics. Everything.

Seventh had studied Montaigne. He had studied Cicero and Seneca and Epictetus. He'd studied all the great philosophers and all the great thinkers from all across time. And what Zero just said, he knew, was the truest thing he had ever heard.

. . .

Zero dropped Seventh off outside his apartment building on the Upper East Side. He asked her to let him know what happened with Third; he would visit him whenever he could. Zero said she would. They promised to keep in touch, and they hugged tightly.

Zero-Hero, said Seventh. Zero my hero.

The driver behind them leaned on his horn.

Zero turned around. Asshole! she shouted. Then, to Seventh she said, See?

Out of the Shadows was published nearly a year later, the story of a young man's struggle to escape his identity.

Mudd would have hated it.

Seventh had written it as nonfiction, as cultural history. Rosenbloom agreed to publish it as fantasy. It had been a difficult year for Rosenbloom; rather than garnering praise for publishing authors of such varied identities, he was excoriated for profiting from their stories, and vilified by the few identities he overlooked. Cannibals, he figured, were a safe political bet.

Out of the Shadows, though, was largely ignored. Its hero was a man who let his people disappear into history, who chose to define himself by what he and his fellow man had in common rather than by what made them different. Or woman.

Typical Libtard bullshit, wrote the first reviewer on Amazon. *One star because I couldn't give it none.*

Replied the second: *Rethuglicans only know how to hate.*

Responded the first: *Get used to it, Jews and homos don't run this country anymore.*

Responded the second: *Go wash your Klan hood, you redneck bible-thumper.*

The assholes continued this for as long as assholes continue these things for, and aside from a couple of customers who praised the fast shipping, that was the end of that.

Seventh didn't mind; writing about his past had been a form of exorcism, and it had served its purpose. A few months later, on the snowy anniversary of Mudd's death, Seventh went for a walk. He would have liked to bring Reese with him, but he never did tell her about her heritage; her story began with her, he had decided, and she could follow it wherever she chose.

She was her own chapter one. No prologue. Why should Adam be the only one born with no past, the only one born without the crippling defect of history? There was nothing for Reese to do but be Reese, as Reesey a Reese as she could ever be.

He walked two blocks east until he came to the large park at the edge of the city. The park was built above the FDR Drive, the busy four-lane highway that runs along the East River, from the southernmost point of Manhattan all the way up to 125th Street. The downside of this design is that at certain points of the park, one could hear the traffic racing and rumbling below. But it also allowed visitors to reach the East River without having to cross the highway.

Not that many people other than Seventh wanted to reach the East River.

The East River was a toilet. For decades, assholes have dumped their waste and sewage here. Not just asshole Americans, mind you, but the asshole British before them, and the asshole Native Americans before them. Asshole humans have dumped so much of what came out of their assholes into the East River that only a complete fucking asshole would step foot in it now.

Seventh looked out at the despoiled river.

Assholes from the very moment we form, he thought.

Finding myself quite empty, with nothing to write about, I offered myself to myself as theme and subject matter.

That was how Montaigne began his famous essays. Thousands of pages later, he had come to pretty much the same conclusion as Zero:

Upon the highest throne in the world, we are seated, still, upon our asses.

Liberal humanist or religious conservative, Catholic or Jewish, courageous philosopher or cowardly politician, this was Montaigne's great genius:

He knew he was an asshole.

That we are all assholes.

Perhaps, he wrote, *we are right to condemn ourselves for giving birth to such an absurd thing as a man; right to call it an act of shame and the organs which serve to do it shameful.*

Maybe, thought Seventh, that was the melting we needed to do, the melting that could save the world: accept that we're all assholes. Maybe then we'd lose respect for our asshole ancestors, and give up our asshole traditions, question our asshole beliefs and asshole nationalities and asshole identities, erase our asshole borders and just live together, as best as a bunch of assholes can hope to.

Seventh lifted up the old valise and rested it on the rail. He undid the old rusted latches, and opened it one last time. He took out the dice, the Monopoly money, and the bubble gum and placed them in his pocket. He would mail them to Zero to give to Third.

And then he reached in, and he took out the Knife of Redemption, and he held it a moment in his hand, heavy and fearsome and covered in the blood of the long-since dead, and he reared back and he threw it, as Samuel the Wise so long ago commanded, as far as he could into the river below, and he watched it sink, and then he closed the old valise, and he latched the old locks, and he threw it as far as he could into the river, too, just as Father wished Julius had so long ago.

With the rest of that ancient bullshit.